LOYALTY OF SEVERUS

THE SAGA OF THE ELAGABAL

LEN BERRY

Copyright © 2024 by Len Berry

All rights reserved.

No portion of this book may be reproduced in any form without written permission from the publisher or author, except as permitted by U.S. copyright law.

To all who have been displaced from their true selves.
You are seen. You are loved.

In the annals of human history, men have always coveted
that which they cannot possess.
This was true when Varia was betrayed by her nephew and
legal son.
This was just as true when Geta and Caracalla visited New
Brasilia.

William Pleiades III
The Modern Ascendancy of Man

A MARTIAL SCOWL HUNG onto Fola's dark-skinned face as she watched the hated wave of occupation sweep toward her. A host of bronze-armored soldiers marched in formation to herald the arrival of the insidious Imperial Assessor. Two banners rose from the diplomatic shuttle in unison, the inquiring stallion of House Geta and the blood red talon of House Caracalla. Between the pair, a final, angular banner crept higher, allowing the two-headed eagle of the Unnamed Empire to menacingly screech at the dignitaries themselves.

Fola stood tall to spite the Assessor's host. Her hand never approached the dull ceremonial sword dangling from her hip. A slight breeze clinked the rings gathering the braids of hair tumbling down her back. The faint wind pushed the mass of her crimson cape hanging from her right shoulder. Yet the gods failed to expose the asymmetrical shape of Fola's chest.

Fola's militant stance clashed with that of her demure companion. Her cousin, the Imperial Widow Bassiana, wore a sleeveless purple dress with angular shoulders and a diamond neckline. Unlike the queen of New Brasilia, Bassiana wore her hair up, tied with interwoven ribbons of violet.

More imperial legionnaires surrounded the stone platform, flanked on each side by a quartet of stern, feminine guardians. The widow licked the shadowy stain of her lips before she spoke. "I don't care for their early arrival."

"There is nothing we can do." Fola kept her brown eyes forward, leaving them fixated on the central banner. "We must abide by Imperial law if you are to succeed."

A worried sigh crept softly from Bassiana's lungs. "Will they ask about Varius?"

"He is still young, and we aren't known for training men to fight." A momentary snarl touched the edge of Fola's mouth. "Even with our present neighbors."

"If they discover—"

"Quiet." Fola shifted her head away from the approaching standard. Sunlight caught the edge of her slender circlet. "You worry too much for your son."

"He's your nephew. Shouldn't you worry for him, too?"

Fola faced the coordinated horde as they approached, further blocking her from all but her closest defenders. "Maybe," she said, just before the regal title hardened her response. "But I am also mother to every soul on this hemisphere, no matter how much blood we share."

The imposing banners closed upon the platform, desperate for any reason to devour any remaining individuality from New Brasilia's soil.

Both cousins remained silent, sharing in their dedication to holding back the Imperial tide.

Fola nodded to a pair of teenage girls wearing matching sleeveless white dresses. The girls lifted sloped woven baskets and walked toward the transport. With every step, they forged a path of lush, tropical leaves upon the otherwise droll path.

Once the fresh scent of ripened melons filled the air, two imperial men emerged, standing side by side. No gust of wind, nor swell of heat, nor burst of sunlight turned either man away.

The taller man wore centurion armor engraved with a relief of a human warrior impaling one of the despicable Nihl. A neutral expression held his face as firm as chiseled stone. Stubble drew a shadow of a scalp upon his skull.

His companion scowled before straightening the Imperial stole around his shoulders and chest. Neatly trimmed brown hair avoided his ears and brow.

Fola and Bassiana lowered their heads in a brief, deferential bow. Their visitors held lower rank but stood with the direct authority of the Usurper. Fola forced the motion only as long as civility demanded.

Fola breathed her last breath of compassion. "Welcome honored guests to New Brasilia. Lord Geta—"

"Dispense with the formalities," the shorter man said after his name was spoken. "I am here to make my regular assessment. I need none of your..." His nose flexed. "Local flavor."

"Patience, friend." The taller man kept his voice low. "At least introduce me to these enchanting women."

"Fine." Geta huffed before opening his hand toward the queen. "This is Fola, warrior-champion and Queen of New Brasilia—"

Before Geta could rush onward, the taller man cordially reached for Fola's hand. She allowed the centurion's grasp as he lowered his head to kiss her palm and wrist. "To visit your lands and your people is a privilege."

Fola gave a slight nod, closing her fingers around the centurion's greeting.

A brief snort burst from Geta's nostrils. "This is the queen's sister, Bassiana, Regent of House Severus."

The tall centurion repeated the motions of his greeting for Bassiana. "My Lady, all of humanity still rejoices at your husband's virtues and victories. I regret never having served him."

Pride swelled in Geta's face, cracking his disdain. "To you both, I present Lord Caium Caracalla, general of the 112th Legion and Military Aide to His Imperial Majesty. Long live Macrinus!"

Stoicism filled the height of Caracalla's martial disposition. "Long live Macrinus!"

The cousins lowered their heads and spoke the reverie in unison. "Long live Macrinus."

Once they'd all spoken their loyalty to the Imperator, the queen cracked the cordial silence. She forged a soft smile before she spoke. "What brings a general of such rank to New Brasilia?"

Caracalla returned Fola's smile. "Highness, my assigned purpose here is to venture onward, to sit in the fabled halls of your neighbor, Sparta. Before that, I wish to observe the young heir left in your charge."

A stern politeness stiffened Bassiana's tone. "What interest do you have in my son?"

"He is a citizen of the Empire and heir to a noble house. I wish to see if he should be recommended to an academy for training and enlistment."

A furious impact overwhelmed Vari's legs. Her ankles burned like the tendons had been cut. Her toes screamed at their unrestrictive leather. The absence of weight stabbed her chest and shoulders. Her scalp whined, having to again abandon her real clothes.

Without a weapon, emptiness absorbed her, enhancing the loneliness that came from changing into a socially acceptable form of dress.

The heiress of House Severus wore a sleeveless white shirt and matching pants while storming through the halls of the Brasilian Royal Palace. She pushed a slight length of midnight brown hair away from her bronze face, tying the short waves into a single knot. Agonizing steps carried no sound as she walked through the arched hallway. It was a horrid side effect of wearing supposedly dignified shoes stuffed with excess cushioning.

More arches rose above the sunlit windows on both sides of the towering hallway. Every slender opening allowed the deep aqua sky to soothe Vari's eyes. For a decade, a similar view of New Brasilia swelled most mornings. It didn't matter that she'd been born on Roma Vatica. If she left orbit, the Usurper's decrees would strike like stray lightning. Despite that, the Severus birthright lay hidden among a million star systems.

A firm, feminine voice spoke in half a whisper. "Varius." A woman slightly older than Vari fast-walked toward her. The deep tan of her skin concealed the lack of Brasilian ancestry in her, even if she stood with the same build and posture possessing every Brasilian warrior. "Someone is looking for you."

"I'm due to attend the official reception—"

"No." The woman drew closer, her voice shifted lower than a whisper. "An imperial general is here specifically to meet with you."

Vari's lower lip stiffened. "Did my mother say why?"

"No."

"Damn." Vari marched in a circle, clenching her masculine fists over and over. Her gaze traced the monolithic tiles along the path she'd walked.

The woman pressed a hand over Varius's shoulder. "What's wrong?"

She leaned close, letting her mouth approach her companion's ear. "I was just in my room, Saran."

"You sealed it?"

"Of course I did." She exhaled sharply, restraining the possibility of panic. "We don't know if anyone sent emissaries ahead of the assessor."

"It's fine." Saran's hand swept under Varius's chin. "Even with Geta arriving a week early, everything is still hidden."

"It still makes me nervous."

"Good." Saran smiled before poking Vari with her elbow. "It should. You're the son of the Imperator."

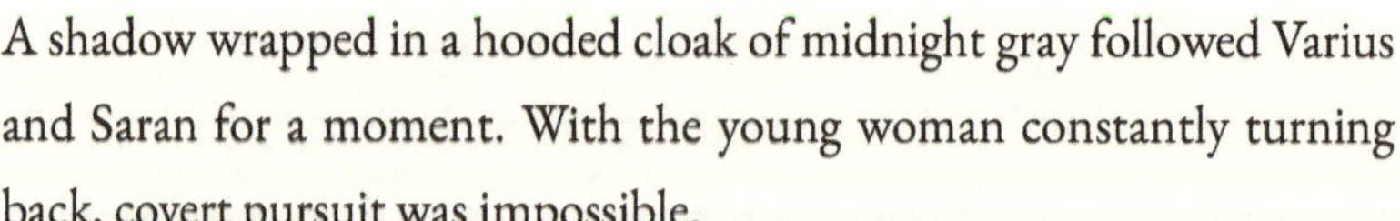

A shadow wrapped in a hooded cloak of midnight gray followed Varius and Saran for a moment. With the young woman constantly turning back, covert pursuit was impossible.

In walking back, the shadow was left to follow the path Varius had taken along the ground floor. After several minutes, there was an intersection without any archways, faintly lit by flickering lanterns. One direction aimed back toward a nest of public areas. A pair of double doors marked the stairs leading into the wine cellar, while the mandatory Imperial statue of Jupiter stood in a carved alcove.

The shadow pressed the button in his left eye socket, humming softly enough not even a cat could hear. "The key to war is here. There is another room, hidden to all but a few. It concerns Severus and the Amazons. Make haste."

With the message finished, the shadow opened his mouth, yanking out the bed of wires and circuits that replaced his dead tongue. He dropped the mechanical mass in front of the statue in absolute silence. The wires wove into the gaps between tiles and the supporting plinth bearing the statue.

Bowing to his removed circuits, the shadow scuttled to the center of the room. He drew a gleaming sapphire marble from his cloak, marveling at the glow for an eternal instant. After recalling his abandoned life, the shadow squeezed the marble to his chest, erupting in a flare of blue light.

There were no prayers to Jupiter. No vindication that a poor man's family slept in peace while the remains of their father fizzled into nothingness.

All that remained were true shadows and scattered dust.

Bassiana loomed in the carved mahogany chair she preferred within the queen's private study. Her eyes stayed transfixed upon the tall, narrow door, waiting equally for hope and doom to arrive. "We must stop this development."

The study was an intimate sealed chamber full of books and scrolls. Such literature concealed a pair of tapestries—standards from a decade earlier, when they'd stood as part of the former Imperator's host.

Fola dominated the square ivory chair, scrolling through a nest of digital details. "If Vari is drafted into one of the academies, she'll get the finest training possible. She may even find new allies."

Bassiana thrust her hands against her armrests. "My child's place isn't at some academy on the opposite side of the galaxy."

"She doesn't belong here."

"No, cousin." Steam rippled from Bassiana's mouth. "She belongs on Roma Vatica, taking her seat on the throne."

Fola's finger stopped sweeping across the tablet. "Calm down."

"I'll calm down once Geta and Caracalla are out of this system." Bassiana clutched the sloped ends of the armrests, her fingers digging into the warm toned varnish. "Calm is dead until then."

Fola looked up from her reports. "Those men aren't our enemy. They aren't even Nihl. They present a threat, but one with advantages."

Bassiana shot to her feet. "You would send my daughter away?"

"It's not my choice. Nor is it yours."

The narrow door opened, allowing Vari and Saran to enter. The latter bowed to the seated queen while the former lowered her head respectfully. "What does Lord Caracalla want with me?"

A cloud of silence hung over Bassiana.

Fola lay her hands over her tablet. "You're a member of a noble house and old enough to be noticed. Caracalla wants to see if you should be enrolled into one of the academies."

"Letting the Usurper's assassins kill me."

"Possibly, but doubtful. Caracalla's pretense is one of military efficiency. I've been reading over his available records. I think he wants your father's legacy to bolster his legions."

"It doesn't matter." Bassiana whispered as she braced a hand on her daughter's forearm. "I won't let you be taken."

"That's only a possibility, cousin." The Queen fixed her eyes upon Vari again. "If he wants to take you from here, we can't stop him without severing your birthright."

Saran tensed her shoulders and lips. "Majesty, how close are Lord Caracalla and Lord Geta?"

"I don't know. Geta is not our friend. Caracalla is a rigid servant of the law."

Bassiana shared a glance with Saran before she spoke. "Then we must stop them both from interfering."

"Which will be impossible until we know what Caracalla is after, especially if he's going to visit Sparta before leaving the planet." Fola's mouth narrowed as she spoke the name of the neighboring nation.

Vari crossed her arms. "When will he want to see me?"

"I'll hold him off until this evening," Bassiana said as she rubbed her son's back. "Stay out of sight until then."

Saran found a way to stand at even straighter attention. "How can I help?"

A strained sigh escaped Fola's mouth before she answered. "Help my Vari find something appropriate to wear for this evening. Make sure neither of you are seen."

Saran bowed. "It will be done, Majesty." When she rose, she hooked a hand around Vari's arm. "The side passages await."

Vari lowered her head. "Your Majesty. Mother."

"See you tonight." Bassiana's finger drifted from her daughter as she was swept away. Her face stiffened as she imagined the impenetrable crossroads Vari faced. A part of her started crying the day her daughter first confided in her. Bassiana swore never to reject Vari, especially since they both wanted justice done upon the Usurper—a justice that could only be performed by the rightful Imperator.

Once the door closed again, Fola rose, pressing a massaging hand over Bassiana's shoulder. "I will do whatever I can for her, but we must remain discreet. A few more years of quiet and we'll have the strength."

"Yes." Bassiana bowed away from her cousin's embrace. "A few more years for the Usurper to grow comfortable on my husband's throne." She backed away in a huff, retreating through the door.

Caracalla would not have Vari. Every quickened step reminded Bassiana of her collected blades. If it ensured Vari would claim the Imperator's Throne—under her birth name, of course—then Bassiana would cut through every nerve in the famed general's body.

Geta sat behind a wide desk in his palace guest room. A sprawl of similar tablets lay in a neat row from one end of the desk to the other. A sunlit window cast Geta as a silhouette in Caracalla's eyes. Geta rubbed his brow before repeating his mantra. "I've sworn to find a reason for the Imperator to wipe this continent from the face of the galaxy, if only so he won't send me back here again."

"Don't care for the tropics?" Caracalla examined a painting of several armed humans standing over an endless field of slain Nihl oppressors.

"No. Nor do I care for these people." Geta shifted one tablet a millimeter, putting it into a more precise position. "I hope you find a reason to hang that boy."

"My informers say Varius Severus is a promising young man." Caracalla turned away from the vision of humanity's ancestral victory. "If I take him from this world, you will not touch him."

"Why pursue him at all? It's pointless."

"You fear rebellion. There is no need." Caracalla approached the desk. "I have allies in every major academy. He will be watched."

"The Imperator's men won't be able to touch him without tarnishing you." Geta shook his head. "You shouldn't diminish yourself like that."

Caracalla rapped a knuckle on the edge of the desk. "You and I have different ideas on what will bring stability to the Empire."

Discourse and dining paired together long before the
Nihl became custodians of humanity.
Still, there was no guarantee that speech or sustenance
would be sweet.

Francine Zemeckis
Searching For Our Roots

A T THE FAR END of the reception hall, Vari stood at attention, offering cordial nods and smiles to anyone she didn't recognize. Brasilians spoke with Imperials, though Vari doubted most of those in attendance knew what Fola had planned for the Usurper. As heralds for each of the honored guests entered, Vari refined the guise of a young man straightening a gold vest over a loose-sleeved black shirt.

Pristine banners and emblems hovered proudly over the spacious reception hall. New Brasilia demonstrated every loyalty to the Unnamed Empire and Imperator Macrinus. None of the tokens had ever tasted dust. Each magnificent cloth hung in defiance of the radiant sunbeams.

Musicians and lookouts filled the oval balcony, all with an unobstructed view of each other and the swelled gathering. Independent centurions patrolled the hall, clad in their signature armor and static-plumed relay helmets.

On the central floor, a table stretched across the middle of the room, segmenting the elliptical chamber. At the midpoint of one side, four gold seats stood in parallel to a single tall onyx chair. The visitors of rank from Roma Vatica wore sleek, layered finery from every corner of the Empire. The native Brasilians dressed themselves in simpler robes and dresses woven from the rarest local cloth.

Saran hovered nearby, draped in a post-fashionable long dress of white silk lined with small gems. "It's funny," she said, hardly moving her lips. "You stand up straight when our enemies approach."

Vari smiled as she leaned toward Saran's ear. "I like to present myself properly." A foxlike grin touched her face for an instant. "It's expected of me."

"There are other things a young nobleman is expected to do." Saran pressed her leg against Vari's thigh. A glance of the immigrant warrior was always a drunken temptation, especially since her dress showed enough of her allure without advertising her martial figure.

"You play dangerous games." Vari loomed close to her companion. A lilac scent clung to Saran's neck. "What if my mother heard you?"

"She would order me to your bed as soon as you decided to retire for the evening."

Vari chuckled and composed her guise. "You're probably right."

An Imperial crier stopped inside the doorway, dramatically clomping both his feet against the marble tiled floor. His arms shot upward as he flared the metallic tint of his fingernails in a wide arc. "Attention. Attention." He fluffed the edges of his white and crimson robe before taking two steps further inside. "I have the privilege of presenting Lord Callium Geta and his Gallae-bride, Lysandra."

Civil applause from Brasilian women and men filled the chamber as Geta strolled into the lavish hall. An echo of a sneer crept over Geta's face. Beside him, his wife stood a head taller, layered in a purple gown that matched Geta's robes.

Another whisper betrayed Varius's desires. "Didn't he have a different Gallae-bride two years ago?"

"Maybe." Saran shrugged. "It's not like she can ever have kids."

"Be nice," Varius said with a somber breath. "It's not her fault she's married to that rat." A drop of moisture softened Vari's lips as he gazed upon the bright emeralds drifting beneath Lysandra's earlobes and highlighted brown hair.

Gallae were said to understand their lover's deepest desires. Their training unlocked insights beyond the analytics of generals and queens. But the Temple of Cybele kept its members close to Roma Vatica whenever possible, only quietly reporting upon the patterns they discovered.

Firm fingers pressed the base of Vari's spine. Saran's wisdom cracked the cloud of curiosity. "There are some things you should not envy."

"You sacrificed plenty to be yourself." Vari's eyes transfixed upon the perfect slope of Lysandra's shoulders. "Why should she be any different?"

As Geta and Lysandra approached one of the gold chairs, the crier bellowed once more. "It is my privilege—" He punctuated the word like it was its own sentence. "—to present Lord Caium Caracalla, escorted by Princess Bassiana."

Caracalla's expression remained stoic under the heightened applause, though he nodded to a few scattered guests. The same cape and armor held him in place as he crossed the oval hall. Bassiana barely touched the general's arm, paying more attention to the shawl of her full-length silver dress. Eventually, they found the unclaimed gold chairs, though none had taken their seats.

Once the applause faded, the crier's voice rang out for the last time, his voice dripping with as much disdain as an Imperial servant could get away with. "Behold now Her Highness Fola Virago, Sovereign Queen of New Brasilia." The crier flexed his shiny fingers outward, lowering himself in a dramatic bow.

Fola entered through a regal archway on the opposite side of the room. When she halted, her brown and black dress fluttered around her like she was a heroine from ancient times. A jeweled stole lay over one shoulder, accenting her Amazonian frame. With both hands, she held a shimmering silver bow.

"In the Age of Nihl, humanity joined together to conquer our hated foe. Our Imperators wielded legendary swords while my mothers defended them from afar." Fola lifted the bow parallel with her eyes. "I swear by my own bow, you are all welcome at my table. Let us share in the meals our ancestors never could." When she lowered her bow, a tremendous applause swelled through the hall. Fola mounted the bow atop the onyx chair, then stood before her seat. She opened her arms to everyone present, especially those positioned by the gold seats. "Come and drink. My blood will be spent in your defense. Come and eat. My body will fall so you may carry on."

As everyone sat at the elongated table, Vari knew she could never make the same promise.

Once the meal was in full swing, Bassiana turned a scrutinizing eye upon Caracalla. "What designs do you have on my son?" She'd trained herself for years to apply leading pronouns with ease.

Caracalla smiled as he chewed a bite of meat steaming with red pepper and cumin. "You don't approve of my presence here."

"General, I wish to understand why you're here." She lifted a goblet of mead to her lips. "I want to know why you're interested in my son."

"Most planets in this Empire are united. This world is not." Caracalla mirrored Bassiana in reaching for his own cup. "Two nations sharing a single world, yours favoring female warriors, Sparta drafting men. You have every reason to unify, yet you don't." After they both drank, he continued. "I want to see if your son has his father's strength. If so, he should accompany me to Sparta. Every citizen must see to the security and stability of the Empire. Your son is no exception."

"You want something in Sparta." Bassiana folded her hands over her lap. "If I helped you, perhaps you would be content."

He gently shook his head. "No, Princess. I will not be bought. Not by our Imperator. Not by you."

Bassiana pierced two colorful bits of seasoned vegetables. "Aren't you a man of the Empire?"

"We are all subject to rightful laws and edicts. None of us can pick which to obey." Caracalla took another drink. "The Imperator carries the Twelfth Quantum Sword. The Eighth is gone with your husband."

Silently, the widow turned to her plate, blocking out any further attempt at conversation. Her words lacked the power to protect her daughter. Her most precise blades lay far out of reach, unable to correct Caracalla's purpose.

Few Gallae embodied as much of their patron deity's grace as Lysandra. Each demure motion from touching her wine cup to biting a small morsel of food exemplified the Imperial definition of feminine grace, even if she were one of the tallest creatures Vari had ever seen. The soft position of her silence among more significant conversations, the ease of every exhale from her sculpted face, every tiny motion eased her closer to a realm of serene divinity.

Everything Vari wanted for herself, but couldn't have. Openly entertaining herself put Vari and her entire family at risk. The price of Vari perfecting herself was any hope of a throne and deposing the Usurper.

Geta caught Vari's gaze and snorted. "Lysandra would appeal to you."

The Gallae made no motion. Bride or not, Lysandra had been positioned to be seen and to elevate Geta's status. No matter how capable of a mind she might have possessed, Vari both envied and pitied her.

"I meant no disrespect, Lord Geta." Vari tilted her head in deference. "I admire your wife's beauty, no matter her status."

A vile sneer appeared on Geta's face. "She works well. If I had a better opinion of you, I would let you watch."

The refined beauty still refused to react. The air around her swelled, broadcasting the scent of Lysandra's customized ritual perfume. If the Gallae had absorbed any wisdom or insights, she made no sign of it.

Saran giggled. "Lord Geta, I believe my date will be indisposed once we have finished this evening." Her eyes flickered toward Varius's waist for a moment, no more.

Geta echoed the laughter. "That's amusing, girl. What was your name again?"

She bowed her head. "Saran of Virago."

The assessor shook his head. "No. I'm sure that's not it."

Only an echo of Saran's playfulness remained. "It's the only name I have."

"Really?" Geta shifted his posture toward Saran. "A Caucasian girl with a tan thinks she's a Virago? Severus, have your pet tell me her real name. I may even give you a few minutes with my wife in return."

"That's not necessary." Vari lifted her hands to distract Geta and defend Saran. "I assure you, Lord Geta, this is Saran of Virago. She is a New Brasilian warrior."

"Are you sure?" Geta glared at Saran's chest, studying her like a six-legged cat. "I could command Lysandra to crawl under the table for you."

A voice gentler than a whisper and softer than a Spring breeze spoke. "If you so wish, my love."

Geta jabbed a finger into his wife's collarbone. "That is devotion. Tell us, Severus, how long has your blonde playmate been playing Amazon? Why would such a girl run to the edge of the Empire in the first place?"

Vari held her tongue. Her throat already stood twisted in the presence of her family name, while totally dismissing her father's towering Imperial status.

"Her reasons are hers," Queen Fola said as her eyes locked onto the assessor's jugular vein. "Saran is mine to command. I doubt I'll ever give her up."

Saran blushed as she bowed to Fola. "Thank you for your faith, my Queen."

Geta snorted. "Keep your secrets." His small eyes shifted toward Vari. "And your gazes."

Caracalla broke from the verbal sparring of the others, watching porters filling glasses and retrieving small dishes for the more demanding guests. "Interesting." Caracalla turned his focus back to Fola. "Your servants are all local citizens."

"Yes." Fola tilted her head and crossed her arms over her chest. "They're well compensated for their services."

"Forgive me," the general said with a smirk. "Many palaces have taken contracts with the Non-Dead to take care of menial labor."

Geta lifted his glass after taking a sip. "More efficient than peasants. Affordable as well."

It was Bassiana who aimed a response at Geta next. "Such things open a cycle of despair. The Non-Dead offer the cheapest contracts for labor, leading more people into long periods of poverty and the need for Non-Dead loans."

Fola relaxed her posture and nodded. "Well said, cousin. I will not permit unnecessary despair among those I am bound to protect. Wealthy families may prefer Non-Dead servants. I prefer to compensate the living."

Every ritual we embrace brings us a step closer to what we
were before the Nihl.

The Unnamed Scribe
Discussion on Human Reemergence

I N THE PURPLE DEPTHS of night, another cloaked figure arrived in New Brasilia. Instead of coming from the sky, this figure walked alone on the only passage leading from Sparta. Infrequent waves from the Greconian Sea muffled the figure's casual approach.

A pair of New Brasilian guards stood at the base of the towering metal door surrounding the city should any Spartans decide to approach uninvited. One woman shifted into a defensive position, while the other raised a cautious hand. "Halt, traveler. Present your passport."

"Yes." The hooded figure extended a hand gloved in black leather with parallel wires circling each finger. His fingers extended a metal and plastic card to reveal his purpose and his identity.

The guard who spoke took the card and scanned it with a tablet she'd taken from her waist. The defensive Amazon braced a rifle on top of a gold-embossed riot shield.

"Roker?"

The hooded figure nodded. "I am Roker."

The guard tapped her tablet. "It says here you're a Non-Dead."

"Some of us still have our wits."

"I see." The guard scrunched her lips and failed to blink her bloodshot eyes. "What business do you have on New Brasilia?"

"I wish to speak with Lord Caium Caracalla. I know he is visiting from Roma Vatica."

"That's an Imperial matter." The guard pulled the card away from her tablet and passed it back to Roker. "I can't help you with that."

"May I pass?"

"Not without permission from the palace. And not until morning."

Roker remained absolutely still for several seconds. "I expected as much."

The Non-Dead's hand stretched farther than possible for a man of his size. He grabbed the guard's wrist, twisting her toward the pavement.

The second guard turned her rifle toward Roker's head. "Let her go."

Roker flashed a grin from the shadows of his abyssal hood. "You may both surrender now."

The first guard screamed from the ground, violently flailing her arms and legs. After an agonizing few seconds, her fingers frantically clawed at the back of her neck.

Roker glided back to a standing position.

Rifle blasts tore into the Non-Dead's body, burning holes in his cloak for an instant after every burst of reddish-pink plasma ate through the heavy cloth.

"I'm already dead." He swept forward like a billowing cloud of absolute shadow, snatching the rifle away before it could fire again. The weapon glowed before dripping into molten slag. "You should have raised the alarm when you had the chance."

The wires surrounding Roker's fingers turned bright as he clamped his hands over the remaining guard's face. Satisfaction rose through

Roker's implants in the certainty that he overwhelmed the guard with the smell of her own ash.

Bells tolled at the onset of dawn, drawing the Virago and those they protected to the Temple of the Elagabal. Priestesses and priests clad in sheer white robes approached the broad stained glass dome, opening every sun-bleached door so all might enter.

As Vari entered, she watched the unstained lens in the center of the dome, the Noon Door. At midday one seeking the Elagabal's solar wisdom would bask in the most intense light of the day. Only the most devout priestesses and priests were allowed to look through the Noon Door, enriching their faith with deeper enlightenment. A sacred sight, one a queen couldn't even ask to experience. Each morning, it drew Vari's gaze through the lens, enchanting her with a longing to see beyond the sky.

Those outside the clergy had to content themselves with a smaller lens positioned to face the horizon. Though the Eye of the Risen was the epicenter of mundane worship, it illuminated with a warm intensity hinting at the day to come. Any wishing to publicly demonstrate the allegiance of their souls gathered to view the dawn through a devout position within the Temple.

With her aunt and mother to the left and Saran to her right, Vari crossed the red-orange carpet of the main aisle, kneeling on a row of pillows arranged before a rail of polished wood and woven wrought iron. Ahead of them, a star sparkled through a vast concave window. Many feet shuffled through the Temple, connected knees pressed into sterile pillows and fresh blankets, allowing all to witness the birth of a new day.

Dawn rose into the window, flooding the Temple of the Elagabal with cleansing rays of light.

Under the vast window, a carved altar framed the underside of the great cosmic eye. Solus, the highest-ranked priest, walked on the opposite side of the rail before laying his hands and forehead upon the stone rim of the altar. "Praise be Elagabal, God of All Stars and bringer of their wisdom." Solus shot up, clapping his hands together. "Thank you for the brilliant day."

A unison of voices responded. "The day is radiant with your light. Let us be worthy of it."

Worth wasn't enough, not for a woman bound by love of her family, duty to her nation, and the craving in her heart. Caracalla's coming punctuated the division that threatened to destroy Vari. The only worth the galaxy saw in Vari was in redeeming the legacy of Sextus Severus and punishing the Usurper's treachery.

Only the throne of Roma Vatica could prove Vari's worth. Without it, she'd only ever be the child of a diminished noble House, the last descendant of the generals who broke free from the Nihl. Seven such Houses had already fallen away from Elagabal's grace, though many in the galaxy claimed that number was eleven.

Bassiana brushed her fingers against Vari's shoulder and whispered. "Is something wrong?"

"No." Vari frowned under a cloud of martial obligation. "Nothing more than usual."

From his guest room in the palace, Geta glared at the trail of bodies pushing toward the domed Temple of the Elagabal. "Heathens. They only keep as many tokens to Jupiter as the law requires."

Lysandra stretched over the bed. Sheets buried most of her body, allowing only an arm, a leg, and her head to sprawl free. "Shall I find a statue and break it for you? Or hide it long enough for you to mark it against them?"

"Hush your heresy, woman." Geta scowled at the ease that he'd responded to a moronic suggestion. His teeth gnashed together while he released an intense exhale. "I refuse to have someone under my banner do anything so ridiculous, no matter the status of your heathen god."

Lysandra rose with a furrowed brow. "Cybele is accepted—"

"Hush." A trembling index finger burrowed through the air, closing in on Lysandra. Geta's face tensed, burrowing deep, enraged lines under his skin. "You will not say such things." He halted his tongue behind heavy breaths. "Invoke the queen of molestation if you want, but do it where I cannot hear. You will remember your place or I will take the lash to you."

"Forgive me." Lysandra bowed to Geta lower than the Amazons bowed to their own queen. "As your wife, you are first in my heart." Lysandra rose again, cloaked in deference. Her eyes beamed with unbroken conviction.

Every damned Gallae offered the same level of loyalty. Utter devotion in their hearts, while their minds wove through hidden plans and deeper strategies. Gallae always tested their boundaries with little efforts and futile comments. Lysandra wasn't stupid enough to think simple vandalism would turn the Empire against New Brasilia. Her purpose was to ensure the Cybeline hadn't sold her to a fool. The true test was to see if Lysandra was loyal to her husband or to her wretched faith.

With a groan, Geta shook his head. "If you weren't protected, I'd make you convert."

Lysandra stood, draping a sheet around her like it was a Senator's robe. She approached Geta, stroking his right ear and jaw with affection. Her natural musk mingled with the remnants of her personal fragrance. "Might I recommend we pry the young man. He appeared enchanted by my presence. I could free his secrets and present them to you."

Geta's eyes widened with curiosity and excitement. "Do you have enough guile to extract such things?" His last Gallae-wife didn't.

A coy expression lifted from the corner of Lysandra's mouth. "I could try."

Outside the window, several armored Brasilian soldiers ran toward the Temple.

A resigned sigh sank Geta's tension. He took his wife's sizable, delicate hand, kissing the soft tissue of her palm. "Something is happening. It will disrupt these heathens." Geta licked the slope of Lysandra's hand and kissed her wrist. "Prove how loyal a wife you are. Spy for me, but make sure he only sees the demure girl he covets."

Despite the warmer climate of New Brasilia, a morning run cleansed Caracalla's senses. Fragrant patches of honeysuckle lined the stone path under his feet. All was calm and peace until a thunder of armored boots rushed through the intersection behind him. A cluster of Brasilian soldiers sprinted for the domed temple surrounded by so many of the local citizens.

He picked up his pace, racing toward the soldiers. When he was close enough, Caracalla sucked in a deep breath before calling to the sprinters. "In the name of Imperator Macrinus, tell me what's happened."

A single soldier glared back, one of the few men among the New Brasilian ranks. "Murder, General. Spies from Sparta may be in New Brasilia."

Caracalla clasped a fist to his chest. "My thanks."

The soldier ran onward. Caracalla turned to the quartet of unarmored centurions meant to protect him. "To my quarters at once. Double-time. I must pen a letter."

A cadre of dutiful soldiers rushed into the Temple of the Elagabal. Sparse whispers shot out as they commanded the worshipers to clear a path through the main aisle. When the soldiers reached the royal entourage near the front railing, Fola and Bassiana stood. The Queen spoke. "What's happened?"

All but one soldier knelt. The remaining soldier passed the queen a tablet before sliding to one knee. "Two guards at the Spartan lane were killed in the night. The dawn shift discovered them burned from the inside out. One of their rifles was melted."

"How many got in?"

The soldier's head lowered. "We don't know. The footage and registration memory has been corrupted."

Fola swept a finger across the tablet screen, skimming the abrupt end to the digital recordings. She played the recording again, squinting to look past erratic lines of electrical interference.

Bassiana solidified her stance, glancing at the screen for a moment. "Spartans?"

For hundreds of years, Sparta quietly wanted to claim the entirety of their planet. If New Brasilia wasn't possessed of ferocity and conviction, no truce would hold back the might of warrior-kings. Cultural refinement didn't deprive New Brasilia of the power to fight. Both nations stared across bridges of trade, exchanging goods and finances. Both held back their strongest commodity, knowing an open war would destroy both of their nations.

Fola passed the tablet to her cousin. "Their king is too busy dealing with Sekht to send spies to kill two guards." The Queen gazed at the soldiers. "Double the posting at the gate. Seal it when it's not in use. See to it yourselves."

The group spoke as a unit and rose. "Yes, my queen." They raced down the aisle as fast as they'd come in.

Fola bowed to the priest and the Eye of the Risen. "My apologies, Solus. It appears the Elagabal has decided to test us early today."

Solus bowed to the queen in response. "I have faith in your success."

Fola left, taking the dawn congregation with her.

Vari marched across the plaza, chasing after the anger in the queen's stride. Every step Fola took echoed with the weight of New Brasilia itself. Vari's attempts to keep up chirped in the echo of a galaxy.

Without turning or slowing down, Fola issued further orders, keeping her reign running like a precise pocket watch. "Cousin, I want you and Varius to stay in my study. I'll send an extra complement of guards."

Bassiana gripped the skirt of her dress with ferocity as she kept up. "What about the Imperials?"

"I'll offer to increase their security, though I doubt our intruder is foolish enough to provoke our esteemed guests. We will have swift justice. By this time tomorrow, I intend to see this murderer swing. Saran?"

The young woman dashed an extra step faster. "Yes, Highness?"

"Take House Severus to my study at once." Formal labels for family sang of the slow boil of rage growing in Fola's heart. "Everyone else, to the gate with me." Fola took any surrounding soldiers on a hard right angle, marching toward the Spartan border.

Vari huddled close to Saran and Bassiana. Rather than focus on her family, she thought about Caracalla. The general's ambitions aimed at Sparta and Vari herself. Was Caracalla plotting something?

A thousand plots from across the galaxy whirled around Vari. New Brasilia blossomed with suspicion and probability. Hatred's lineage reached between stars, desperate to ensnare Vari, her family, and the small morsel of inheritance she'd been allowed to keep.

"Macrinus." The hushed whisper of the Usurper's name squeezed Vari's stomach. Her enemy had to be at the heart of the growing doom.

A centurion marched away from the guest wing of the palace, his crested helmet aimed toward Bassiana. With so many fighters in the Imperial retinue, any of them could be the killer. Even this one. The centurion clasped his fist against his chest before snapping a folded envelope toward Bassiana. "Princess Bassiana, a message from my lord."

Bassiana took the envelope, pulling loose the unsealed flap. "Geta or Caracalla?"

"Lord Caracalla, Princess."

Bassiana lifted the cream-toned paper, pressing her thumb beside the freshly inked signature. After a few moments, she closed it once more. "Thank you, Centurion. Tell your lord I understand and accept."

The centurion clasped his chest again, then turned about. He returned on the same path he'd came.

Dread weighed upon Vari's mouth. She strained against the possibilities, forcing herself to confront the future. "What is it?"

"Caracalla wants to see you in an hour. He requests your private counsel on New Brasilia and this morning's activities."

Saran scowled. "I'll go with him."

"You'll do no such thing. Your queen left you direct orders. The only way for you to attend Caracalla's meeting would be to invite the general into my cousin's study." Bassiana let Saran's mind absorb the reality of their situation.

Vari already struggled to process the facts of the moment. Any request for her counsel was nothing but a pretense for Caracalla's still-hidden goals. The trap waited to claw deep into the concealed young woman. "You intend to have me meet with him."

Bassiana beckoned them to continue their journey to Fola's study. "It would appear so."

In the first meetings that formed the Unnamed Empire,
anyone who advocated for peace was killed.
Such is why Varia embraced war in all its forms.

The Clarion
Shaping The Imperatrix

FOR HER MEETING WITH Caracalla, Vari wore a fresh black shirt over a pair of tan pants. A tight band kept her dark hair away from her face. Since Caracalla was a guest of Imperial stature, he'd been provided chambers befitting that rank. Vari glared at the centurions posted in each corner of the spacious anteroom. All of them wore full armor, complete with war-ready shields and spears.

The general wore a centurion's uniform pants and tunic, both garments crafted in a durable weave of white trimmed with red. Caracalla rested a hand over a portable weapons rack. An energized smile grew from the large man's chin. "Young Severus. Thank you for coming."

Vari approached before giving a respectful nod. "No thanks are necessary, Lord Caracalla."

Silence hung between them, clawing at their ears and voices. The threat of a shared future repulsed them both as much as it drew them together. Caracalla nodded. "What are your preliminary thoughts on Sparta's encroachment of the outer gate?"

"It's not necessarily from Sparta."

"I trust you have good cause to defend the enemies of your maternal lineage."

For Vari, it was enough that Fola didn't suspect Sparta. But Caracalla made it known he wanted to study Vari for some undisclosed purpose. Any questions from the general were clearly part of a deeper test.

"Spartan tactics are based on positioning and cooperative reliance." As a noble heir or neighbor to a martial nation, Vari had her own studies to call upon. "Spartans rarely allow single combat, nor do they work in subterfuge."

"Perhaps they've changed tactics."

"No. Spartans use fast, decisive strikes. If they wanted to attack New Brasilia, they would come in force or not at all."

Caracalla took a casual breath before relaxing his gaze. "Who would attack your nation, if not Sparta?"

The ease of the question slapped Vari like a sweaty blanket on a hot night. If the previous questions were a test, there was no reason for that test to have already ended.

"The answer depends on your motives, Lord Caracalla."

The general stepped behind the weapons rack, resting his palms on the top corners. "My motive here is to observe you, Young Severus. No matter the political climate, you are still part of a noble lineage and represent potential for humanity. Our species has too many splintered sects and heretical factions. Even now, Imperial and Spartan forces stand against Sekht. Such a division would allow the Nihl to destroy us, should they ever return."

Vari smirked at the general's dodgy answer. "Who did you fight for ten years ago, Lord Caracalla?"

"Humanity, Young Severus. And the Unnamed Empire." Caracalla tapped his fingers against the weapons rack. "Draw a weapon, any you prefer."

Caracalla's test collided between insight and action. Or the general wanted something outside the factional or political.

The rack held a long and short staff, a history of knives, a javelin, a spear, a whip, and two swords, one curved, the other short. No guns waited to blaze with life. Nothing present resembled one of the greater swords, though Vari would have avoided such a weapon. Every centurion shuffled as Vari examined her choices. Each blade was forged to atomic sharpness. Only the most durable woods composed the handles of either staff.

Caracalla frowned. "You're stalling."

Vari favored length and reach while fighting. She snatched the spear from the rack, sweeping the tip upward. She rested the dull end on the floor. "Satisfied?"

The general hooked his finger at Vari and stepped back. "Mitchell, Kell." Two centurions converged from their defensive positions. They rang their spears twice on the floor and held their shields high. Caracalla held his left hand toward the centurions. "Strike the armor on either of these men. They will defend."

With no offering of armor, Vari crouched into a defensive stance as she prowled around the centurions. A promise of defense was not a refusal to attack. Vari bent her right arm to brace the back of the spear while supporting the shaft between her left thumb and index finger.

Her targets shifted, lining their shields to make a defensive barrier. Both centurions altered their stances, watching like hunters behind the broad, rectangular shields.

The left centurion's eyes shifted frequently, lacking the stability of his partner.

Vari steadied her posture with stoic rigidity, locking her strategy in place. She took a few short steps closer, making to attack. Instead of pushing forward with the spear, Vari locked her vision with the left centurion before making an air kiss that puckered against the air.

The centurion recoiled for half a second. Vari jabbed the spear downward, aiming at the man's feet. Both centurions slammed their shields down, blocking the spear tip. Vari dropped the spear, clamping her right hand over the top of her target's shield. By using the shield as a fulcrum point, Vari swung her left hand around. A quick jab bounced off the left centurion's chest plate.

"Hold." The centurions composed themselves and stepped back while Caracalla approached. The general glared down at Vari. "What was that?"

"Distraction." Vari gave no satisfaction at her performance. She did not need to pass Caracalla's tests, nor did she care about failing them. Only her own pleasure mattered, along with the pride of her lineage. "I used the moment to create a slight variance in how one centurion held his shield. That let me use my spear to create an opening where I could close the distance fast enough to strike."

A half-irritated grin filled Caracalla's face as he nodded. "I didn't say to strike with the weapon you'd chosen. Clever." Caracalla's expression eased. "You give pride to your father's name."

No Imperial ever hinted at the former Imperator's pride. For Caracalla to do so might belie an ally or reveal a powerful enemy. Under the endless web of obligations, Vari knew only a single response. "Thank you."

The general lifted a finger. "I'd still like to see how well you fight, not just your tenacity for strategy. When I have the chance, I will have to compliment your mother and the queen on your education."

Distant clashes echoed through the halls at a volume only Roker could hear. Every conversation, from mundane to administrative, chimed through advanced Non-Dead ears. The metallic clashes proved odd compared to every other sound throughout the palace. So much of the structure was restrained and peaceful, especially for a nation of warriors and archers.

New Brasilia wasn't the focus of any collective concern. It was a step to climb on the path to the greatest prize. The Unnamed Empire was an oyster waiting to be prised open, allowing the pearl inside to be claimed.

To clear that path, flames needed to be fanned and old fires stoked to a howling roar. The old enmity of the previous decade hadn't died out. Bitter conflicts only needed an excuse for rebirth, a reason never applied.

Roker's scouts had fulfilled their duties, paying off the meager debts of their mortal lives. The incinerated remains of a Non-Dead clung to the gaps between tiles. Digital stains saturated geographic wounds into the armor of Virago. Roker planned to wound Severus, if only to ignite the coming battle.

Across from the palace wine cellar, a digital radiance washed toward the hallway. The sole mandated statue of Jupiter sparkled before the sensors of Roker's eyes. Amazons always thought Non-Dead nothing more than pathetic servants trapped in an eternity of servitude. No warrior nation would revel in the ultimate victory to come.

Roker stroked the proud statue. No switch lay concealed in Jupiter's muscles. The Imperial god offered no access lever, nor did he present a card reader.

The arched indentation behind the statue stood with more pride than the supposed god. Roker pushed against the sides of the arch. His foot tapped along the digital stains marking the plinth below the statue. An echo rolled lower than the distant clanging, so Roker pushed his foot against the floor tiles while shoving against the arch.

With a click, the entire section of wall shifted to the right, opening a tunnel full of secretive darkness. Such a passage was too tempting not to follow.

Caracalla paced around the room, examining Vari from every angle. The general's stare wasn't like the measured analysis the frequented Mhati's training lessons. Something sharper waited within Caracalla's gaze.

"I have only a single test remaining for my evaluation." Caracalla snatched the spear from the floor. His fingers pressed where Vari previously held the weapon. The general signaled a third centurion to hand over a pistol.

"Mitchell. Kell." A heavy breath ran away from Caracalla. "Kill Varius Severus."

"What?" Vari shifted backward, bracing her fists and arms for combat.

The pair of centurions lifted their shields and angled their spears. Both moved in opposite directions, ready to flank Varius.

"Young Severus." Caracalla lifted the pistol and spear parallel to each other. "Do you know the fundamental reason why humanity adopted archaic weaponry when fighting the Nihl?"

A spear thrust shot toward Vari's abdomen. If she'd been any slower to evade the strike, she would have already been impaled.

"It's not a taunt, young Severus. I expect an answer."

The test continued outside of raw assassination. Both centurions shifted to herd Vari against a wall or corner. Their eyes fixated with unyielding intensity, especially from the soldier Vari distracted before.

"Standard firearms didn't work against the Nihl." The other guards blocked the door leading away from Caracalla's guest quarters. Vari had even odds of finding centurions or her aunt's forces once she reached the hallway.

"We have beam weapons, many stronger than this pistol." Caracalla held the weapon higher. "Why don't we use those?"

"They don't deal damage fast enough."

A centurion shoved forward with a spear thrust, followed instantly by a shield bash. Vari spun on one heel, rolling her body against the shield and its bearer. She twisted behind the soldier, hooking her foot around the centurion's ankle. A shove dropped him to the floor.

Caracalla paced along the perimeter of the room. "We could bear more guns against the aliens."

The standing centurion used the melee to thrust his spear at Vari. The young woman caught the weapon by its shaft—only for the centurion to release the spear. Vari fell. The floor slapped her shoulder blades.

A gladius snapped into the standing centurion's hand. The sword's tip shot toward Vari with repeated thrusts.

The other centurion stood, bearing both spear and shield.

"Young Severus, answer me or I will order another of my men to kill you." Caracalla's voice remained steady and analytical as he continued pacing. "What is the real reason why we didn't use mass produced weapons?"

Vari parried another spear thrust as he twisted up to a crouching position. The gladius rapidly jabbed at her. She swung the stolen spear at the stocky sword. The refined edge sliced through the pinky side of Vari's hand. A wince smothered her lips.

If a greater sword had been on the rack, Vari could have used it to keep her distance from the centurions and destroy their weapons. Perhaps Caracalla knew Vari had trained with the largest type of melee weapon—a practice common for anyone born the son of the Imperator.

"The Nihl had Quantum technology." Vari shifted right, making occasional thrusts through a widening web of wet agony. Her wounded hand seared against every emphatic motion. "We stole what we could and used it against them."

"Excellent." Joy flooded Caracalla's rising smile. "You finally pieced it together. Why are you still fighting?"

"Because they haven't killed me."

The general nodded. "True, but you haven't killed them."

If Vari killed a centurion, it wouldn't just be a scandal, it invited charges of treason.

Both centurions closed ranks, bracing their shields against their bodies, eliminating the space between them.

Vari struck back, swinging her spear like an elongated club. When the centurions slowed for an instant, Vari rammed the spear into a shield.

The protective plate turned unwieldy and fell from its owner's grasp. The shieldless centurion shifted his spear, much like Vari had before.

Another series of thrusts shot from the gladius. Vari pivoted away from the sword and rushed for the shieldless centurion. Vari clamped her hands around the spear. The soldier refused to surrender another weapon. Vari punched the spear shaft with the base of her palm. Bits of wood pierced Vari's hand as the spear broke, knocking the shieldless centurion backward.

Still unarmed, Vari darted for the weapons rack. She pulled loose the first thing she touched. The long staff in her hands warded back a centurion, but wobbled too much to fight off hardened soldier. A centurion's boot locked the staff against the floor, depriving the weapon of any worth.

Vari snatched a short sword from the rack. She turned, needing a hasty defense. Her arm and foot bumped the rack, toppling it to the floor. Every remaining weapon lay trapped under a web of folded metal and wood. Metallic chimes and heavy lacquered ricochets echoed against the tiled floor.

"What a mess." Caracalla shook his head. "Poor form, young Severus. That's exactly what killed your father."

The low fire sat close to dormancy for a decade before erupting into a fresh burst of steaming magma. Rage had no place in the void left by a lost father. The sudden inertia came from the unrealized ambitions in Varia's soul.

Vari hacked half of the long staff free. The cleaved stick parried any attacks from the centurions. A gladius jutted at her abdomen. Vari saw the blade with her eyes, but her heart imagined the Twelfth Quantum Sword. For an instant, the Usurper mocked House Severus from the safety of a plumed helmet.

Vari's short sword thrust upward, stabbing through any available metal, flesh, or bone.

A wet, reddened blade hung in Vari's grasp. The shieldless centurion mirrored the young woman's posture. Both prowled closer, ready to spill the other's intestines across the tiled floor.

"Did poor combat skills get your father killed, young Severus? Is that why your House no longer holds a Quantum sword?"

The words jabbed through Vari's mind. Again, the Usurper mocked her with only an armored glare.

Years of permitting false faith weighed upon the young woman's shoulders. A single statue was too much, no matter what purpose it served. Vari was no mere noble prince. She was the Heir of the true Imperator, even if countless legions saluted the fiction of Macrinus.

Vari didn't need luck to fight a single soldier. Over a decade of lessons, physical and mental, surged within her body. Every being had an opening, one a quick fighter could exploit. A combatant slowed by armor, even agile centurion armor, begged for someone to strike.

Wrists remained protected. Faces lay in a nest of metal, communications, and padding. But none of those things defended a soldier from an accelerated strike. Especially not when Vari exploded with unrestrained fury.

The shieldless centurion scrambled backward, clawing at the short sword embedded in his helmet and face. Deeper shades of red drifted over the centurion's neck and chest.

"I don't know what happened with my father." Vari wiped sweat from her brow. "I was a child."

"Not good enough."

Vari shook her head and stomped toward the door. "I don't care."

A searing blast shot the tiles ahead of Vari. Bitter ozone teased the young woman's nose.

Caracalla lowered his pistol. The general refused to blink. "I did not give you permission to leave."

Blood dripped from Vari's wounded hand as she closed her fists. After several deep breaths, her voice softened. "If I had my father's sword, I'd never need your permission."

Caracalla nodded. "A truth I'll not question. I hope you'll reflect on that. I know I will." The general gestured for the remaining centurions to stand down. "We will speak again, young Severus."

A snarl pushed Vari's lip toward her nose. "Animal." She left.`

In the course of history, someone always stands in the
path of greatness. Humans and Nihl served this purpose
to each other. Diadumenian stood in Varia's way. Sparta
blocked New Brasilia's quest for vengeance.
There is no guarantee of success when this happens.

Lucian Ateius
Insights in the Age of Quantum

V ARI STORMED AWAY FROM the guest wing of the palace. She
scowled through time at her mother. Stress furrowed her brow.
The gash in her hand lit with a burning itch. None of it would have
happened if her mother had forbidden her from meeting with Caracalla.

The general had invoked the memory of Sextus Severus enough for
Vari to recall her father's face. Dark hair, kind eyes, a pale smile to reassure
a curious child. Macrinus forbade such visages in the Unnamed Empire.

Early edicts from the Usurper forbade public displays honoring the
former Imperator. In the decade since, Vari hadn't been allowed to see
her father's face. Scavenged images lay hidden within Vari's room, the
least of the crimes she maintained in secret. With the assessor nearby,
such places were too dangerous to visit.

A tall, fashionable woman appeared before Vari. Luminous shades of
jade drifted over perfected curves. A veil of whispers floated before the
pleasant outline of Lysandra's sculpted face.

Vari couldn't evade the Gallae. Rage boiled within her moistened hands. Desire stiffened her movements. The woman had spotted her. Ignoring Lysandra would offend all of House Geta.

Once she was close enough, Vari offered a polite bow. "Good morning, Lady Geta."

"Good morning, young sir." Her voice remained soft, a perfect emblem of her training. "I seem to have lost my escort."

"There was a disturbance earlier." She'd never reveal her aunt's stresses, especially not to the assessor's wife. "More guards should have been sent to your quarters."

A delicate hand touched the woman's mouth, separated only by her translucent veil. Even her fingernails bore a shade of green to match the rest of her outfit. "I had taken a walk just after breakfast. I've seen people running from a distance. Was that the disturbance?"

"Responders, most likely." With no one else around, decorum presented Vari no other option, even after her meeting with Caracalla. "Should I escort you back to your chambers?"

"Please." Lysandra's smile glowed through her veil. "I would be most appreciative."

Vari smiled back, unsure of how much to restrain or express herself. Her infatuation with the Gallae was already public knowledge, though she wasn't the first person to look at such a woman with visual and emotional curiosity. Vari admired Lysandra's bravery for transforming into a complete Gallae. Not needing to hide herself, but allowing it to come into the open always filled Vari with amazement and envy. She loved the ability of someone to become their truest self. Such explorations were impossible for Vari. She would never be herself in public spaces, nor would anyone ever see her as she was. Always a noble heir, hopefully an Imperator, but never simply a woman.

As Vari lifted her arm to act as escort, Lysandra winced. "Oh my." Her eyes matched her mouth, sloping into a worried pout. "What happened to your hands?"

The wounds on Vari's hand remained fresh and flowing. A few spots of clotting dotted the edges of the long cut. "It's—it's nothing."

"That's far too much blood to be nothing." Lysandra's gaze darted though her exquisite blossom fragrance. "I wish I knew where to find some bandages."

"It looks worse than it actually is." Vari pulled her hand back, not wanting to mar the lady's jade dress. "I'll escort you to your quarters then see to this scratch."

Lysandra cupped her fingers around Vari's arm, even after she'd withdrawn. "There's a sink in my quarters. I will tend to your wound."

Bassiana watched the steady flow of soldiers from the relative safety of her cousin's study. Both local and Imperial forces increased their patrols, blocking sunlight from every doorway and arch. Hundreds of eyes searched for some killer from the night.

"My lady." Saran spoke in a softened tone. "Please sit. I can make you some tea."

"I don't want tea." Bassiana's stern whisper spoke of her deeper concern, a focus greater than any spear or sword might ever manage.

"There's nothing either of us can do. As you and our queen have said, we must cooperate with the Imperials." A heavy sigh rolled from Saran as she flopped onto a chair. "If the Usurper stations a permanent garrison here, nothing will work in our favor."

Without a word, Bassiana sat. The cuffs of her favored Temple dress billowed out as she pressed her hands over an antique reading desk. Her palms squeezed over the lacquered smoothness of the surface. After contemplating the space between her thumbs, an even softer whisper emerged. "They hate us. Our mothers and aunts shot down the ships. Greater swords tore directly through the Nihl, only because of the vigilance of New Brasilia. Since Imperial hands worked the filthy business, they stole the glory. They named themselves protectors of humanity."

"Vari is heir to those protectors."

Bassiana rang her left fist against the table. "Her father had some sense. Sextus was the first rational Imperial in centuries. He married me to keep Fola happy."

A pale, young hand pressed over Bassiana's fingers. Saran leaned close, possessed of a stern mouth and a determined spirit. "My lady, you're being too hard on yourself."

"Am I?" The princess spoke at the volume of the queen she was raised to become. "After all this time, the Unnamed Empire has come to my home intent on telling me I must give them my son so my husband's enemies might be happy." Her darkened eyelids tensed with a hatred beyond her words. "We are nothing to them."

Saran folded her hands upon her stomach. "I'm sorry, my lady."

Bassiana breathed deep before massaging Saran's coarse, tanned wrist. "Why should you feel sorrow for my words?"

Saran held joined her hands to Bassiana's, shattering any barrier between their ache. "I share your pain, the terror that something might happen to Vari. Neither of us can do anything about it now, no matter how deeply it stings our souls."

Silence hovered between them, but neither broke even a finger of contact. "You're being quite familiar today, Saran."

The bronzed blonde smiled. "If it puts your mind at ease, I'll be your best friend."

"Are you that desperate for friends?"

"Are you that desperate to cling onto Vari?"

Bassiana snapped to her feet and snatched her hands away. "Do not mock me."

"I'm not." Saran clasped her hands and lowered her head. "Nothing is for certain. You know that."

The door swept open, allowing Fola to march inside. "What do we know?"

Bassiana steadied herself. "Saran believes Vari will pass, even if much of me wishes she would fail."

"Then Varia would die," the queen said. "Did Caracalla call for her?"

"As soon as you were called away." Bassiana sighed. With a glance, she ordered Saran to prepare the suggested tea. "Have we learned anything new about last night's attack?"

Fola took her ivory seat, stretching over the chair. "No. Signs of a struggle." She shook her head. "Those poor girls. Someone melted their entire nervous systems."

"Melted?" Bassiana scowled. "What an awful way to die."

"Whoever did this may or may not have a connection to Caracalla. If they do, we must discover their purpose." Fola stroked the carved edges of her right armrest. "If they have no connection..." Another instant of hesitation locked Fola's mouth. "They must be found."

Vari followed Lysandra into Geta's guest chambers. The rooms bore the same layout as Caracalla's, but lacked any of the martial intent. Centurions hadn't even guarded the door. Vari assumed they'd gone off with the assessor during the commotion.

Lysandra towered beside the lavatory door as she swept back her veil. Unimpeded, her brown locks and luminous highlights glowed like a heavenly trophy. "Thank you for escorting me."

"My pleasure." Vari eased cautiously into the lavatory. From the corner of her eye, she saw the mussed bedsheets, certain they'd been used for more than sleep. She twisted the knobs of the faucet, drowning her senses for a saturated instant. Decorum demanded she clean her wounds. Something primal screamed for her to stay.

Vari gently lifted her hands. "I still need to tend these wounds."

"It will take more than cuts for you to offend me." Lysandra's words glided like a spring breeze.

Vari doubted Lord Geta would share his wife's opinions.

Lysandra took a single step into the lavatory. "Do I need to find you some bandages?"

The Gallae's perfectly calibrated fragrance swept around Vari, beckoning her with unspoken possibility. She squirmed excitedly within the measured allure, no matter the purpose Lysandra intended for her scent.

A splinter fell loose from Vari's palm. The wound was a blessing, so long as it kept her focused.

Lysandra quietly observed. Verdant grace surrounded her. Her softest breath hinted at her flawless waist and her delicate neck. Curiosity begged Vari to touch Lysandra, or even the emerald seams of her dress.

The Gallae stroked the door facing with her middle finger. "Do I offend you, Varius?"

"No." Warmth ran through her cheeks at the unfiltered sound of her legal name. "Why would you offend me?"

"When you watch me, your eyes cry with curiosity." Lysandra smiled. A brunette wisp tumbled over her cheek. "Every twitch of your brow craves to undress me. Your fingers curl to touch the fullness of my rank."

The water stung. Steam rolled into Vari's nose. A faint hue of red swirled into the drain, making the flowing water shimmer brighter. "I'm not sure what you mean."

"Don't be coy." Lysandra grinned. She eased a second step closer. "You want to touch me, if only to make sure I'm real."

"If you weren't real," Vari said between increasingly deeper breaths. "We wouldn't be talking."

Another step forward from Lysandra compelled Vari to join her. Lysandra moistened the edge of her upper lip with the tip of her tongue. "Then call me your desire. Imagine what you want. We can make that real."

Between Lysandra's impressive height and fashionable shoes, Vari had to look upward, even as seduction curled closer. Greater needs filled the young woman, a craving to see herself that had never been realized. "I have other desires."

Lysandra reached around Vari, shutting the water off. The Gallae's body wedged between Varius and the sink. Their hips brushed together.

"Do I intimidate you, Varius?" Her hands braced against the edge of the sink, feigning submission. "I'm not much taller than you. And you clearly stand taller than my husband."

Vari wasn't pinned in the lavatory. She had at least two ways out, only needing an excuse to escape. "Perhaps we should find him. It would be poor form to allow an honored guest to be hurt."

The Gallae leaned in, entwining her lips with Vari's. Her kiss tasted of cherries and scandalous acceptance. Lysandra's mouth opened with an unfiltered invitation.

But the psyche of an ambitious heir yanked Vari away.

Lysandra flexed her lips inward, suckling on the remains of Vari's contact. "I'm made for perfection, Varius. There's no reason to force a distance between us."

Curled fingers cupped over Vari's mouth. She suddenly envied the shape of Lysandra's lips. "You're married."

"Your sex drive is more active now than it will ever be." She drifted two soft fingertips down the side of Vari's face. "You can't impregnate me, so I'm perfect for satisfying you."

Vari lowered her hand without meeting Lysandra's face. "Your husband would be offended."

"No. He wouldn't." Lysandra tilted Vari's chin upward. "We discussed it this morning, before the commotion started." Lysandra leaned for a kiss, but refused to make contact. "I want you, Varius. Take me once, make me your mistress, kill my husband, and claim his property for yourself. Any way suits me." She kissed Vari for an instant, her teeth and tongue drilling with desire. "This is my purpose in life."

Vari clamped her eyes shut. Questions gnawed her, threatening to emerge into conscious thought. Ideas swelled within her, things she wanted outside of the privacy of her concealed room.

A whimper creaked from her voice. "I can't."

Lysandra pressed a finger over Vari's lips. A clean fragrance of petals and wonder hooked into every sensation Vari possessed.

"There's nothing you have to do," Lysandra said. "Leave all the work to me."

Lady Lysandra said nothing to suggest Varius Severus was
capable of such an atrocity.
Could we have missed something?

Only the Non-Dead.

Stray Message Sent by Gallae Priestess Cybeline

R OKER TOOK NOTHING FROM the hidden room after confirming its contents. Others needed to discover its wonders without interference. When he examined the concealed treasures, he studied every wrinkle, analyzing each criminal shape before committing it to digital memory. In time, Roker would load each image onto a data card, if only to motivate interested parties.

He left the secret room behind, stopping at the first arched window he reached. Several centurions paced around the perimeter of the palace, though their speed matched a regular patrol rather than a force dealing with a crisis. None of the Brasilians were in sight. Roker entertained the possibility that the Amazons were still hunting him.

Other locations still waited for his examination. None of them would have half the wonders he'd witnessed. The katas, the clothes, the chamber as a whole was more than Geta and Macrinus could imagine.

It would cost them to get such evidence. Roker knew the Imperator would pay.

Vari coiled her arms around her body. Every second reminded her of her wrongness, the incorrect shape of her bones, the cruelty of her wayward hormones. She'd been touched for a pleasant moment, torn away from herself. Her breathing refused to steady.

Bliss wasn't typically found leaning against a lavatory countertop

She'd meant to clean her wounds after applying the decorum of a noble host. Instead, her bloodstream thickened with a bouquet of cravings she'd never considered. Lysandra hadn't needed to insist on a prying tease. The Gallae's mouth had danced in shattering perfection.

If she'd been in Lysandra's place, Vari was certain a blinding tide of bliss would consume her.

Just as Lysandra promised, she'd dazzled Varius with her efforts. A plying kiss. A graze of teeth upon skin. The options were more boundless than rumors suggested. Vari needed to breathe in Lysandra's hair, massage her neck, taste her wrists—

A wily smile curled upon Lysandra's face. The shade on her cheeks and lips hadn't smudged. "Still stunned?"

The last flakes of decorum forced Vari to nod. "I've never felt anything like that before."

"You should imagine what we'll do next." Lysandra turned, resting a palm on the sink while two fingers traced the shape of Vari's jaw. "When should I find you? Tonight? Tomorrow?"

At the edge of holding her breath, Vari clenched her teeth closed. "It's not that easy."

"Of course it is. You know why I'm here." She slowly withdrew her hand. "You kneel at the sunrise, I embrace the shape of my flesh. If you can pray to your god, why can't I do the same?"

Vari's jaw slipped open. Her eyes crept wide at the notion of Lysandra sharing her faith. Stepping from an imperfect body into living artistry was an achingly impossible dream for Vari. "I-I didn't know it was like that."

Lysandra giggled, playfully touching Vari's arm for a moment. "What do you think makes me a Gallae? My body is only the first step of my worship and devotion."

Vari sobered. Lysandra wasn't some idealized fantasy, not even her own. "I didn't realize that."

"Most people don't." She teased a lock of hair that tumbled free from her drawn veil. "They think we're all just pretty girls with elegant clothes and an immunity from most Imperial statutes on religion."

"But that..." Heavy breaths escaped from Vari. Lysandra's seduction wasn't just worship. It teased another mystery, one sealed away from decorum and ambition. Vari didn't understand enough. "Does that mean you're a nymphet?"

Lysandra laughed. "A little. I'm telling you this because, Varius Severus, I like you. I want to explore you, and to let you explore me."

A ray of conviction filled Vari's chest. She saw truth behind what Lysandra said. There was a wonder behind Lysandra's words, enticing Vari to salivate.

"You still haven't answered my question," Lysandra asked. "When should I find you?"

Chills crept over Vari's shoulders. A newfound curiosity swelled in her core, enticing her close to places she'd been told never to approach. Some writings suggested it was the Gallae who first discovered how to overthrow the Nihl. What greater wisdom—or sensations—were they hiding?

"In the morning."

After revealing a soft grin, Lysandra leaned close, delivering a chaste kiss on Vari's lips. "How is your hand?"

Thin towels twisted around Vari's wound. "Fine for now. I'll have a friend look them over."

"As long as you're certain." Lysandra lowered the thin veil over her face, but failed to block her devoted smile. "Take care of yourself, Varius."

Close to sunset, Roker wove his way through the city, straying further from his pre-dawn activities. In the less wealthy areas, he'd expected to see residences marked with the power glyph of the Non-Dead. Instead, he saw the seals of mortal financiers. Nothing in the vicinity hinted at the drones his order used to populate the galaxy.

To his aged sensibilities, Roker found the scene archaic and quaint.

When he approached a checkpoint leading out of the city, he shifted left toward a region of nested warehouses. Several Amazons patrolled the nearby alleys. One warrior woman stood on a rooftop.

Then another appeared.

Roker pressed himself into a shadowy corner. It could have been a shift change, given the hour. There was as much of a chance the Amazons had found him.

He still had places to witness and records to take. As he continued, Roker kicked an empty can out of his path. Amazons watched as he moved from one alley to the next.

Sensors left by Roker's scouts scurried through nearby pipes and drains. Their wiring eased through stones, spying on whatever lay under the city.

Roker pulled a panel away from his left forearm, twisting it into a recording screen. Thermal sensors and IR spectra were a standard part of his existence. Most Non-Dead were recycled parts, a chassis to apply sensors and motors, possibly a defensive platform. Roker wasn't like them. He'd ascended to his position. If he hadn't, someone else would have taken his place, leaving him to rot where the Nihl had killed him.

Everywhere, the results were the same. Layers upon layers of stone, enough to keep any satellite from ever seeing a deeper structure. Imperial assessors would never spot any anomaly, unless they had help.

Such things worked as long as the ground stayed intact. Once the hidden sectors tasted open air, the assessor would swoop in without fear.

Roker closed the panel on his arm, leaving the prying eyes of Amazons behind him. Somewhere, he'd found a passageway to the secrets below. Most beings would only see a sewer. For Roker, the latent levels of Quantum were too much for him to ignore.

Bassiana charged into Caracalla's quarters as the sun drifted below the horizon. "General, I would have words with you."

He rose from his desk and clasped his fist to his chest. "Of course, Princess. How may I assist you?"

"My son returned with wounds on his hands."

"And no further wounds. You've done well with him."

"Don't placate me." She stomped close, the hem of her temple dress still fluttering around her. Rage stiffened her spine. Her upper lip tensed as her nostrils flared. "He was unmarked when he left me. When he returned, he was injured."

Rigidity held Caracalla in place. "One of my men slashed him with a gladius."

Bassiana stomped closer with heated breath. "You put swords to my son?"

The general remained unmoved. "Spears and shields, as well. He dispatched both of the centurions I'd ordered to kill him. You should be proud."

Bassiana's voice hollowed. "You ordered men to kill my son."

"It was the only way to test his abilities. I only did so once I was certain he could handle direct combat tactics. You have nothing to worry about."

Without a sound, Bassiana drew a knife from her sleeve and sprung forward. The slightly curved tip pressed against Caracalla's throat. "You have no right to touch my son."

"You're faster than I expected, Princess." His eyes traced down Bassiana's arm. "Also."

A dagger snapped against the underside of Bassiana's breast.

Caracalla kept his voice even, "I don't wear my title for show."

The Regent stepped back, slipping the knife back into her sleeve. "I never thought your title was ceremonial."

The general sheathed his dagger. "The people of the Empire often forget the debt all humanity owes the archers of New Brasilia. I sometimes wonder how many arrows killed Nihl during the war."

Cavernous breaths shifted Bassiana's arms against her chest. "What do you want?"

"Stability." Caracalla returned to his desk and sat. "Right now, the Imperator keeps things stable. It isn't perfect. Nothing ever is. However, anything might change that. I would prefer not to send my subordinates into battle, much less war. If change comes, humanity must rise victorious once more.

"Just because your husband's sword is lost doesn't mean your son is worthless. Varius has a strong name and two potent bloodlines. He is the reassurance that peace will endure."

Bassiana's face hardened. Caracalla was no traditional loyalist. If the general meant to take Vari as reassurance, that meant positioning for a greater ploy, one adjacent to the Throne. "You would have my son become the Imperator's pet?"

"We are all subjects, Princess. Our freedom comes in deciding to help our brethren or leaving them to their own fates."

Stomach acid ate into Bassiana's throat. Few creatures wanted war. Fola didn't. Nor did Caracalla. But justice couldn't be abandoned so the Empire might enjoy consistency and stability.

"That is a fair statement, General. I remind you that people do not take kindly to others forcing conditions for the common good, especially when they are often trampled on as a result." Bassiana walked for the door, turning back after a moment. "May I ask about your business with Sparta?"

"I have no business with Sparta. I want to see how your son handles an adverse environment."

"You accomplished that without leaving this room."

"A single cut does not make an adverse environment, nor do a pair of soldiers operating under my direct orders."

"Leave my son be." Bassiana glided toward the door.

"He doesn't belong to you, Princess. He belongs to the Empire and to all humanity. His father's bloodline saw to that."

Saran sat on a cushioned bench, resting one arm on the windowsill behind her. With the sun in retreat, the plaza outside lit the world. Conical roofs, low spires, and distant domes sparkled in the late dusk.

Vari rubbed the tightened bandage around her hand, never clawing at the medication working within. "The assessors are still here."

"That might be the most casual I've ever heard you mention our annual visitors."

She shrugged. "Maybe I'm used to it."

"With the general here as well?" Saran shook her head. "I doubt it. Something's changed."

Vari pulled the confining hair tie away from the base of her skull. Loose, short curls drifted around her face as she flopped onto a broad couch. "I don't want to talk about it."

Without pressing the issue, Saran's eyes bored into Vari. She studied the bandage, the looseness of Vari's shoulders. Her chest remained tense with every breath, even as her fingers absently circled her abdomen.

"I can't tell if you're relaxed or more constricted than I've ever seen you." Saran braced her elbows on her knees. "Something else happened—something you didn't tell us about."

Vari's chin twitched for an instant.

"You can tell me, Vari. Tell me why you're so... excited."

Vari turned her gaze, leaving the rest of her body frozen. "What makes you think I'm excited?"

"Your pants are a little tight."

"Huh?" Vari still wore the same drab tan pants. She deserved a livelier color, especially if she ever wanted a closer rendezvous. An unformed idea stiffened her arousal. "Dammit." Vari hurled a pillow toward the bench as she pulled her legs together. "Mind your own business."

Saran batted the pillow away. "It's my job to be nosy about your business."

Vari draped an aching hand over her eyes. "Leave me alone."

Saran strolled from her seat, passing where Vari had to see her. She draped her arms over the back of the couch and leaned over her covered face. "Talk to me."

The concealed woman groaned.

"Was it the heat of battle that got you going? Did you want to get an intimate peek at the general?"

Vari growled at the thought of making a flirtatious distraction.

"Dreaming about Geta's succulent Gallae?"

Vari's lips remained tightly clenched, restraining an answer, an understanding, perhaps even more. Teases prodded into Vari well enough, but this was more of an emotional stab.

Saran moved around the couch again, kneeling beside Vari. She lay her head so her hair brushed against Vari's chest, dismissing her teasing. "So... it is the Gallae."

"Go home, Saran. I'll be fine."

"I sleep in here. Your bed is in the next room."

Vari sat up, nudging the Amazon back. "I should go in there and lock the door behind me."

"Without telling me your secrets?" Saran cocked an eyebrow and shook her head. "You want me to break down the door and force you to tell me? Would that be fun?"

"You wouldn't dare."

Ranks divided most people, but Saran had witnessed all of Varia. She'd applauded Vari's secret training and applied lessons she'd discarded to become a New Brasilian. Saran refused to let Vari's lust ruin her, not when she concealed things Macrinus would crown Saran to reveal.

"Someone has to sort you out." Saran stood, dropping her belt to the floor. She stepped out of her shoes and walked toward the closed doors leading to Vari's bedchamber.

"Where are you going?"

"To bed."

"You said you were sleeping out here."

"I was going to, but you're busy dreaming about that Gallae." Saran loosened her off-white tunic and uniform skirt, letting both fall from her body. The young woman stood prideful in her underwear. "The way I see it, I'm going to get some sleep or I can distract you from your scandalous fantasy."

Vari sat at the edge of standing from the couch. Her thoughts lay trapped in the Gallae's web. Reluctantly, she stood like a scolded child.

"Don't act so somber about it." Saran took Vari's hand, guiding her into the bedchamber.

———◆O◆———

Geta tired of counting grain stores and examining munitions depots. Every article stayed within the parameters established by the Senate. If just one thing was in excess, he could request a garrison be stationed on New Brasilia. It would allow Geta get back to organizing the affairs of the Empire instead of wandering along the far edges of the galaxy.

Every time Geta returned to Roma Vatica, he burned the same prayer. *May the gods expose Amazon treachery.*

Each year, he returned to the same result. No stores of Quantum, no ship factories, nothing to imbue Amazon arrows with enough force to pierce an atmosphere. Let them waste their chests out of some ancient adoration. Let the Brasilians make medicines and weave fine fabrics. No matter how much they acted like good citizens, they still prayed to heathen gods. They begged the stars to let a covetous boy steal the throne from a proper leader.

Such heathens were foolish enough to fracture the Empire. If they had the chance, they'd start another war. The Imperator, wise as he may have been, may have doomed the Empire with his mercy.

Geta set aside a tablet bearing the latest tally from the local bricklayer's union. His balcony offered a night sky, full of foreign constellations and roaming drones. Crisis be damned. If some invader wanted to kill him, it'd be a welcome sacrifice. Legions would ravage New Brasilia and build a proper protectorate. Geta's lustful wife would inherit all his titles if that happened. Lysandra had the potential to become a worthy Lady Geta, even if she couldn't bear children.

Hot wind stung the side of Geta's face, turning him away from the city. The only structure of note was the Temple of the Elagabal, a worthless, opulent mound filled with eye-shaped windows. It needed to be torn down and sanitized. A Mother temple to Cybele would be preferable to any Brasilian star worship.

A dry voice coasted from above. "They seek the wisdom of the soul."

Geta mistook the silhouette for a statue at first. The outline was shaped with shadowy fabric and the faint glint of sensors and surface wiring.

The figure jumped to the balcony, staying at the edge of the light. "I am Roker. I speak for the Non-Dead."

Roker's stillness echoed confidence, not servitude. Geta shook his head, glad to see a hint of the familiar. Anyone other than a mechanism would have inspired fear. Geta bribed the animated corpses for protection annually. "There are few Non-Dead on New Brasilia."

"True, Lord Geta. I came from Sparta. Galis before that. I have been to many places, heard many voices, conscripted many lives."

Geta allowed himself to smirk for an instant. "You are the invader."

"I am." Roker bowed with acceptance. "There are things I have been ordered to examine."

Familiar or not, the Non-Dead served a role within society. They did not rule. "How do such things concern me?"

"I was told to see you in the event I discovered something of interest."

Geta crossed his arms. "What, pray tell, did you find?"

"I cannot say, assessor. I can only tell you where to go before asking that you look for yourself."

"Why?"

"Because there is an uncertainty in the galaxy. We know the Eighth Quantum Sword was lost, not necessarily destroyed."

Anger snapped Geta's fists shut. The Eighth Quantum Sword defied discovery. Macrinus wanted the weapon to solidify his reign as Imperator, yet every attempt to find the Severus weapon failed. "Have you seen the sword?"

"No. I have seen records. Someone knows the whereabouts of the weapon—but that is not why I am here."

"The Eighth Sword still exists." A trembling whisper couldn't ease the possibilities in Geta's mind. "I need to know more."

"No." Roker pulled back his hood, revealing a hairless head with gray-green skin. Alternating sensors with changing lights rolled within the glossy black metal of his eye sockets. "We offer the information you need, not a slight verification."

"Verification?"

"If we knew the location of the sword, we would have already retrieved it. Do you wish for the information, or would you prefer to return in a year for another assessment?"

Buried within a scowl, Geta shook his head. "I never want to see this damned rock again."

"Good." Roker drew a sliver of reflective white from inside his cloak. "Take this."

The assessor turned the data card between his fingers. "What's on this?"

"Coordinates and instructions on how to reach each location. The rest, I leave to you." Roker lifted his hood once again. "In return, I wish to speak privately with Macrinus."

Geta wore a fulfilled smile. "If you know anything about the Eighth Quantum Sword, he'll want to speak with you as well."

"Excellent. I'll return tomorrow evening. We'll discuss Roma Vatica more then." Roker climbed atop the railing and jumped upward into the night.

Geta allowed himself a moment of contemplation. His wife had insisted she had nothing worthwhile to report. Yet a miraculous Non-Dead appeared offering bountiful evidence. He'd investigate, but only with the strictest of defenses in place.

The Clarion
The Presence of the Imperatrix

MORNING RETURNED. DAWN LIGHT inspired temples and prayer. Tired souls scavenged for secrets or pleasure.

Vari and Saran lay beneath a feather-soft sheet that glowed in the sunlight. While Saran slept, Vari let her fingers drift. Her hand absorbed the slope of Saran's abdomen and chest, avoiding the nest of ceremonial scars. Light blanketed Saran's loosened hair and slumbering face, draping her with angelic radiance.

Saran chose to carve away her original shape for the hope that others would accept the honesty of her spirit. She achieved what she wanted to become. Her body and spirit were the same, the embodiment of New Brasilian might. Such power lingered in ages past, present in case humanity craved an archer's fury once again.

As morning grew stronger, time and peace ran thin. The Gallae would offer herself without limitation. Nothing Saran would care to see.

Vari whispered into the tiny half-oval of Saran's ear. A fragrance of dried sweat reminded Vari of a field of butterflies. "Saran. It's morning."

"Mmm..." Without opening her eyes, she smiled. Only after stretching her arms and shoulders did Saran fully wake. "Good morning."

"Did you sleep well?"

"Perfection." Saran sat up. Her callused, tender fingers drew Vari into a warm, heartful kiss. "You didn't send me away."

"I'd never do that." Vari ran her fingers through Saran's hair. Her index finger dabbed the top of Saran's ear. "You're my best friend."

She giggled. "I'm your only friend."

The joke pierced Vari with widening sobriety. "They're going to take me away."

"Then leave something behind. I can't promise much, aside from good standing with your family."

Vari kissed her again. "You deserve more than that."

A delicate whisper lifted from Saran's heart. "One day."

Vari absorbed as much as possible from Saran's presence. The taste of salty skin excited Vari, but it lacked the overwhelming tenacity of breathing in Lysandra. Every second drew the Gallae closer. The towering woman exuded confidence and grace from her throne within Vari's thoughts. Every power Vari wanted for herself already existed within Lysandra's presence.

Saran laughed again. "Again already? Or is that for the Gallae?"

A truthful half-smile defined Vari's face. "Maybe it's both."

"Downgraded before I can get out of bed." Saran frowned. "You know how to charm a girl."

Vari shrugged. "I can't lie to you."

Saran turned away, covering her face. "I don't want to feel used."

Vari stroked the Amazon's bare back. "You're my best friend—no matter how many I have. Why would you be used?"

"Because you're still curious about Geta's sex machine." Saran's voice turned to razors. "You like what she is as much as what she does."

"Saran, did you ever consider I might want you more?"

"No."

In the wake of the crippling syllable, Vari kissed Saran's shoulder. "Have someone bring us breakfast and I'll prove it to you."

The assessor's escort of a hundred soldiers marched narrow alleys as Geta followed the instructions from the digital card. Caracalla walked beside him, wearing full armor and cape, along with his relay helm.

"Soon we'll have them, my friend." Geta pointed to a slimmer alleyway to his left. "This way."

Caracalla stiffened under the crest of his impressive helmet. A centurion's role was to defend an assessor's approach rather than follow. "Left turn." As the centurions obeyed, the general tilted closer. "What are you hoping to find?"

"What we've always been looking for." The assessor grinned. "Treason."

"It isn't our place to create enemies who aren't there."

"But they are here. They've always been here." Hated memories curled around Geta's brow. "They stood against our Imperator. If they have the opportunity, they'll do it again. All they lack is the means to pull it off. When I find they have those means, I'll crush their opportunities. They will know their place."

"Sounds quite zealous."

Their path twisted along hard angles. Any formation would crumble trying to follow.

"Zealotry is the nature of my position. Anything less is a failure of my duty and my allegiance to Macrinus."

"I serve the Empire." No threads of hot wind broke Caracalla's rigid resolve. "I need no zealotry."

A pair of Brasilians withdrew from the corner of a neighboring rooftop.

Once they reached a round sewage plate, Geta glanced at the digital card and nodded. Centurions slammed prybars into the plate, grunting as they lifted it. A cloud of musty rot blew out as soon as the thick metal circle slipped away.

Caracalla spat acid from the back of his throat. "Congratulations on locating yesterday's waste."

Geta paced around the dingy hole until he found a ladder cut into the stone. Without warning, he descended.

"Callium, wait."

"No time." Geta's elation echoed to the surface. "We have two stops on this journey."

Caracalla followed with a fraction of his centurions.

Insect-shaped survey probes fluttered from Geta's hands, flying in opposite directions through the curved tunnels. He checked his tablet, watching the view from each probe. He touched the image of a door as it appeared on the corner of his tablet.

"There." A map of the sewers scrolled over the bottom half of the tablet. "This door is not on our maps."

"Send down four men to defend the bottom of this ladder." Caracalla pointed at the present centurions. "Everyone else, with me."

The probe fluttered thin metal wings in front of the discovered door. Two centurions tried forcing the passage open before pressing small gray globs into the edges. "Step back, my lords." The soldiers all locked their shields to form a reinforced wall. Six bangs ripped through the tunnel, leaving drips of fire scattered along the chosen path.

"Move, move." Geta shoved between the centurions. "I want to see."

One centurion moved in before the assessor. "Arrows, my lord. There have to be thousands."

The centurion passed an arrow to Geta. He stroked the silvery-blue shaft of metal, tapping the notch at its base before flicking the tip. A scowl sank his entire body. "Arrows."

"This isn't just an arrow." Caracalla rotated a projectile, checking every angle possible in the dim light. "There are hollow nodes near the head and tail, consistent with Quantum infusion ports." He pointed at the openings in Geta's arrow. "You should check all these arrows for such nodes. Check any arrows carried by ceremonial archers, too. I suspect you'll find this a significant stockpile."

"All I want is to find one undocumented drop of Quantum." Geta rubbed the nodes, gritting his teeth. "I'll buy that man a title and a Gallae all his own."

An uncharacteristic knock signaled Saran's return with breakfast. She'd insisted on taking care of it herself, giving Vari time to dress. Vari laughed at the brusqueness of Saran's return. A woman of surprises.

When she opened the door, Vari gazed deep into the parallel curves forming his tall guest's cleavage. Lysandra wore a circlet of silver with matching floral pins throughout her piled hair. The low neckline of her crimson dress was amplified by the slender green trim that danced over her body. She licked her lips, the top painted ruby, the bottom stained emerald.

"Lysandra." Her name was eternity. It was the only title that encompassed what Vari desired, the flesh she was still desperate to entangle.

"I promised." The Gallae eased Vari back, closing the door behind her. Feline eyes swept over Vari's tan shirt and brown pants. "You've dressed? Are you challenging me?"

"Habit." Vari should have said Saran was coming back. Her resistance lay eclipsed by Lysandra's shadow.

"No matter." She traced her fingers along Vari's face, just like before. For a moment, she let her fingers play with one of Vari's loose curls.

She hadn't bound her excess hair. If she'd cut it, Lysandra couldn't play with it, but neither could Saran.

"Perhaps you need a reminder of my zeal." Lysandra's graceful touch led Vari toward the bed. Her hands clamped against the front of Vari's shirt. The dual shades of her lips pressed over the surface of the young woman's mouth. Her tongue pushed inward as her arms thrust down, tearing the shirt in half.

Once her hands were free, they set to loosening Vari's pants. Her kiss shifted into a lunge deep enough for her tongue to tickle the back of Vari's throat.

She fell onto the mattress.

Lysandra yanked the last ribbons of shirt and pants away.

Vari lay naked, powerless. All she had to do was say Saran's name. The mood would shatter, the game would end. Instead, her eyes followed the ruddy color capping Lysandra's fingertips. A faint grasp and a flick of her wrists loosened a set of laces along her back. The angular red dress tumbled like a swaying feather, floating to the floor.

Aggression filled Lysandra's eyes as she transfixed upon Vari's desire. "Praise to my goddess, Cybele. My lover has risen for me to mount."

Vari said nothing. No words wove her thoughts away from her shamefully prone excitement.

Lysandra unclasped the red lace around her chest, freeing her ample bosom. Such full amazement, luscious and absolute. The Gallae climbed over Vari's waist. Her right hand opened for Vari.

"Give me your hand."

It wasn't a question and Vari did not answer. She put her hand in Lysandra's, massaging the soft palm and fingertips. Lysandra's smile scaled toward her cheeks before she pulled Vari's fingers downward. No cloth kept Vari from stroking Lysandra's moistening flesh or breathing in a tickle of her finest hair.

"What most arouses your curiosity?"

Still unable to speak, Vari bent into Lysandra's nipples. She kissed pristine skin and rolled her lips over Lysandra's sternum. A guiding hand encouraging her to nurse.

"Taste." A deep whisper lifted Lysandra's chest.

She bent her knees, falling onto Vari. Lysandra's hips and hands supported Vari's waist, letting the younger woman enter and drink from the Gallae.

Warmth spurted into Vari. A drip, nothing more. The sour enticement thickened within her mouth.

As she swallowed, the Gallae shoved them both onto the mattress. Words slithered from her lips directly into Vari's ears. "Resist your impulses. Focus on our bodies. Entangle our pleasure."

Lysandra pumped her body up and down, back and forth. Vari reached for the Gallae's hips, only to be pushed away. Sharp breaths kept them flowing together. If Vari sped up, Lysandra rolled her fingernails over her abdomen, pinched her elbow joints, or tugged her scalp. Lysandra's face curled with pleasure without generating a single bead of sweat or allowing a thread of hair to fall out of place.

Vari breathed deep, holding her own chest in place. Her lungs flooded with excitement. Her instincts screamed to move onward. In the nest of lust and desire, she found a steady calm. As they churned from one pant to the next, Vari bit back a whisper of her own. Her eyes explored the refined softness encircling Lysandra. A desire erupted from Vari's true self, begging to release every painful inhibition.

Amid the pumping, Lysandra let a loving exhale roll from her lower lip. "You are lovely and sweet. Perfect and superbly strong." Her hands squeezed their way up Vari's ribs, fusing with shared breaths. The Gallae slowed, almost stopping. "What's this?"

Vari had failed. She hadn't lost herself, yet still managed to disappoint Lysandra. "Is something wrong?"

"Touch my breasts." Her command purred with curiosity, but lacked any lustful impulses.

Vari ran her hands over each mound, rolling over the curves before resting her palms over exposed nipples. Such a simple feature was dynamic upon a woman's body, yet lacking in Vari's own flesh.

"Mmm, yes. Now look into my eyes."

Vari lifted her head. Her gaze met Lysandra's. Their eyes remained focused, blinking as one. Every eyelash on the Gallae's face curled at an identical arc. Tender creams filled her pores, luminous shades tinted the idyllic symmetry of her skin.

"It was not desire in your eyes." Lysandra held her breath as her wondrous eyes flooded with life. "It was admiration."

"Aren't those the same?" Vari lay on the altar of the Gallae's religious experience, lost to the sway of the moment.

At the instant when Vari was certain Lysandra would pull away, the Gallae took deep, thrusting breaths. She pressed herself against Vari's waist. Her chin rubbed massaged the curve of Vari's neck. Her forehead pressed against Vari's chest. She licked the skin around Vari's nipple, only to pull back, licking her lips. After returning to lick the nipple itself, Lysandra grinned.

"I see you." Lysandra stroked her knuckles down the sides of Vari's face. "Sister."

"What?" Vari froze, exposed—yet accepted.

The Gallae hadn't run, even as she spoke Vari's secret. Vari never had a chance to admit who she was to her father. Her mother only accepted after accidentally discovering the truth.

Lysandra remounted, pushing Vari's confused desire as deep as possible. "Do as I say, sister, and that general will never claim you."

Faster breaths rushed through Vari. Blood pumped, fueled by rage as much as the clarity of touching Lysandra. Her perfection offered the unbelievable. Escape. Control over Vari's own purpose. An untempered curiosity softened her lips as she matched Lysandra's gaze and the cycling of their flesh.

"I... I can't."

"Stop hiding." Lysandra's hips squeezed to absorb Varius's body. "Let me show you the way."

Vari committed to Lysandra's movements. There'd been no guidance before. Acceptance was a grudging gift. Lysandra somehow saw into Vari. A Gallae priestess offered Vari a place at their unattainable altar.

If Lysandra saw Vari and still wanted her, Vari would gladly stay entwined.

The Gallae scratched a finger upon the fold above Vari's lips.

"Embrace sister goddess, one trapped in a prison of flesh."

Lysandra was such a confined creature. Her conviction, her demeanor, her strength—all gave power to a greater being. Such a being lingered behind Vari's eyes, screaming to be free.

"Call sister goddess, a mother of shadowed shape."

Vari saw Lysandra's towering perfection. Her body begged to embrace Lysandra's exactness, to know the fragrance of freedom. Each Gallae had her own tailored scent, demanding control of herself and others.

"Summon sister goddess, a daughter of desire."

The Gallae pulled her hand from Vari's mouth and tapped her throat. Each word was an intent prayer enchanting the fabric of the galaxy.

"Summon sister goddess." A tremor shook Vari's jaw. Her voice wavered. "A daughter of desire."

"Sister goddess, give her spirit the shape she chooses."

Choice was everything. Saran chose for herself. Fola chose for herself.

Lysandra was the ideal guide. Following her opened choices and ideas unforeseen.

"Sister goddess, craft a body worthy of her soul."

Lysandra quickened herself, accelerating toward a climax they'd both forgotten.

Vari shivered in confusion. Her mouth flexed, grinning in the shape of freedom. She could leave all her imperfections behind.

The Gallae tapped Vari's throat as she revealed the next line. "Sister goddess, I discard my deceptions."

"Sister goddess," Vari said in a gasp. "I discard my deceptions."

The syllables slipped loose. Vari deflated.

Only a Gallae could free someone from a militant grasp. Everything about Lysandra sang of perfection. The hint of cherry on her lips, the absolute purpose behind her slightest touch.

Escape from Caracalla was possible only through a Gallae. Lysandra prayed to a daughter of desire and a discarding of deceptions. Lysandra's devotion grew from the instant her salivated tongue traced circles against Vari's skin and chest. Devotion swelled in the towering woman, replacing over overtly sensual graces.

Another panting tap struck Vari on the throat.

"Sister goddess, I give you my true name, Lysandra." The Gallae's eyes transfixed on Vari, ready to witness absolute acceptance.

Lysandra was the Gallae's name. Vari had expected to hear another. Their recitation prompted Cybele, channeling obedience to an order willingly subservient to the Usurper.

Vari shook her head, wincing. "I can't." A Gallae served, she could not rule.

Lysandra scowled at an angle that echoed Saran's irritation. "You're going to lie now? Why keep hiding yourself?"

A bead of tears drowned Vari's eyes. "I'm not you."

Lysandra pinned Vari to the bed. "Climax and call out your name." She bent forward, kissing Vari with a sisterly grace. "That's all you have left. Do it and you'll be protected and free, forever."

There was no freedom in a galaxy held by the Usurper. Only Vari could reclaim her ancestral throne. Her head shook, aching in the gap between ambition and desire. "I'm not like you."

"I tasted prosthetic glue on your chest. The residue lingers for several days afterward." Lysandra stroked Vari's hair, filling her eyes with sympathy. "You must have torn your breastforms off as soon as we reached orbit."

"Stop it." Vari hated herself and her duty. She'd said no. She had to.

"Do you have a closet of dresses somewhere?" Lysandra's fingertip curled a lock of Vari's hair, pulling it over her earlobe. "It's not just fabric and fragrance. There's more to you, sister." Lysandra leaned in to whisper. "Let me take you away from your pain. You deserve to be yourself, to have every wonder you've always craved."

The door slung open, its handle knocking against the wall. "You finally snuck in." Saran crossed her arms and glared through Lysandra. "There's nothing for you here, Gallae."

"The guard, returned at last." Lysandra angled herself like a willful vixen. "Are you a discarded date? A woman desperate to demonstrate her worth?"

Saran opened her fingers over her belt. "You should leave. New Brasilia, not just the palace. Run back to your temple on Roma Vatica and pray I never burn it to the ground."

Lysandra lovingly stroked Vari's face. "What say you, sister?"

Vari flicked her gaze toward Saran. Such a beacon of truth and conviction. She didn't deserve Saran.

With one arm freed, Vari pushed the Gallae away, forcing her to the foot of the bed. "I said I'm not you."

Lysandra made a single huff. All pleasure crumbled from her body. "As you wish, young Severus." She pulled her dress on and tightened the laces in a handful of seconds. A wolfish grin appeared on her face. "We will see each other again."

Lysandra's grace remained unbroken as she glided toward the door. She stopped next to Saran, sweeping a hand where the young Brasilian once had a second breast. "If you're devoted enough to keep her secrets, tell me. I'll see you get this back."

Saran's eyes continued burning. "You need to leave."

"I'm certain you know my sister's name." Lysandra withdrew and fluttered away.

The shell of Varia Severus lay exposed in a bed of unattained desires.

The Virago war room analyzed every piece of data connected to New Brasilia's affairs. At its heart, the Oval Desk dominated the room. Its warm, crystalline surface lay marred only by tablets and digital projections. A guard from each of the Six Founding Sororities stood in the corner of the room. A warrior of rank always monitored the desk.

Whenever possible, Fola preferred to monitor her nation personally. The responsibilities of rule, defense, and public trust circled her head, regardless of any crown she wore. Her cousin sat with her, offering additional eyes and a familiar voice of counsel.

As Fola switched between reports on her tablet, she peeked up for an instant. "Something troubles you, cousin."

Bassiana held out a tablet layered with surveillance recordings. "Geta's wife." The Gallae, draped in layers of green, stood in an intersecting hallway. Her poise remained constant from one clip to the next. "She stood there for an hour and a half yesterday. She didn't move until she encountered my son."

Fola nodded. "I'm surprised you have a problem with a Gallae."

"Only that one. There's no reason to say she's not loyal to her husband." Bassiana lay the tabled on the Oval Desk before pressing her arms together. "She might be recruiting for her damned religion."

"They cannot take what they cannot prove." Fola tapped on her tablet. "Look at this." Light ripped over the Oval Desk, curling into a schedule of that day's assessments. One row glowed brighter than the others.

"Why are they rechecking those warehouses?"

"That's what I'd like to know," Fola said. "Do we have a cache there?"

Bassiana shrugged. "Arrows."

Fola dismissed the schedule with a gesture. "Go find Vari. I want her with us in case they track down the Quantum."

Saran's fists stayed locked in the same death grip from the moment Lysandra touched her through the endless silence that followed. She glared through the floor, having been discarded at a whim. If she'd caught anyone else with Vari, she'd worry some form of assault had taken place. But deep pools of envy noticeably drowned Vari every time Lysandra drew close.

Any jokes crumbled away. Saran's loyalty never faltered, even when anyone else's would have dissolved.

Vari tended to her room, gathering the soiled bedsheets that meant peace so recently faded. She collected some torn remains lying on the floor before putting on a lightweight sleeveless black shirt.

"She called you sister." Saran didn't break from the scolded floor, nor did she release her tightened fingers. "How did she find out?"

"I don't know." Vari only managed a whisper. She looked out the window, unable or unwilling to look at Saran. "She was going like…"

Words escaped from Saran's clenched teeth. "I didn't tell you to stop."

"Fine." Vari nodded, cupping her hands over her eyes. "She had her own pace. It was… I haven't got the words."

"Try."

"Saran…" Her face desperately broke away from her shame. Her lips fumbled for an answer she failed to create. "In the middle of it all, she paused. She started looking me over, like a doctor or a priest. When she licked my chest, she said she could taste…"

Vari crumbled. She sulked against the window, staring at the base of the wall.

"You were going along with her." Saran rammed her arms outward, unwilling to punch her frustrations. Agony spewed from her voice. "Dammit, Varia, I heard you reciting along with her."

"It was the sex."

"No. Not for you. Maybe if it had been me instead of her." Saran scowled. A tremor ran through her face. "She found your weakness, and she almost had you."

A short breath filled Vari with life. "I stopped." She faced Saran, bearing the spirit that kept her close and bound her soul. She never tried to shape the spark of life when it flared in her eyes, no matter how she dressed or fought to kindle that light. "When I realized what she really wanted, I stopped."

Saran reached for his shoulder, but stopped herself. She couldn't give in, not when he didn't understand what she'd almost lost. "You wanted to go with her."

Vari winced. She met Saran's eyes for half an instant before snapping away. "Yes."

"How much would you have lost if you would have followed her?"

"Everything." She sat on the corner of her bed, wiping her face. "Nothing. No matter what I do, I'll only ever be half of myself."

Saran touched the side of Vari's face, making sure she was understood. "If you take the throne, you can make what laws you want. But only if we conquer the Usurper." She pressed a wounded kiss upon the top of her lover's head. "A Gallae can't do that. Only the Imperator can."

A barb of strength visibly pulled Vari from the ruins of despair. "I know."

Saran's hands opened. Bruises lingered from where her fingers stayed tight for so long. Once she flexed her palm, she slapped Vari hard enough to knock her off the bed. "If you know it, then act like it."

Raw vulnerability flooded the blood vessels in Vari's eyes. Gravity finally set in around Vari, putting her breathing back to normal.

Saran took a deep breath and sighed. Her hand reached down, ready to pull up the scolded heir. "Lecture's over," Saran said. "Let's eat."

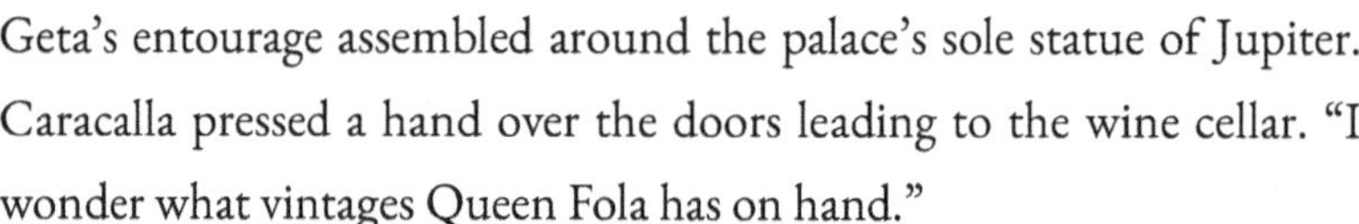

Geta's entourage assembled around the palace's sole statue of Jupiter. Caracalla pressed a hand over the doors leading to the wine cellar. "I wonder what vintages Queen Fola has on hand."

"That must wait." Geta lifted a hand to match his winding grin. "My contact says our prize is behind the statue."

Centurions prodded the walls and banged on bricks. They kicked tiles and shook on nearby windows. One found bravery enough to approach the visage of Jupiter, pushing on the plinth holding the great god. A hidden plate clicked along the base of the statue. Hidden gears rumbled beneath the floor.

"My lords?" The centurion snapped to his feet.

The protective arch around the statue sucked into the wall, rising out of sight. Chilled air rose from the exposed passage. No sigh of dust or decay shrouded a shadowed set of steps.

"Excellent work." Geta clapped a hand over the successful centurion's shoulder before smiling at Caracalla. "Are you ready?"

"Yes." The general stepped toward the opposite side of the opening. "Would you like to enter first or shall I secure the chamber?"

"Oh..." Geta grinned like a spoiled boy opening birthday presents. "I'll take this honor for myself."

A short descent led Geta and his party into a wide chamber divided between two realms. Delicate arrangements consumed the left side, balancing a wardrobe, a canopied bed, and a vanity, all wooden and polished into a matching shine. Rigid combat charts and aged wooden chests bordered an expansive cushioned rug.

Geta rushed to the wardrobe. His rib cage lifted, bristling with anticipation of the prize he'd craved for so long. Instead, a wealth of dresses and blouses hung in anticipation. Skirts and gowns froze, desperate for a casual or formal moment to shine. A bare mannequin lay abandoned at the bottom of the wardrobe. The vanity was consumed by the creams and fragrances that absorbed women of wealth and power.

"Where is it?" he asked. His sweeping hand snatched the canopy open, revealing only a plush bed fitted with soft sheets.

Caracalla turned away from the charts. "Callium, there are combat katas here."

Geta marched toward the general. The assessor showered the drawings with his signature scowl. No scandals lay within the charts, only illustrations of a man swinging a greater sword in different poses. "Women's clothing and fighting techniques. Hardly worth hiding, even on New Brasilia."

"These aren't plausible fighting techniques," Caracalla said. He mimed several of the movements. "The speed necessary isn't possible with a greater sword. Even if it was, there are too many defensive gaps, especially at close range."

A fine script ran along the bottom of each illustration. Every hair-thin letter shaped a name for the corresponding move. "Dispersal arc. Distortion wave." Geta shook his head. "Burst slash."

The assessor's lips trembled. "These katas..." He pressed against the wall as a trembling grin swallowed his face. Intensity and fury locked his eyes open. "These are Quantum Sword techniques."

"Then they're in violation."

Excitement charged Geta's nodding. "Oh, yes."

A solemn nod confirmed Caracalla's understanding. "Is there any-thing else of note?"

"Clothes and trinkets. Probably a place where young Severus can show off for that pet of his."

Heels clipped on the steps, echoing through the chamber. Lysandra stood at the entrance, beaming with pride.

Caracalla lifted a hand. "Lady Geta, please wait outside."

The Gallae pointed at the wardrobe. "I should look through those clothes."

Geta waved a dismissive hand. "Do so quickly."

"That would be inappropriate." Lysandra glided past Geta and Cara-calla, her demeanor swelling as though she commanded those present, not her husband.

Rather than taking offense, Geta shrugged as his glee enlarged. "It seems my wife wants to shop for rare clothes. Appropriate since the Houses Severus and Virago will soon be a memory." Geta lifted his voice toward the passage. "I need two men down here for an inventory."

Caracalla kept dwelling over the kata sheets, taking pictures of each. A pair of centurions descended, each opening a wooden chest.

As Lysandra mingled with the dresses, Geta approached. Such a se-ductive body appeared graceful in the presence of others. Geta planned to unveil the whore inside her as soon as they returned to his estate.

Lysandra stroked through the pages of a handwritten journal. "Hus-band?" The Gallae licked her lips. "Did you examine these things?"

"I did. Take any you like."

"I intend to, so I may present them to the Cybeline. These are all designed for a woman with two breasts."

The clothes weren't meant for the supposed Amazon. Or any Amazon. "What are you getting at, woman?"

Lysandra adopted a demure pose. A soft smile rose over her two-toned mouth. "I did as you suggested, learning a great deal. Young Severus will surely cry when she realizes we've gone through her things."

"Her?" Geta tilted his head at the oddity of Lysandra's words.

Lysandra's cheeks puffed as joy filled her face. "Yes. She craves to become Gallae." Her index finger pressed against a sequence of feminine scribblings. "Young Varia wrote her true name for us to find."

A galaxy of amazement filled Geta's thoughts. His discovery was a definitive political maneuver. His wife's claims ended any threat House Severus ever posed to the Imperator. "Lysandra, if you could give birth, I'd make you my first wife."

"Officially, I'll be ranked second." She draped a few of the dresses over one arm. "Excuse me, husband. I should report to the Cybeline. at once."

"Please do."

Geta stared lustfully at his wife's legs as she ascended the steps.

"Lord Geta." A centurion lifted his hand. "You should see this."

As Geta moved toward the opened chests, a centurion lifted a clear box with reflective metal edges. Inside, a swirling sphere of blue and white glistened with power.

The Non-Dead's intelligence had been perfect. Everything fell in place to shatter the hint of dissension within the Empire. "Arrows, forbidden katas, a Quantum Battery, and a Gallae heir."

Caracalla's eyebrows twitched. "What?"

Geta didn't bother answering. "Confiscate everything. Photograph it all. Prepare my ship to leave. I want off this planet within the hour."

To strike at the banner of the Unnamed Empire is an act
of Treason.
Yet Macrinus did the same a generation earlier, just as
humanity did ages before.
We are all traitors. None of us is blameless.

Diary of the Grand Lady Julia Maesa

T HE NUMBER OF BRASILIANS around the Oval Desk tripled as internal surveillance reports flooded the war room. Images and statistics poured from every part of the city, all bound by Imperial activity. Fola crossed her arms, letting the details float in front of her.

An armored soldier clutched her chest as a salute. "My Queen, the Imperial transport is fueling to depart."

Fola gave a silent nod in response. There was still too little data to act upon.

Bassiana whispered beside her cousin. "Someone found our caches."

A slender uniformed man rose from the far side of the Oval Desk. "My Queen? Something's happening outside the palace."

A live image floated above the crystalline table. Pairs of centurions marched from the palace toward the spaceport. Weighted wooden chests bobbed between each duo of soldiers.

"Broken lock." Bassiana pointed to a dangling latch on the center chest. "They've stolen something."

Fola pressed a fist against her mouth. Her lungs filled with a blistering air. She closed her eyes, not needing to see any more. "Call Geta."

A woman with side-shaved curls tapped a console. Repetitious beeping chimed across the room. The rhythm chimed for a solid minute.

Fola tilted to her cousin. "Where's Vari?"

"In her room. With Saran."

The Queen's eyes snapped open. "Bring me my armor."

Three warriors bowed and fled the room.

"Call in all off-duty personnel. Signal for reinforcements. Prepare an interstellar relay to our allies." The Queen turned around, shoving a ceremonial banner aside like it was a loose curtain.

A glossy black door with a palm reader stood exposed. Fola pressed her right hand over the square scanner sealing the door. Furious air filled her lungs again, she announced herself. "Fola of Virago. Queen of New Brasilia." The door hissed as it opened like a waking eye. Three racks of shimmering metal arrows mounted on one side. A rack of elaborate gleaming bows hung with absent anticipation. "Anyone who doesn't have to be here, grab a bow. Take arrows. Run to the spaceport."

A wealth of Brasilians, armored or not, moved from their positions, collecting the forbidden weapons.

"Bassiana?"

The Severus Regent stepped closer, bowing her head. "Yes, my Queen?"

Fola took out a bow and several arrows. "Get these to Saran. Be ready to escape."

Bassiana bowed, taking the weapons. "I will." Bassiana clutched the bow tightly in one hand, an echo of the warrior she never became.

Only a second for two cousins to hug before the end of all things.

As Bassiana departed, Fola measured the resolve of the soldiers she armed for battle. "Steady yourselves. Today will be a bloody day."

Caracalla marched across the plaza, surveying the convergence of several legions. Rows of centurions escorted the confiscated goods to the spaceport. A bare showing of the locals witnessed the parade of Imperial movement. None of the Amazons was present to watch.

"They know we've found something." The general triggered the relay within his helmet. "Bring my sword."

"The heathen Queen just tried to contact me." Geta stomped along at a harried pace. His wife copied his pace but not the rocky cadence. "Given our discoveries, I thought it best not to answer."

"It wouldn't matter. They suspected before they called."

Lysandra stood tall. "Then it's best we left."

"It is." Caracalla kept this tone low. With all efforts centered on Geta's personal departure, sacrifices were in order. "I'll defend your retreat."

Geta shook his head. "There's no need for that."

"By now, Fola has coordinated an attack. If she has the means to assault your transport, she will ground us. The battle will come fast and bloody."

The assessor lost all animation. "You are the general."

"I've ordered a contingent to remain with you. Everyone else will stay with me. Signal Sparta when you reach orbit. Take the evidence to the Imperator. We will restore justice to New Brasilia."

Both men clasped arms. When Geta let go, he reached for his wife. "Come along, Lysandra." She took his hand, and they sprinted away as fast as Geta could manage.

As the Getas reached the opposite side of the plaza, two centurions presented a long glossy metal case in front of Caracalla. The general pressed his fingers over a security plate, allowing the case to open with a fragrant hiss of Vatican air. Inside, a shimmering sword lay equal to Caracalla's height. Sunbeams caught the atomic edge, imbuing the weapon with restored life.

Caracalla lifted the sword overhead before signaling every remaining centurion. "All soldiers loyal to the Empire, stand fast. Ensure our assessor escapes. Destroy the Brasilian caches and converge on the spaceport."

Every centurion drew weapons before assembling into battle formation.

The knock-pause-triple knock sequence at the door told Vari her mother had come for dire purposes. After a two-second pause, Bassiana entered with regal ferocity. Vari and Saran both stood.

Bassiana lay two bundles of metal on the closest couch before facing Saran. "Arm yourself."

Saran sprinted to the couch, leaving Vari behind without question. She tossed a quiver of arrows over her shoulder. Part of the bow detached from the handle. Saran clipped the separated portion over her left ear. A transparent yellow rectangle rippled over her left eye.

Agony filled Vari. Her intestines knotted around a dying hope. She was powerless to keep Saran safe. "What happened?"

"Geta discovered at least one of our weapons caches." Bassiana clamped her arms around her ribs. "He also found your other room."

"So, he has my father's kata charts."

Saran shook her head. "To say the least."

"Remove that tone before you leave this room." The princess sighed. One of her many immaculate braids tumbled away from the pristine pile. "Vari, where is your greater sword?"

Vari sank further, having failed to protect herself from Imperial prowling. "In my other room."

"We'll assume they've confiscated it. Saran, you and I will open an escape—"

"No." Vari stood. She'd been told to act like an Imperator. "You mean for me to run away, Mother. I won't do it."

"Only you can take the throne." Bassiana frowned. "The rest of us are expendable so long as you reach that goal."

"My father stood with his men." Vari watched Saran more than his own mother. "I won't assume another standard."

Saran tugged on the bow's dense metallic string. "You have to escape, Vari."

"If Geta gets away, it'll be the same as everyone being dead." Years of dedication crumbled faster with every sliver taken from Vari's private chamber. A kata damned her, a greater sword convicted her, a tailored dress condemned her.

Her only path was forward.

Vari walked for the door. "Let's go."

Bassiana sighed before following.

Saran's lips abandoned any anger that may have lingered. "Spoken like an Imperator."

Geta kept his hand clasped to Lysandra's. Centurions sprinted beside them. Shields thundered together as they slammed into angled walls.

"For once," Lysandra said, "I regret wearing heels."

"Leave them. I'll buy you more when we return to Roma Vatica."

The Gallae kicked one shoe away, then hopped to discard its companion. Her pace quickened enough to speed ahead of her husband.

An explosion ruptured ahead of their escape. Dust and broken bricks blasted through the air. Debris clattered on the shields, rolling like distant thunder.

A voice cried out from ahead. "Amazons!"

Pistols and rifles snapped forth, pushing through the fine gaps between three or more shields. Centurions braced spears against the remaining gaps, ready for the New Brasilian scourge however it arrived.

Another furious burst scattered over the shields. Arrows zipped into the mass of soldiers. Lines of gleaming silver rippled in too many directions.

"To arms! To arms!" Centurions yelled orders. Guns aligned, blasting toward vacated buildings. Each volley struck with waves of heat, raining molten rock and steel onto the soldiers.

In the distance, a woman howled a battle cry. "Leave none alive." More arrows barraged the group, digging every drop of magma from the core of New Brasilia. The rotten heart of the world boiled Geta's nostrils.

The assessor tore a pistol from a centurion's belt. Rage spewed from his throat, growing every time he squeezed the trigger.

"Create a perimeter." The shaking ground failed to stagger Caracalla. "Keep the path through the plaza blocked. Do not let a single Amazon through."

His men stood in solid rows, the first bearing spears with their shields, the next holding their shields at a defensive angle. A third row lifted rifles that demanded both hands to operate.

The palace doors erupted with a flood of Brasilians. A line of archers shifted to one knee and fired. The next line rushed past the first, unleashing their own volley. Arrows clattered against the shields, a collision of the galaxy's finest metals, nothing more.

From behind his legions, Caracalla saw his men standing, enduring the assault. "Advance ten march." He counted up from one. The centurions moved a step forward with each number. At the end of the count, he called, "Halt."

More arrows speckled against the barrier. None exploded. For all their discoveries, they'd only found a single Quantum Battery.

Caracalla realized why two waves of arrows failed to explode.

The Amazons had lured them into assuming there were no more Quantum Arrows. Centurions pooled together to endure standard arrows.

Waves of his men were flung through the air when the third line unleashed their arrows. Smoke and charred meat filled the general's lungs as he dove for cover.

Vari lashed her belt to a cable extending from one rooftop to the next. When a wave of Quantum arrows struck the centurions below, bodies scattered through the air. When the dying echoes hit Vari, she slid down the cable.

Fola had forced the general close to the palace. The first wave of centurions had no escape. Explosions flung more centurions than Vari expected. Had Caracalla forgotten that Brasilian archers shot down Nihl ships? Most of the Empire allowed that fact to escape them.

Saran slid down the cable behind Vari. The fierce blonde sprang to her feet, ready to fire upon the centurions.

Vari clapped a hand over the nocked arrow and shook her head. A single shot would tell Caracalla where to attack.

Bassiana descended last. She rolled onto the roof, rising ready to fight, even if she wasn't dressed for battle.

Vari could not allow her mother to play regent, not when battle swelled beside them. "Stay out of the fight. We'll use the rooftops to circle behind Caracalla's defensive line."

Calmly, Bassiana asked, "To what end?"

"Depends on what it's like when we get there. We can open a path for our forces at the palace or rush toward the spaceport."

Below, Imperial guns roared to life.

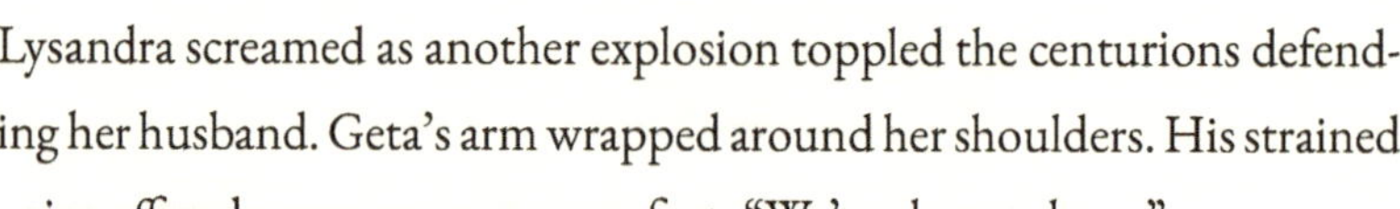

Lysandra screamed as another explosion toppled the centurions defending her husband. Geta's arm wrapped around her shoulders. His strained voice offered an uncommon comfort. "We're almost there."

An Amazon in a skimpy white uniform jumped behind Geta, swatting the closest centurion with her bow. She shoved another man back before grabbing Geta by the neck. Her swift, wiry fingers coiled around his throat.

Geta kicked at the Amazon. His pistol blasted at the sky, unable to press against his assailant.

The Amazon kicked his knee from behind, toppling him to the pavement. Her position let her throttle Geta while crushing his throat.

Each brick scratched Geta's brow as he rose and fell. His arms turned limp as his blood-stained vision blurred.

Air flooded his nose and mouth. The fiendish woman crumpled from a single pistol shot.

Lysandra shoved the barrel of the gun against the Amazon's head and fired a second time. All intent faded from the soldier's dark, murderous eyes.

"Perhaps I should be first," Lysandra said.

"Quite a progressive scandal." Geta took his wife's hand, curling close to her.

Together, they followed the dwindling centurions to the spaceport.

The glass of Artaxata was molded from the bones of all
children of the Unnamed Empire.

F IRES RISING FROM MOLTEN pits and burning bodies locked the
centurions into a narrow approach. If he was to keep his men alive,
Caracalla needed them to evade the bulk of the forbidden Quantum
arrows. The general's rank cape wrapped around his massive sword,
keeping it across his back and easier to access.

Far beyond angry women and battle-hardened men, Queen Fola stood
at the entrance to her palace. She did not cower beneath the robed statue
of her heathen sun god. Instead, the amber-skinned vision stood proud,
just as capable of violence as those in her service. The wings of her helmet
spread above her head. A dress hued in elegant purple cushioned her
from the segments of bronze armor outlining her muscles. She raised
a silver bow etched with gold, shaping her into an even more glorious
target.

The general fired his pistol, flinging concussive shots over the shoulders of his own men. He ordered his soldiers onward, even as the Amazons braced their own shields.

Sunlight washed over Fola, making her glow beyond the range of human beauty. Regalia was beneath such a being. If she hadn't stood against the Empire, Caracalla would have confessed his admiration.

His words defied his instincts. "Lock shields. Raise spears and javelins. Death to the Amazon Queen!"

The centurions echoed history's unending demand. "Death!"

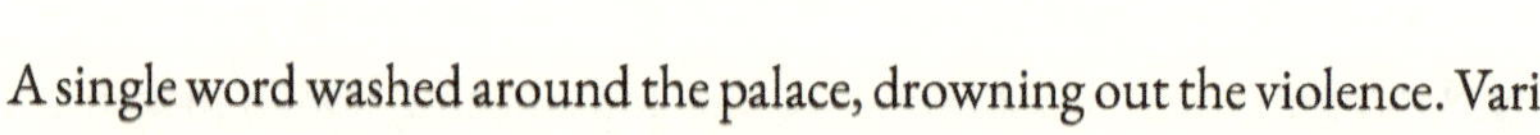

A single word washed around the palace, drowning out the violence. Vari refused to surrender to it, even though so many had already fallen.

Three Brasilian warriors jumped from their places on the plaza rooftops, rushing toward Vari, Bassiana, and Saran. Each warrior placed a hand to their heart and bowed their heads for an instant.

Targeting eyepieces hung on many of their faces, yet none of them lit with active data. Vari stood with as much presence as safety permitted. "How many Quantum arrows do you have?"

"None.

"I just ran out."

"I don't have any."

Vari touched Saran's wrist. "How many do you have?"

"Six."

"Give them each one."

Saran nodded once, passing an arrow each to the others.

Bassiana pulled her arms close to her body. Her dark, regal eyes narrowed with visible scrutiny.

"We'll keep following Geta." Vari clapped two of the warriors on the shoulder. "I need the rest of you to move in behind the centurions attacking the palace. Use those arrows to break through their lines."

The warrior Vari hadn't touched looked deep into her eyes. "It will be done, Imperator."

Such a label was not hers to carry. It belonged to her father. It had been stolen by the Usurper.

Yet those who stood for New Brasilia used the term freely.

A solemn breath sank into Vari's chest, though she defied the weight of such an anchor. Thank you," she said. "Mother, Saran, let's go."

The warriors rushed away with a drumming of footsteps.

Vari ran for the spaceport, the Imperial battle cry echoing behind her once more.

"Death!"

As the distance between them closed, Caracalla locked eyes with Fola. He freed the greater sword from his back, visualizing its mass ripping through the queen's armor, her flesh, even chopping her bones apart. His shoulder pressed against a centurion entering the third row.

An explosion shook the air from behind Caracalla. Centurions cried out. "Amazons at the rear."

The general turned back. Another arrow tore through the soldiers following him. Putrid magma blistered the air.

Someone howled over Imperial channels about Quantum arrows.

Caracalla gasped when he realized the voice was his.

A third explosion rippled through the ground behind Caracalla. Fractured screams echoed off the palace walls. Centurion shields melted under the explosive wake.

Any effort to claim the palace crumbled like the structured formations of Caracalla's men. Taking Brasilian prisoners of note meant nothing if Geta failed to present evidence to the Imperator.

Caracalla studied Fola's gaze. The statuesque woman never budged from her position at the front of her palace. New Brasilia was her world. It would take more than a parade of centurions to drive her loose.

"Fall back," he commanded. "To the spaceport. Double time."

Stimulant boosters throughout Caracalla's armor injected his muscles with a furious flood of synthetic testosterone. His legs propelled him toward the plaza. As he dashed, two women and a young man appeared in the distance. Amplified strength shot the general through the air in a single bound.

The flat of his sword crushed one Brasilian. Caracalla twisted in an arc. His speed smashed through the bow of a young archer. The taste of ozone filled his nose and mouth. Caracalla swung again, tearing through the Amazon's remaining breast. He slammed his sword downward, cleaving the remains away from his weapon.

He pointed the tip of the blade back toward the palace, hoping Fola noticed.

Guns blasted every direction, each shot echoed off the one before. Amazons stopped pushing through centurion defenses, but it didn't keep Geta's pistol from snapping at any potential enemy.

The enemies of the Unnamed Empire were less than human. Anything less than human was not entitled to any respect.

Flags rippled overhead, filled with pride for House Severus and New Brasilia. The planet may as well have been New Nihl for all it mattered. Macrinus showed pity to the orphan and his—her—mother. An Imperator ruled with any power he saw fit. Macrinus began his reign with wisdom and justice. The Amazons only offered spite when they should have given gratitude.

An elaborate archway loomed behind the towering flags. Such a great curve of stone and steel, wasted on a heretical populace.

Imperial soldiers surrounded a grand oval spacecraft. Immense cannons hung from the widest points of the man-made ellipse. Orange bolts shook the air before tearing through their pursuers.

Between explosions, many women screamed in woeful agony. Pride filled Geta at the sound of his victory.

One centurion turned. "Lord Geta. Captain Novall says the path is clear."

"Then run, damn you. Run."

Geta hand locked tighter with Lysandra's as they both sped up. The sides of his mouth curled in anticipation. The truth finally bubbled to the surface.

He planned to thank the Non-Dead spy, if such a thing ever proved possible.

Orange plasma flared from the spaceport. The plaza intersecting much of the city turned into a living hellscape. Infernal carnage tore through bodies and sculptures alike.

Vari crouched on the opposite side of the plaza. Her face twisted at the stink of liquefied stone and molten bones. "What madness is that?"

Bassiana pressed her left sleeve over her nose and mouth. "Narrow-beam assault cannons. They aren't atmospheric weapons. They melt everything they hit."

Clouds of smoke obscured most of the city, including the palace. Guns and arrows fired in both directions. An intersection of decorative fountains in the heart of the plaza bubbled with boiling water and bulged with toxic mud. Stray trickles of water turned gray from the ash flooding the air.

Saran tapped the targeting display tucked over her ear. "I can fire from here. Getting closer won't help."

Within a swell of dingy air, the regent glared where the palace should have stood. "No one's come through." She tugged the hem of her skirt, freeing a leather strip from her leg. As she pulled the strip apart, a pair of thin, curved blades emerged. She held one toward Vari, who shook her head.

If Saran fired, the next rupture of plasma would wash upon them. A ship wasn't their target.

Geta was.

Vari shook her head again. "Hold a moment longer."

When humanity faced losing their history or destroying
their shackles, the choice was simple.
The husks of Nihl warships littered the cosmos.

The Unnamed Scribe
Discussion on Human Reemergence

GETA RUSHED THROUGH THE confines of the Imperial starship,
still clinging to his wife's hand. He dropped her into a plush passenger seat before strapping himself into the next chair. A sharp exhale
rushed from his mouth. "I'll never have to set foot on that abysmal planet
again."

"It's wonderful to be done with it." Lysandra latched the safety harness over her lap and shoulders. Sweat poured down her brow, leaving
a lock of hair matted with perspiration. Despite the imperfections of
the moment, the Gallae appeared more beautiful and sensual than ever
before.

Geta gave his restraining harness a tug, ensuring its tightness. "You
should know, I intend to ravish you once we reach cruising speed."

She offered an exhausted smile. "I would expect no less."

"Good. Prepare your reports. I shall do the same. We'll transmit when
we reach orbit."

"Yes, my love."

Geta pressed a switch on his armrest. "Captain, how long until we lift off?"

A voice puffed from the speakers. "Two minutes after the rest of the centurions board, my Lord."

"Seal the door now. Have the remaining men transferred to Caracalla's command."

He shut off the communicator and triggered a data terminal to lift from the floor to his right. Lysandra plucked her fingers through an extensive report, striking each letter with a wealth of speed and grace. Geta typed at his own pace, detailing the discovery, noting specific quantities of Quantum-capable arrows and matching sword katas hidden from public scrutiny.

The ship shook all around as the engines fired. As the ship rose, it roared with turbulence and thunder, lingering gifts from the Amazons and their overheated planet.

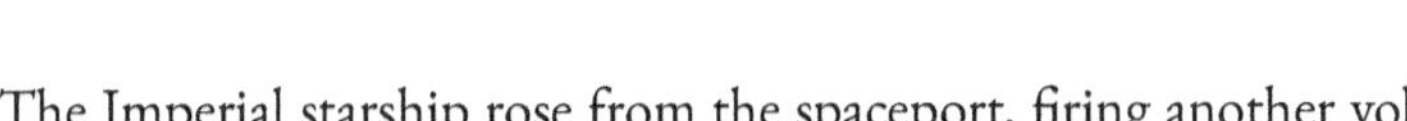

The Imperial starship rose from the spaceport, firing another volley of orange beams at the Brasilian architecture. Little more slag boiled the planet's surface following the stray attack.

Arrows rushed upward, knocking the ship sideways. The Quantum impact wasn't enough to deflect the craft from its ascent into the clouds.

"Locking now." Saran squeezed two fingers against the side of her targeting reticule.

"Get it." Frustration tensed Vari's mouth. She wished she'd let Saran attack while the ash was thicker.

Tiny lines and minuscule numbers zipped across Saran's eye. She pushed Vari back. "I'm about to blast Quantum all over this place."

The ground shook with storming footsteps. Hundreds of armored feet proceeded from the palace at a hard march. Bassiana braced herself in an attack position, ready to take a few men with her to the grave. "We are about to have guests."

"Target locked." Saran extended her bow, letting the angular metal arc around her body. She lifted the weapon, keeping the handle pointed at the Imperial ship rising beyond the clouds. When the ship moved, Saran's hand followed it. Her free hand eased over her shoulder, grasping the end of a Quantum arrow. As the shaft slipped into position, the rear node glowed with white and blue swirls. The same glow engulfed Saran as she pulled back on the string.

A scattered wall of centurions raced through the combative cloud around the palace. Speed compelled them more than any defensive craving. Spears and rifles edges over their disconnected shields. Every man howled his own battle cry.

Seven centurions charged at them. Rifles fired toward Saran.

Vari dashed at the closest shooter, shoving the warmed weapon up before diving onto the soldier.

Bassiana slid under a centurion's shield, slashing upward with her blades. She rose above the shield, chopping into the soldier's neck. The limp body tumbled in a wet crash, depositing his weapons.

Using the fallen rifle, Vari shot ahead of charging cluster of centurions.

Rather than halting from Vari's attack, the centurions stopped as swirls of blue and white light blossomed over the plaza.

Quantum flowed through Saran's bow and arrow as she drew the string. A single arc stretched upward, twisting into a thin line rising toward the escaping starship. Saran's arrow snapped free, blasting upward. Clouds ran from the gleaming bolt. The atmosphere screamed through the shimmering approach.

An explosive burst of pale aqua spread overhead, knocking the ship into a spin. Smoke spewed from one end of the flattened metal ellipse, yet the craft remained in the air.

Another arrow snapped into Saran's hand. Her head and bow remained in line with her target. She kept her legs locked at an open angle, her back curved like a reed in the wind.

Her muscles would have been delightfully strong. Her skin would pull and press beyond the delight of nocturnal contortions.

Rather than make such sweet contact, Vari rushed another centurion, twisting her body so the soldier would shift at a vulnerable arc. Bassiana swept behind the centurion, slashing the soldier's calf muscles.

Vari stole the fallen man's gladius, immediately blocking a spear thrust from another centurion. She chopped away the tip and rolled against the incoming shield. When Vari elbowed the man's skull, Bassiana thrust a blade through the man's face.

Saran drew back on her drawstring. A deep breath lifted her shoulders as she adjusted her bow. Her lips parted, letting her release the air in her lungs and the tension in her string. The arrow rocketed upward, bending into an arc as it raced after the Imperial ship.

Saran drew another arrow, ready to fire as the previous struck the escaping craft.

Blue, red, and yellow blistered the sky. Air rumbled in a shower of debris. A second explosion grew from the cacophony of color, breaking the ship in half before it shattered into a thousand pieces.

A prideful grin grew across Vari's face. Her heart quickened at Geta's defeat. Her lungs trembled in glee since Saran's hand delivered the decisive blow.

Before any cry of joy emerged from Vari, a crimson cape fluttered into her path. A massive centurion landed next to Saran. A shining metal curtain as long as the centurion swept down. In a single stroke, Caracalla swung through Saran, dividing her weapon, her last arrow, and her body. A line of gore shot from her left shoulder to her right hip. Threads of blond hair drifted in the sudden breeze.

The Amazon fell in twain, landing with a wet slap against the pavement.

Caracalla spun, lifting his greater sword in an easy salute. "You have fought well, young Severus, but your ambition should have given you prudence."

Prudence was impossible. Vari's legs pushed her toward her enemy. The size of the general's weapon didn't matter, only the bloody band angling over the blade. Death lived in Vari's fingertips, doomed to eternally crave Saran's vibrant touch.

An arrow struck Caracalla from the side. Another drove into his shoulder. The massive man lost his balance, falling to his knees.

Caracalla dropped his weapon and lifted his hands. "We are defeated. I cede victory to House Severus and the warriors of New Brasilia. As spoils, I seek to parley with Queen Fola."

Screams scratched inside Vari's throat. She kicked the general down, pinning Caracalla on his back. The damage was already done—on both sides. But Caracalla didn't surrender until after he'd attacked Saran. Vari turned the sword tip downward, ready to pierce the general's heart.

Bassiana grabbed Vari by the wrists, dragging her away from the general. "You cannot kill him. He may know something important."

Steam hissed through Vari's teeth. "He... he killed..." Vari didn't glance to the side, nor could she allow the words to mirror reality.

"I know, Vari. Fola held me back when your father died."

"He killed—"

"Stop." Bassiana pushed herself in front of her daughter. "Breathe."

Vari screamed. The impotence of combat shook the gladius she held. Vari pulled herself from her mother, throwing the sword away.

Within a widening pool of blood, Saran's lips held a satisfied curl. The expression echoed the same humored smile she wore when she poked fun at Vari.

She wanted to hold Saran, know her warmth and presence one last time. Such a sensation was impossible at the angle of Caracalla's strike. It left Vari frozen with the frigid impossibility of reality coiling around her eyes and heart.

After all Imperial spite had been swept from the city, Caracalla sat in a dungeon. Caged alone, the general still wore his chest armor, though his cape, belt, helmet, and weapons had been removed. He glared through the bars.

"You cannot win." Caracalla did not thread spite into his voice as he spoke. "Reinforcements will come."

Fola stood away from the cell. She too still wore her armor, complete with all her regalia. "Your men have been disarmed. They will be cared for until a suitable opportunity allows them to be sent home."

Caracalla shook his head. "It won't matter. Your Spartan rivals will heed the call of their Imperator."

The Queen was not moved by her adversary's boast. "Then why surrender?"

"To bargain for your life." He rubbed his buzzed scalp. "Do as I say and I can protect you from what's coming."

"You were the one who surrendered, general. Not I."

"I offer clarity to accompany your wisdom. The full might of the Unnamed Empire will soon fall upon you. What can you do when an armada of Imperial warships blockades your planet? What can you do to hold off the tide of soldiers who storms your homeland? In a week, you'll be attacked from every direction. In a month, you'll be under siege." Caracalla hardened himself and approached the edge of his cage. "Who will feed your people if the Imperator brings his sword upon you?"

Fola locked her arms across her chest. "You're failing to scare me."

"I bring you the reality of your situation." Caracalla sighed as he retreated from the bars. "You cost me more men than I expected. You'll make anyone pay dearly for attacking you, but you cannot fight the entirety of humanity."

"What noble advice."

"Think of your people, not some duplicitous Gallae or her mother."

Fola tensed at the venomous reference to her second cousin. Such malice whispered beyond Vari's peculiarities. They needed a male Imperial heir, not a Brasilian woman confined within a boy's flesh. "I lived through the last war, general. I'll walk away from this one as well."

She left the dungeon, letting Caracalla stew in solitude.

Fola returned to the war room, making no effort to remove her armor or loosen her burdens. She flopped into her chair, pressing both hands over her face.

Bassiana loomed beside her cousin, blocking any of the steady gathering of analysts from monitoring their queen instead of their stations.

Anger lines betrayed Fola's age when she lowered her hands. "He played us."

Bassiana kept her voice low. "How?"

"He made us waste time. He says he's pleading for our lives." A rigid breath crumbled from Fola's nose. "The Spartans are already on their way."

"Then we trade him, or at least the centurions."

Fola rubbed her forehead. "I have no desire to kill a thousand men."

"Then call in our favors."

The Queen audibly slapped her hands against her armrests. "This wasn't supposed to happen for at least another five years. You were supposed to find a wife for Vari who could bring us ships. Now, we have nothing and we have to fight a war."

Bassiana stroked the knuckles of her cousin's hand. She closed her eyes and drifted into a solemn nod. "What do you want us to do?"

Fola sighed. She ordered men killed, but Bassiana actually performed the fatal act. "Honor the newly dead. We should pray the Elagabal grants us the wisdom to find a path to the future."

Let them bury or burn their dead, if they like.
They'll have to do it again tomorrow.

King II Leonidas

WHEN THE DAWN RETURNED, smoke still lingered over New Brasilia. Streaks of ash and fire kissed every building, including the Temple of the Elagabal. Around the grand dome, hundreds of pyres had been erected, each bearing the empty flesh of a Brasilian warrior.

Within the temple, the queen's inner circle stood around a steel casket. Fola had dressed herself in a simple dress of loose black fabric trimmed with the darkest shade of red. Her thumbs pressed the edges of the open vessel containing the remains of the late Lieutenant-General Saran in full armor and regalia.

The Queen faced her entourage with dry eyes. Her tears fell in a deep solitude of the loneliest night. "The sisters of our flesh will be offered unto the sky. This sweet sister of our soul, a Brasilian not of New Brasilia, will be returned to the family of her birth. Let her name be noted first among our honored dead."

Tears hadn't stopped pouring from Vari's eyes. She'd cried all night, passing out from the heartache. When she woke, her cheeks were still wet from sadness, even though she'd slept following the battle and the long night after.

Saran lay in her casket, her wide eyes closed to the living universe. Blond hair framed her face and cushioned her neck. The armor of her posthumous promotion fit her as though she were born to it. Bronze plates mimicked her frame, gold and silver inlay traced the shape of her muscles. Poised between her hands and feet, she held a bow identical to the weapon she'd fired at Geta.

The temple priest lifted his hands from the altar, exalting the sun's rays as they washed over Saran's body. "Let us now give our sisters the awe of silence." His hands smashed together without making a sound.

The quiet temple drew sobbing from deeper within Vari's soul. Others echoed her anguish with restrained sniffles.

In the presence of the Elagabal and all of New Brasilia, Vari defied the holy offering. "No." Vari snapped her hands into fists. "Saran is not a woman of silence. I don't know a single Brasilian warrior who is best honored by quiet, especially not Saran."

Bassiana's stifled voice shot a glare in response. "This isn't the time."

"When is the right time?" Vari didn't restrain herself, not by words or motion. "Are we supposed to stay quiet while everyone else decides how to kill us? We've been quiet for ten years, Mother. Now, the fire is lit. Let us burn across the galaxy. Every world will see our dawn. The Elagabal rests within every star, so let's show them what's been in front of them all along."

Stern, dark eyes fumed from many faces. Of them, Bassiana spoke. "Varia, you're upset—"

"Saran deserves better." Serenity enveloped Saran's eternally still face.

Solus stepped down from the height of the altar, opening his hands to Varius. "You speak of her with conviction, but what better could we give her?"

"For Saran—for all our warriors?" Varius watched Fola's rigid expression. His mother's rage grew too loud for any sound to express. "I promise a gift to the fallen we honor today. I pledge to take for them the only gift worthy of their lives—The Throne of the Unnamed Empire."

Broke gasps and voices processed Vari's words. A swelling of murmurs filled the temple.

Vari touched Saran's lips. They had the right color, but felt cold and unnaturally smooth. "Saran, for you, I'll take it all."

Aside from a few lights at the end of the hall, the only sights for Caracalla were bars and bland walls. He glared at the drain in the middle of the room, while sewer gas hissed from the small slots.

If his position and Fola's had been switched, he would have allowed her to take part in the funeral rites for her soldiers. Instead, he sat alone, without a single word about the welfare or condition of his centurions.

Pyres surely filled the city streets. Thousands of families would ignite flames and blend their loved ones with refuse and ash. All because the New Brasilian government hid Quantum batteries and arrows capable of piercing the heavens.

Sedition was inevitable in Geta's eyes, but Caracalla hadn't listened. The Imperator and the Senate legislated away any path to backwards ascension. If Sextus had been half as shrewd, the women outside would still be alive. Macrinus would only have a distant claim to ruling humanity.

Instead, Fola and Bassiana engaged in treachery. They plotted mass genocide, just as they concealed the young woman's true gender.

Yet it was Macrinus, not House Severus, who carried the Twelfth Quantum Sword. As the highest-ranking weapon, its owner automatically gained the rank of Imperator. Every human war commander knew they needed to protect their weapons from being exploited by the Nihl. The genetic security system ensured executive ranking throughout the Empire.

When Sextus was lost, the Eighth Sword was lost with him. Even if Varius killed Macrinus, the Twelfth Sword would never obey him. Her. Whatever the foolish child wanted, they could study all the combat techniques in the galaxy and never assume the Throne of Humanity.

A dried voice spoke. "Such a waste."

Caracalla's brows lifted. There were only bars, bare walls, and distant lights. No one was present to speak with him.

Still, the voice spoke again. "The drain."

In the floor, the brickwork took on a subtle slope, leading to a slotted metal plate stained by whatever fluids had been deposited by the room's previous occupants. Even the seams between bricks bore similar stains of aged yellow and desiccated brown.

The faint outline of a face twinkled between the slots. A pair of eyes watched him. Tiny lights flickered in sequence along the speaker's head.

"A Non-Dead cannot easily walk into a New Brasilian dungeon, General," the speaker said. "Especially, with a prisoner as distinct as yourself on hand."

"I didn't think there were many Non-Dead on New Brasilia."

The Non-Dead sighed. "There aren't. I and my colleagues came specifically to help Lord Geta complete his assignment."

"You identified the caches."

The Non-Dead bowed. "I discovered young Severus's secret room as well. I was most surprised to find evidence of his Gallae persona."

"I care not for a child's desires."

"Which makes you a rare man of quality and honor, General. I would like to be your friend."

Caracalla was trapped waiting for Imperial retribution. "Instead, I am a prisoner."

"Then I should help you escape."

"I will not sell my flesh to you, Non-Dead."

"Nor do I want it. I want a meeting with the Imperator."

"Impossible. One does not command an unrequested audience. Your kind aren't even commoners. It's beyond you."

"You can arrange it."

"I just told you it's not possible."

"Lord Geta thought it was. Perhaps he knew something you didn't." The Non-Dead brushed his fingers over his brow. "I'll let you think about it. We'll talk again once the Spartans are closer."

Fola remained at the Temple of the Elagabal throughout the day, watching the pyres dwindle against the sunset. Within the temple, Vari stayed at Saran's side, unwilling to move for food, for drink, for a hint of relief.

"She won't leave her."

Bassiana glanced inside before letting her head sink. "Eventually she will, but a part of her will stay tied to Saran."

"When Saran first begged to train here, I didn't believe her. The only thing she wanted more than to be Brasilian was to stand beside your daughter. None of us will ever know how deep her loyalty or fondness runs, not even Vari."

The cousins nodded in acknowledgment of their shared lack of understanding.

After a moment, Bassiana wedged her fingers against her mouth and nose. "When it comes time for us to prove our quality, will any of us measure up to Saran?"

"You suggest the impossible, cousin." Fola hugged Bassiana with one hand around the Regent's waist. Their shoulders and heads pressed together without mournful decorum. "The best we can do is measure up to ourselves."

One thing that haunted Varia was the unknown horrors
committed in her name.
The Imperatrix preferred to know her demons personally.

The Clarion
The Presence of the Imperatrix

F OUR BRASILIANS IN FULL armor marched in front of Caracalla's
cell. Three aimed pistols at the general, while the fourth Brasilian
opened the door. "Lord Caracalla, come with us."

He rose and nodded. Surrounded by the warriors, he walked through
the dim halls with his head held high. Rather than ascend away from
the dungeon, they wound through deeper passages flanked by vacant
closet-sized cells. Two more armored women stood beside a thick steel
door. One pulled it open as the general approached.

"Inside, please," the other Brasilian said. Despite her concise assertion,
she maintained a respectful tone.

Caracalla said nothing as he walked into the room.

The door slammed shut behind him. A slab table dominated the
room. Cabinets with clear doors lined every wall, displaying the customized surgical tools ready for expert use.

Bassiana stood on the opposite side of the slab table. Her arms crossed
over the front of a plain crimson shirt. She'd twisted her braids into a bun
piled high along the back of her head.

"Shall we talk?"

"There is nothing for us to discuss." Caracalla crossed his arms in a defiant echo of Bassiana's position. "You violated your oath of nonaggression. You conspired to teach your son forbidden Quantum Sword techniques. You coerced your cousin, the queen of New Brasilia, to commit treasonous actions against a lawfully positioned military force. I have nothing to say to you. May I return to my cell?"

Bassiana flicked two fingers at the general. A tiny barb soared across the room. Caracalla caught the slender metal fiber before it could hit him in the face.

"Do you know why I still have two breasts, General?"

The barb slipped from Caracalla's fingers, bouncing along the darkened concrete floor. "You never had enough exposure to Quantum Arrows to melt part of your body. Such activities are inappropriate for an Imperator's bride."

An insidious smile crept over Bassiana's face. She approached a cabinet and an audible lock snapped open. "My family's trade is information. My mother and father both served House Severus this way. When Macrinus conspired against us, he lost his brother. Luckily, I found him—for the few days he survived."

Suddenly, strength abandoned Caracalla's knees. He stumbled, catching himself against the edge of the slab. His lungs flexed in an anxious, unwarranted panic.

"I did not train my son in this manner. Until he was nine, he studied the katas you saw, along with tactics, economics, and social policy." Bassiana took a curved scalpel from the cabinet. "You can fall on the floor, if you like."

"The barb..."

"Contact inhibits equilibrium. It maintains muscle function without impairing any function above the shoulders. As big as you are, you might even be able to shrug."

The general collapsed onto the floor.

"You saw my son's private room. This is mine."

Bassiana flowed around the table and unfastened the straps of Caracalla's armor. He swung an arm to push her away—but lost all strength as soon as he lifted a hand.

"Before we begin, I want you to think about Quantum Swords, especially where Macrinus keeps his."

"No."

"Don't be so coy about it." Bassiana pushed the large man against the table. With several grunts, she lifted him onto the slab.

Once Caracalla was on his back, Bassiana used a scalpel to puncture a muscle close to his spine. Knives, spears, bullets, and stones had pushed their way into Caracalla's flesh at one point or another. He'd fought to maintain himself to keep such wounds from severing his certainty in battle. A calm mind was often triumphant in his experience. Responding to pain, no matter how deep the eruption, begged one to lose themselves to the weakness of disloyalty. The most wounded creature always howled against their rationality. Despite knowing this or possessing decades of endurance training, the smallest grunt escaped Caracalla's restraint before the interrogation truly began.

"What did you tell the Spartans to do?"

"Attack."

Bassiana pulled back. "Cooperative already?"

A strained sneer rose along Caracalla's face. "I already told the queen."

She pierced the scalpel along a higher band of muscle, cutting where Caracalla's ribs connected to his vertebrae. "If you intend to be flippant, I will inflict every measure of destruction you visited upon the warriors of New Brasilia, starting with Saran of Virago."

The name echoed with familiarity, but Caracalla couldn't place it. "I don't remember the name."

"That was the young woman you chose to cleave before you surrendered." Bassiana plunged the scalpel into another nerve cluster, lighting the general's lungs on fire.

———◆○◆———

Vari entered her aunt's study with her head low. Her hand clutched a white handkerchief colored in two tones with heartache.

Outside the window, several pyres smoldered against the dusk sky.

Fola's hands remained in her lap as she watched the fleeting embers of her devoted followers. Her armor lay over her desk, adorned with hundreds of scratches and burn marks. There hadn't been time to note which were new.

Without turning from the pyres, the queen spoke. "When you are Imperator, will you leave a Quantum Blade sitting unattended on whatever ship last carried you?"

Vari's lip sagged. "No."

Fola's voice hung in a whisper. "Then why..." She glared at a pyre as it crumbled into stagnant ash. "Would you even consider—" Her voice spiked like a crash of thunder on a clear day. "—leaving your secret room unlocked?"

"I didn't think—"

"No. You didn't. There are things your mother should have taught you after your father died."

Even if she was Queen, Fola didn't have the full picture. Vari had locked the room. It was secure. But the implications were too abominable for Vari to consider. "Aunt Fola, you don't—"

"I didn't tell you to speak." The Queen hammered a fist on the edge of her desk. Her eyes turned, lined with the ruins of a thousand earthquakes.

Vari shook her head, a frustrated tremor more than a denial. "I never meant to put anyone in harm's way."

The Queen's aching eyes aimed fury at Vari's face. She emptied a sharp breath. "At least you have the sense to recognize what's happened because of you."

Vari tasted Fola's unquenched rage. "Too many are dead."

Fola opened a hand toward the dying pyres. "How many will die because of this?"

"I haven't heard the current tally."

The Queen popped her knuckles. "I'm not asking how many are dead. Tell me how many more will die because of your negligence."

It was impossible to count how many would come from Sparta. There wasn't a way to estimate who would follow Geta. If Fola's allies joined the fight, how many would fall? Did House Severus have secret allies waiting to prove their loyalty? The response to all those inquiries reached the same point in Vari's mind. "I don't know."

"Of course not. You couldn't keep a door locked, so, in a week, thousands will die. You can't keep a Gallae out of your bed, so in a month, a million will die. How long will it take for a billion to die? How long, Varia?"

Endless anger fueled Fola's questions. Nothing said the lessons of a queen couldn't be as painful as those taught by a general. "The longer the fighting goes on," Vari said, "the more likely we all die."

"Every time you make a decision, ask yourself how many more people will die."

"I understand."

"Good." Fola turned back to her previous position. "If you don't mind, I would prefer to be alone."

Vari quietly lowered her head, then stepped out. After Fola made a point, she never cared to litigate it again.

There'd been truth in the queen's questioning, but a lingering fact gnawed at Vari. She'd locked away all her secrets, yet they'd still gotten out.

<hr>

A thousand tiny cuts scattered around Caracalla's spine. Bassiana set aside her latest tool, a two-pronged jagged hook slathered in dark blood. Specks of the same darkness danced over the Regent's fingers and hands.

Beside the slab, half a lemon lay in a nest of bloody instruments. Puddles of diluted fluids pooled under the cut of fruit. Bassiana pressed the lemon against the fresh wounds in the general's back. The large man whimpered behind his locked jaw.

"No need to restrain yourself." Bassiana rubbed the fruit in a firm circle before pulling it away. "I have no intention of letting you die."

Caracalla opened his mouth. Words ran from him. "She killed an Imperial official."

"At last. Caium Caracalla speaks from his soul." Bassiana put the lemon back with the used tools before taking out a stubby blade sprawling with tiny serrations. "This is the point where quality answers rise from the subconscious."

"Anyone who attacks the Imperator's banner forfeits their life." Caracalla sucked in quick, searing breaths. "Execution is the law."

"I don't recognize your Imperator. He stole everything he values from my husband." She pressed the small blade into a clean patch of skin between Caracalla's neck and shoulders. "Service to the Usurper should be punishable by death."

⎯⎯⎯◆O◆⎯⎯⎯

Vari took Caracalla's greater sword to her room—the same room that Geta and the Imperials had ransacked. She hadn't cleaned the weapon. Instead, her eyes fixated on the erratic crimson line that dried on the blade.

With both hands locked around the base of the sword, Vari shifted through her favored kata. The tip aligned with some imagined target, a version of Caracalla, bound to a wall, unable to evade. Vari shifted the weapon parallel with the floor, wincing at a familiar strain in her wrists. She swung upward, letting the sword's inertia keep the weapon in motion. As she twisted in a spiral, the tip swept across the center of her ethereal target.

Vari didn't need to project Quantum to kill. Her steaming anger fueled each thrust. Grief burned a path behind every slash. Her body moved through every step of the kata, even if it lacked the full exertion of her family's weapon. If she had a Quantum Sword at that moment, it would have given her no joy.

Each muscle boiled with lactic acid. After endless minutes of stinging agony, Vari dropped the greater sword.

"I can't..." Vari huffed against her screaming lungs and the stickiness of her parched mouth. "I should have protected her."

Vari closed her eyes.

Saran's sarcastic smile lingered close. Her hair glowed as it caught the wind on a sunny day. Vari had kissed the diagonal scar on the right side of her chest. She moaned deliciously when Vari touched the intimate line.

Lysandra laughed from the shadows. The Gallae ensnared Vari in a web of allure and sculpted perfection.

If Varia wanted perfection, she would have been with Lysandra when her ship exploded.

The pretty scar on Saran's chest never wavered. It was a line that, once crossed, could never be escaped.

Vari steamed at her inability to take vengeance. The dungeons were off limits for her presumed safety, even if her mother went there to quench savage desires. Vari could not drag Caracalla onto the plaza, nor order the general drawn and quartered for killing Saran.

An exhausted young woman had no one specific to defend.

No one except for a determined young heiress who wanted vengeance for Saran's death.

Nascent days of violence

Tears upon her cheeks

The Usurper eternally knows

A Fire Upon The Deep

Sister-Priestess Toivoa

Rhythmic Axioms of the Elagabal

AFTER HOURS OF WANDERING and consideration, Vari ventured to the war room and bowed while Fola read reports on a tablet. Several aides went about their duties, monitoring security and reviewing intelligence assessments. For at least two minutes, the queen remained locked upon whatever data rose to a ruler's gaze. Anything except for Vari's presence.

A would-be Imperator humbled. But a rigid pose was a small price for a meaningful request.

Fola passed her tablet to an aide. "Vari." There was no lesson or inquisition. She was far too busy for that.

Vari deepened her bow. "Queen Fola, may I make a request?"

She leaned closer. Her eyes drilled through the space between them. "You may."

"Thank you." Vari rose. Her heartbeat steadied for a chance to make things right. "If I may, I would like to escort Saran's body, if only to the spaceport."

Fola breathed in. "Might I ask why?"

Vari steadied the words in her mind before possibly sending them to her mouth. The Queen would scrutinize every thought and action. Others would search Vari's demeanor to the justify the loss of their loved ones.

"I want to help." Simplicity wasn't enough. Vari needed to deliver clarity. "I loved Saran. This is something I can do for her."

Fola turned to one of her aides. "Mhati, bring me the funeral transfer data."

An aide with a scar curling from her jawline brought a tablet to the queen. To call Fola's closest confidant and one of Vari's earliest combat teachers simply an aide undercut the woman's quality. Mhati gave a polite nod before stepping back to her duties

After a long, quiet glance, Fola gave the tablet to Vari. "Sister, daughter, or love, treat her the way she should be treated."

Vari lowered her head with gratitude more than respect. "I'll make sure those who take Saran will care for her as well as we would." She rose with an additional nod. "Thank you."

"Thank you for considering your words."

Back in his cell, Caracalla lay on his stomach. Every part of his body stung, especially along his back, where every cut pierced him with a deep, undying ache. He drifted at the edge of consciousness, but a voice kept calling for him.

"General Caracalla? General? Are you there?"

He hurt, but such pain didn't cause delirium. "Who's there?"

"General. Good. You're alive."

"I have felt too many obscure knives to call myself alive."

"You killed a popular woman." A stringy thread of blood ran from Caracalla's arms to the drain where the Non-Dead had spoken before. "Have you ever killed a popular person before?"

"I killed a soldier during a battle." Caracalla winced as his cuts stung him in unison. "Why are you here?"

"The same reason as before. I want to help you. In return, I only ask you to arrange for me to meet with the Imperator in private."

"Such a thing would endanger the Imperator."

The Non-Dead softened his tone. "If words are such a threat, then I fear for the Empire."

Caracalla's lungs strained as he breathed. He needed the wounds to heal if he hoped to hold up his end of a single conversation. "I can hardly move. Let me rest."

Laughter echoed from the drain. "There won't be much time later. Also, I need to demonstrate my good will."

Beneath the Temple of the Elagabal, Vari loomed within the storage crypt. Her stomach rolled at the notion of leaving Saran in a basement.

When she wasn't checking the funeral transfer data, Vari hugged the tablet against her chest. She'd read the basic details enough times to recite them from memory. For her journey to Gaulius, Saran's casket would lay solemnly in a cargo hold. After that, her family would take her, even though Saran hadn't mentioned them after she took a Brasilian name.

Vari enclosed the steel casket within a storage crate. Had she eaten, Vari would have vomited at the thought of anyone confining her closest friend into cargo. The act of heat sealing the crate should have been the only direct cause of nausea.

Solus walked into the crypt, carrying a pair of cups. The priest wore only a simple robe, having left all the intricate vestments upon the altar. "Are you well, Vari?"

"Well enough."

"Please don't lie, not when you are so troubled."

Vari lay the heat sealer aside and wiped her brow. "I don't know how anyone can feel well after the past few days."

The priest extended a cup to Vari. "You aren't supposed to feel well when you lose someone."

"You're right." Vari took the cup, watching warmth swirl into a low cloud of chocolate.

Solus wrapped his fingers around his own cup. "How do you see Saran?"

Vari stumbled through labels to find one that fit. "Legally, she was my cousin, at least on New Brasilia. She was my bodyguard." She sank over the cup of sweet steam. "She was my friend."

"Just your friend?"

Vari sipped the hot chocolate. "We loved each other. Friends, not exactly family. The night before she died, we spent the night together."

"Had you done that before?"

"A few times, usually at her urging."

Solus gave a soft smile. "I'll ask again. How do you see Saran?"

Vari took another drink. The chocolate appeared bright compared to the looming pit of gloom. Such hesitation was a pity, since Saran loved hot chocolate, even if she spurned most sweet things.

"I always thought of her as my best friend. No matter what we've done, that'll always be true."

"Let that be your guide," Solus said. "Your heart is the only box that can hold her spirit."

Mhati stiffened. Her eyes widened. "My Queen." Her fingers thrummed over a layer of buttons.

The Oval Desk shimmered with a new image. The bridge connecting New Brasilia and Sparta held a broad line of soldiers. Each approaching soldier held a round shield bearing the simplified arrow of Sparta's eternal advance. Every face lay under a helmet with oval eye holes separated by a spear-shaped nose guard. The soldiers all held up spears, locking into formation until they attacked.

A heavy sigh burrowed into Fola's throat, but she choked it back. "We knew they would come. Everyone to arms. Assemble near the gate." The queen pressed her hand against the plate on her chest. "Remember our sisters. Strike in their honor."

The warriors in the war room thrust fists upward. In unison, they all cried out. "To arms."

Every voice turned to their communicators. Orders spread like water, signaling the defense of their city and nation.

Alarms blared overhead, spurring every Brasilian soldier into battle positions once more.

A sleek hearse drifted to a stop once it circled the scorched pits tossed throughout the plaza. The elongated car hissed before landing on its six parking legs. When Vari got out, she faced only the spaceport.

Solus pointed toward a small ship with wide wings perched above the fuselage. A dust-stained cargo ramp lowered, allowing a lone spacer to file out. His protective suit encased him with red and black trim. An elliptical bubble shield retracted since New Brasilia's atmosphere favored human life.

The dark-haired spacer approached the hearse with a tablet tucked under his left arm. "Brother Solus? I'm Captain Lucan. I understand you need the *Enchantment* to transport something to Gaulius."

Solus bowed his head. "Yes. It's a funeral matter. Will that be an issue?"

Vari checked her own tablet, verifying the ship and its captain. The choice came from necessity, since the ship was already passing near New Brasilia.

"Shouldn't be. Is someone going to accept the... I don't know the right word."

Vari swept through the tablet and nodded. "Planetary Administrator Julius Pollus or his daughter, Julia Pollus."

"Pollus. Got it." Lucan tapped a gloved finger on his tablet. "Name of the deceased? So I can say who I'm bringing."

Pride refused to fill Vari's tongue. She needed to say Saran's name. She could even say her full posthumous title. No one after Lucan would ever again ask who Saran is. They'd only ask who Saran was.

Solus touched Vari on the shoulder. "I can finish, if you want."

Vari shook her head. She breathed in. The words defied her. Another breath squeezed into her lungs.

Impatience flooded the tapping of Lucan's foot. The captain's eyes remained steady and patient.

Forcing the captain to wait endangered his life. The Spartans would come. Or a fleet of Imperial ships. If that happened, Vari's own hesitation would cost a decent-seeming man his life. It would cost a family knowledge of their fallen daughter.

"Lieutenant-General Saran of Virago."

Lucan's eyebrows perked up. "Wow. Nice rank." He tapped on his tablet, then tilted his head. "Saran of Virago is an Amazon name, right?"

"That's her name." Vari kept any spite from her voice.

Solus folded his hands. "Is there a problem, Captain?"

"Well, yeah." Lucan shrugged with his tablet. "Between recent events and Gaulius never being a grand travel destination, I don't know that anyone, especially a planetary Administrator, will accept your friend. Warriors with royal names don't get shipped off world to get buried. Not to mention any Imperial detachment might confiscate her, uh, remains in case there's a weapon on board."

Solus gripped his fingers around the folds of his robe for an instant. "Vari, is Saran's birth name listed?"

"An adopted Amazon?" Lucan smirked. "You guys are full of surprises."

Vari said nothing as she swept through the details. Pages swept under her fingertip, spinning past in a breeze. Dozens of names appeared, scattered labels of Saran's next of kin. One possibility had Saran's birthday and no further details. "Judith Pollus?"

"Is that it?" Lucan's finger hovered over his tablet. "Judith Pollus?"

Vari scanned over the details again, nodding. Before Vari spoke, Solus answered. "Yes, Captain."

Lucan's head bobbed in acceptance as he typed Saran's dead name. A label she'd abandoned in life shrouded her in death. "I can work with that. No offense, but alliances with this planet are about to get thin."

"Glad to have someone like you on our side," Vari said with a smile.

"Our side?"

"Captain," Solus said, "this is Varius Severus, heir of Imperator Sextus Severus."

Vari internally cringed, but maintained her composure near a hospitable traveler.

Lucan's eyes swept from Vari's feet to his face. "You seem a bit more tan than the last Imperator."

"This is my mother's home world." Vari planted her feet. She'd given Lucan too much information, but her deceptions weren't nuanced. Vari could only lie to herself.

Lucan held his hand out. "I'd like to shake your hand. It's not every day when a man gets to meet real royalty."

Vari took the man's hand.

At the end of the silent exchange, Lucan nodded. "I'll take care of your friend."

Finally taking easier breaths, Vari mirrored the captain's gesture. Peace was possible for her again, even in a universe without Saran. Vari exhaled, taking on a greater calm.

A scattered formation of birds zipped overhead, racing inland.

Alarms brazenly squealed throughout the city.

On the First Day of Exodus, the Sekht exalted their home
star, Rah. They openly prayed, despite the rain of Spartan
warfare overhead.

"Rejoice, rejoice," they sang.
"A daughter is born of the sun.
"A son rises into heaven."

No one understood this omen, not even the former Gallae
who led the chorus.

Whisper John McClard
Annals of a Fractured Humanity

B ASSIANA ROUNDED A HALLWAY corner close to the war room.
Shrieks swelled every corner, shook every set of ears. A group of
warriors flanked the queen as she entered the hall, triggering Bassiana to
call out. "Cousin? Cousin?"

The group halted when Fola turned. "What is it, Bassiana?"

"I heard the alarms, but I can't find Vari."

Fola released a slow exhale. "She's at the spaceport."

"What's she doing there?"

Fola approached her cousin, bracing a hand against Bassiana's spine. "She's being responsible. She asked to handle the arrangements to transfer Saran's remains back to Gaulius."

Without another breath, Bassiana's eyes sprang open. She sprinted away from the queen and past the warriors. The skirts of her flowing dress whipped behind her.

The muted tones of an alarm whispered into Caracalla's cell. He sat up, bracing his hands on the edge of his cot. Every breath dragged against his rib cage. His sides burst with inflamed nerves. Every cut on his back boiled, even though the tiny wounds had all sealed. The taste of copper dripped down his throat.

"Madwoman."

The general stood, whining against the agony chewing through his muscles. No one guarded the end of the hall. No one arrived to change the watch. He'd been abandoned.

"Are you there, Non-Dead?" Caracalla tapped a foot on the drain. The soft pat of his boot echoed through the connected pipes.

No one responded. Only Sparta could cause such a reaction.

Queen Fola approached the gate. A pair of weighty binoculars pressed against her eyes. The image that had loomed over the Oval Desk remained unchanged as she appeared in person.

The wealth of Sparta's planetary forces stood at the gates of New Brasilia.

Mhati tugged on the straps of her armor. "They wait."

If such a mass waited, words might still halt the loss of blood. A last chance for peace before the battle began. "Train two arrows on my position," Fola said. "I will speak with them."

Gears squeaked and crunched as Fola stepped onto the wide bridge. She refused any transport to move her faster. Cars might carry bombs or hide soldiers. On foot, Fola flaunted her resolve for everyone to see. She never shifted her weight to account for the quiver slung over her shoulder, nor did she touch the sword on her belt or the bow on her back.

The Spartans remained still. Each spear remained held high. Every shield defended its owner and the next man in line. Their gazes were impossible to see. None of them spoke.

Halfway between the gate and the army, Fola stopped. She rested her hands on her hips. If someone wanted to speak with her, they needed to prove themselves.

A bridge of stones and pavement stretched between Fola and those approaching her gates. Seawater sloshed far beneath her feet, swirling around hundreds of small, empty islands. With air travel maintained by an isolated network of Imperial satellites, the bridge was the only connection between the two nations. In an hour's time, that path was shut by a defiant queen and the fiercest army humanity offered.

The center of the Spartan line parted for an instant. A hulking soldier stepped forward with an arched relay mounted on his helmet to command the others. He carried a spear on his right, a shield on his left, exactly like every living Spartan. His olive-shaded arms and neck were exposed to the open air. The remainder of his flesh was covered only by a maroon vest and pants. A braided beard extended down his chest, woven with bits of colored glass. He stopped far enough back for Fola to be safe, though not far enough away to let Fola use her bow.

"I am Dion." The Spartan's voice was gravel thrust in the air and ignited by thunder. "I carry the burden of leadership in my king's absence."

"Your king still battles the Sekht."

"He will continue until he is satisfied."

"May he strike swiftly to their heart."

Dion clanged his spear against his shield. The other Spartans followed his example. Their shared clash echoed over the water.

"We have come for the Imperial General Caium Caracalla. He was to visit Sparta. He has not been heard from."

"We have him."

"We will take custody of him and his men."

"No." Fola held her assertion. "He will stay."

"Is he your guest?" Following the last word, Dion spat through his helmet and beard.

"No longer. He conspired against my family and my people. He murdered members of my household." Though she was queen, Fola would never allow Varius to monopolize Saran's loss.

"Did they die in battle?"

"Yes, but an unwanted battle."

"My king craves to battle New Brasilia."

"Our truce stands."

Dion's mouth crunched. He leaned on his spear like he'd been wounded. Foam oozed out of his helmet. "Treachery," was the last word he spoke before falling on the pavement.

Fola commanded all those present, having heard Dion muffled words. "Do not fire." She approached the Spartan envoy, resting on one knee as she pulled off his helmet.

Dion's eyes rolled inward. Foam gushed from his lips, coating his thick beard. Bubbles popped out of his nose. Fola touched his wrist, feeling only ice.

Steam and wires rang out from behind the Spartan lines. Shapes bobbed up and down, forcing the spears to waver. A horde of black-shrouded figures tumbled over the front line. Wires and panels smeared over each figure's body. None had living faces, instead wearing pale masks with a uniform seam running down the center. The horde rushed at Fola. Their faces split open, revealing crimson conductors.

Fola ran for the gate. Dark red blasts chased after her, searing the pavement where she'd just stood. A cloud of pungent tar clogged her nose.

"Archers. Prepare to fire."

Fola jumped from side to side. Disrupted voices cracked through her relay. Explosive bursts showered her with the dust of annihilated cement. In the pause between bursts, the scuttle of feet scraped on the surface behind her.

"Count to three. Attack my helmet."

She took off her helmet. A vermilion streak ate through one of the sculpted wings armoring her relay.

One. Fola hurled the helmet ahead of her. The half-melted helmet clattered against the bridge.

Two. More reddened blasts struck the nearby pavement. The bridge started bubbling in spots surrounded by molten blasts.

Three. Fola jumped forward. Her body curled as she skidded along the surface.

A pair of arrows struck the bridge, annihilating her helmet in a surge of blue-white light. The impact shoved Fola closer to the gate. Her cape caught on fire, forcing her to release the blazing flag into the wind.

Brasilian soldiers raced around the queen. Their shields braced together, buckling against the horde's continued blasts.

When Fola burst through the gate, she braced her left arm against the broad wall. "Report."

Mhati made no salute. A line of red zipped far overhead. "Defensive arrows struck their target. A section of the bridge has been destroyed."

"Good. Call back our forces. Consider the bridge lost."

"Yes, my Queen." Mhati relayed the orders before bracing her wrist against her brow. "Were those things...?" Confusion curled the aide's mouth.

Fola drew in a deep breath. She tasted venom at the rising answer. "They were Non-Dead."

"It's illegal to weaponize Non-Dead."

The queen snorted a laugh. "So is stockpiling Quantum Arrows."

Captain Lucan gazed at the distant end of the city. "Quantum Arrows?"

Smoke rose from the wall and the coastal bridge beyond. Anything closer would have been inside the gate.

Solus clamped his fingers over his mouth.

Lucan's mouth twisted as he faced Vari. "Was that a Quantum Arrow attack?"

Vari turned from the rising plume to the spacers on the docking ramp. Her eyes refused to turn from a drone pushing Saran toward the docking ramp. Softly, Vari said, "Yes."

Smoke drifted outward, reaching for the plaza, the city, and the spaceport.

"Dammit." The captain pressed a button on his wrist. "Prepare for emergency liftoff."

Vari snapped a glance at her tablet. There were procedural details she needed to finish to uphold her responsibilities. Every note served as the last embers of proximity with Saran. "Captain, we still haven't processed everything."

"We'll do it in the air." Captain Lucan slapped a hand against Vari's shoulder. "In the Imperator's name, you need to get on the *Enchantment* right now."

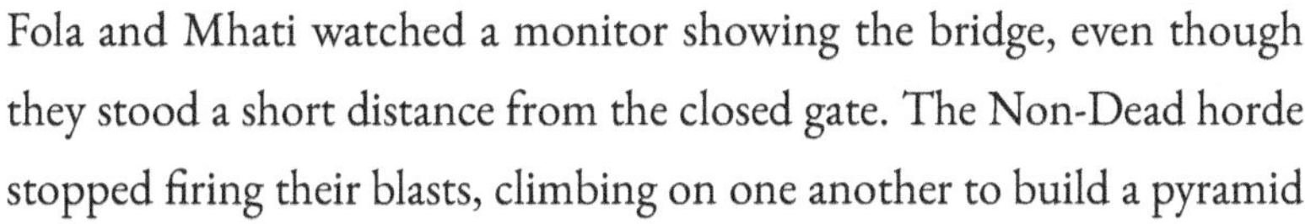

Fola and Mhati watched a monitor showing the bridge, even though they stood a short distance from the closed gate. The Non-Dead horde stopped firing their blasts, climbing on one another to build a pyramid of bodies.

The queen braced her arms against her chest. "I have never seen a more absurd demonstration of futility."

"I have seen Spartans commit fantastic physical acts." Mhati shook her head. "Why would these... things be allowed in the way?"

"They haven't tried to set out any cables." Fola frowned at the growing formation. "Why don't these Non-Dead let the Spartans patch the bridge?"

A Brasilian warrior approached and bowed. "My Queen, shall we attack the enemy formation?"

"No. I want to see what these Non-Dead are doing. Don't waste our arrows unless we need to."

On the display, the Non-Dead pyramid wobbled back and forth. Segmented faces inched closer in waves over the top of the wall. The blank expressions fell faster than the dull faces exposed their heretical weapons.

Mhati pressed her thumb and index finger against the image, comparing the flimsy height with the rest of the landscape. Eventually, she shifted her hand ninety degrees, both halves of the bridge gap without changing the spacing of her fingers. "The Non-Dead are the Spartan's bridge."

"Elagabal protect us." Fola exhaled sharply. "Attack the Non-Dead at once."

Arrows fired upon the mass of bodies. The pyramid toppled within the explosive cloud. A few Non-Dead who fell grabbed the edge of the gap. Other Non-Dead who remained intact scattered into a loose formation before climbing over those who gripped the broken bridge. As the formation swung across the gap, a few grabbed onto the distant side. The head-mounted blasts Fola dodged fired again, heating the makeshift biomass and the jagged edges of the gap.

The Spartans lowered their spears and charged forward, stopping before they reached the gooey patch. Each spear tip in the front two rows spewed a coat of green sealant over the hot sludge.

Dion, the fallen Spartan envoy, rushed out of the Spartan line. His head sloped downward like he was always staring at his feet. He ran ahead of the group. A glow of rusty red enveloped his joints, a color that grew brighter with every step the Spartan took.

When he reached the gate, a surge of blue-white light exploded away from Dion's flesh, evaporating the stone walls into a cloud of crimson dust.

Lucan froze, staring at the swell of azure rising above the far edge of the city. "That was a Quantum bomb."

Vari hesitantly stepped closer to the glowing orb blazing from the distant gate. It was the same light that shrouded the fleeting ship Saran had destroyed.

Long gloved fingers caught Vari's arm. "We have to go."

Solus yanked a pistol from under his tunic.

Lucan drew a larger pistol from his own waist in less than a blink. "Don't. It won't end well for you."

Solus scowled. "I won't let you harm him."

"I said he should come in the name of the Imperator."

Vari punched the captain's collar and pulled free. Lucan dropped the pistol. Vari kicked the weapon away.

"Wait." Lucan pushed his open hands into the air. "I don't invoke Macrinus." He unlatched the glove from his suit and pulled back the cloth sleeve inside.

Lucan lifted his exposed hand. A tattoo sealed the captain's wrist. The design illustrated an Imperial Eagle bearing one head, not two.

"Do you know this mark, Varius Severus?"

Such an aged emblem had been archaic for most of Vari's life. A decade, in fact, even though it once stood all around Vari. "Absolutely."

"Then, in the name of the Imperator, your father, Sextus Severus, I beg you to come with me."

Vari shook her head. "My family here needs me."

Lucan restored his sleeve and reconnected his glove. "In the next twenty minutes, there's a good chance your family will be dead. Would you like to die with them?"

"How? You don't know that."

"The truce is broken." Lucan's glove locks snapped shut. "Spartans have attacked your gates. A Quantum bomb just went off. How long will it take for Imperial fighters to fill the sky?"

Imperial ships laying waste to New Brasilia always posed a threat. The possibility loomed closer to reality, especially with so many spikes of escalation. Macrinus would love to have Bassiana drawn and quartered in Colosseum Titan. The Usurper would crucify Fola to send some perverse message to all of humanity.

Fola's ideas filled Vari's mouth. "The longer the fighting goes on, the more likely it becomes that we all die."

Solus whispered from Vari's side. "Do you mean for us to surrender?"

"Everyone dies," Lucan said. "Just because New Brasilia is under fire doesn't mean all Amazons are in the same state."

Vari tensed her lips. "There are no others."

"He speaks of the Disgraced," Solus said. "Warriors who broke their bows and turned their backs on New Brasilia."

"You can wait for everyone to die or you can get on board and find an ally." Lucan shrugged. "Your choice."

Possibilities swirled ahead of Vari. She'd triggered so much fighting already. A perfect soul lay in a crate, dead from her heroism. Spartans violated their truce to attack New Brasilia, even using their own forbidden Quantum weapons. If there was a chance that loyalty to her father could gather more allies, Vari wanted to take it.

After all, adding a second head to an Imperial tattoo was easy. With such ease, Lucan hadn't bothered to profess his loyalty to the Usurper.

Captain Lucan had the heart of an ally.

Vari nodded. "We board."

A countenance must be paid
A price taken from our souls, our lives
And those we leave behind.
All debts must be settled.

Vaticus Jupiter, the First Imperator
Sermon of the Swords

D UNGEON WALLS SHOOK. SLATE floors quaked.

From the drain, the Non-Dead spoke. "Isn't it magnificent?"

Caracalla clenched his teeth. "What?"

"My surprise. All this shaking comes from a drop of Quantum congealing within a Spartan. I'm sure the Amazons never suspected such a thing."

The general shook his head as disgust swelled upon his tongue. "I cannot condone such actions."

"If you are so displeased, you may stay here when I depart." The Non-Dead's factual tone remained unbroken as he shifted topics. "What evidence of New Brasilia's crimes do you still possess?"

"We have the katas—"

"Which are in the palace."

"The Quantum Arrows—"

"Your men are here, and Geta is dead."

"There was a Quantum Battery."

"Which was aboard Geta's ship. If the battery is still intact, the Amazons have reclaimed it."

Such a loss, losing Geta to Amazon treachery. The assessor had grown fond of his wife, more with every passing moment. Lysandra even committed herself to actively serving her husband's ideals.

The truth seized Caracalla by the neck. "What of the Lady Geta's claims?"

"Regarding Varius Severus's undisclosed proclivities?"

No matter how well the young man fought, Lysandra had proof that Varius longed to be a girl—and ineligible to become Imperator. "Yes."

"Much of the evidence was destroyed with Geta's ship." The Non-Dead smirked. "But not all of it. I've concealed a few incriminating items, samples from each category. They are sealed in a preservation case, which I will grant to you."

"When I present you to the Imperator in private." Caracalla sneered at the swirl of machinations. Give him a weapon and tactics, so he might honor the ancient gods. Such whispers served only the insidious.

"If that is your wish, General." The Non-Dead lowered his head, echoing deference. "The case is coded. If our enemies tamper with it, the materials inside will melt. I fear this may be the last evidence you have. Without it, our actions will appear as an overextension of the Imperator's will."

The Non-Dead's head rose. Faint indicators flickered across the creature's face. "Do I have your word that our interests are aligned, General Caium Caracalla?"

Every aching breath steamed through Caracalla's nose and mouth. A single light upon the Non-Dead's brow remained steady, even as others swayed on and off. If such a being betrayed Caracalla, the general would thrust the creature fully into death. "You have my pledge of honor."

Caracalla silently pledged the Non-Dead would remain in the Imperator's service until the evidence was delivered.

"Climb on your cot. The floor will not be safe to touch."

As soon as Caracalla curled upon the cot, he reflexively groaned at the strain from his assorted lacerations. Such pain drifted away an instant later as a glowing blob appeared on the floor. The amorphous shape slid into the loose shape of a hand. Steam rose from each fingertip. The palm bubbled. Plumes of stone gray smoke curled around the drain, grasping toward the ceiling. The general clamped a loose sheet over his nose and mouth. His coughs tasted like blood and gravel.

A thick thwump erupted from the floor. The drain dropped before widening into a pit of wet stone.

Dust billowed away from the Non-Dead, leaving a black cloak and hood to mark the shadow's presence. "Come. Our exit awaits."

Caracalla jumped into the shallow tunnel. Every burrowed slope had the luster of melted rocks that cooled in the past. "You dug this tunnel."

"I widened it. It was originally a sewage drain. Perhaps it will be again."

The Non-Dead crept down a tunnel of melted stones, and the general followed.

Bassiana sprinted toward the spaceport. Spiraled leather straps on her shoes squeezed her ankles. When rays of blue and white eclipsed the horizon, she kept her gaze forward. Upon the spaceport.

Upon Vari.

She was Bassiana's pride, the one reminder she had of a lover who cared. What had it mattered if the marriage had been arranged? Bassiana's heart and soul would always be Brasilian. Yet a piece of her, something entwined with wisdom, thoughtfulness, and hope belonged to Sextus Severus.

That part of Bassiana echoed in Vari, no matter how her daughter might react.

She had to find Vari, even as an explosion knocked her off her feet.

Some vanguard of Spartan ferocity blasted through the streets. Whatever caused the impact faded, even though so much Quantum wash still streaked over the sky.

Nearby shop owners peered out their windows. A well-dressed clothier emerged, tugging at the ribbon snap accenting his immaculate suit. He crouched beside Bassiana, trying to help her up. "Princess, what's happened now?"

Too much fear confined the eyes of the people. Not just the clothier. Anyone watching shared the same expression of awe and dread.

"Thank you." Bassiana pressed a gentle hand upon the clothier's silk jacket. Why hadn't he fled for a safehouse? "I must go. You should do the same."

Her ears blotted out any sounds that followed. Bassiana moved as fast as she dared, darting from one intersection to the next.

In time, she saw Solus's hearse. The rear door was still open.

A broad-winged ship rose above the port.

No sign of Solus remained around the car. Saran's remains weren't in the hearse or lying nearby. Nothing told Bassiana where to find her daughter, leaving the regent as powerless as the day Fola and Saran first explained how Vari wasn't a stupid little boy.

Bassiana's throat shook in her grief. Her daughter had to be protected. "Vari!"

Half of Fola's face burned. Her grimace easily implied pain more than the disgust churning within her stomach.

Any archery seemed foolish under a bed of rubble and segmented rock. Too many lay dead, no matter if their bodies lay submerged in circuitry, muscle, or Quantum scarring.

Mhati relayed orders while a medic bandaged Fola's face.

"What's going on?"

The medic tugged on Fola's bandage. "Be calm, my Queen."

"Not while we fight." A crater of heated slag opened New Brasilia to attack. Exposure to the blast tore at Fola's intestines.

Mhati screamed into her own helmet. "Stand fast. Our Queen waits for word of your glory."

Fola pulled away from the medic, shifting toward her lieutenant. "What's happened?"

Mhati lowered her head to the queen. "Another wave of Spartans is crossing the mass of Non-Dead. They're continuing to push our warriors back."

If the Spartans successfully crossed the bridge, nothing would hold them back. Yet the Brasilians kept falling back, one step at a time.

"I need a helmet. Mhati, tell the front line that I will stand with them."

A voice called for Fola by name, shuffling through the assembly of warriors. "Fola? Fola?" Bassiana's pile of braids dangled erratically from the right side of her head.

"Let my cousin through."

The crowded warriors parted, allowing Bassiana to approach. She stumbled, failing to kneel or bow. "They took her, Fola."

Fola pulled Bassiana up. Another blast shook the air. "Cousin." A sharp exhale raced from Fola's nose. "I can't chase Vari right now. I have a gate to hold with bodies alone."

Bassiana faced the queen, gasping through her panting. "Cousin, your face—"

"I'll heal. Go back to the palace." Darkened specks loomed in the distant sky, growing closer to the battle. "If we live, we'll worry about Vari tomorrow." Fola shoved her cousin into the medic's arms before drawing her sword. "Archers, fire at the incoming fighters. Everyone else, with me."

The Queen, slow in her first steps, marched toward the gate and the Spartans beyond.

⬤

The inertia of liftoff still locked Vari to her seat.

Solus clasped both hands to his chest as the *Enchantment* thrust higher into the atmosphere.

A holographic ripple floated in front of the sealed hatch leading to the cockpit. Lucan's voice crackled through a speaker. "Thought you should see what's outside."

Two formations of three-winged Imperial fighters shot across the ripple. A stretched discus loomed behind another swell of fighters, dwarfing the similar craft Saran had destroyed. An even greater mass of Imperial ships loomed at the edges of orbit, absorbing solar strength.

Solus grasped his mouth. "Elagabal protect us."

Vari offered a whisper of sympathy. "He will give us patience."

The priest's fingers concealed even more of his face. "We'll be captured."

A moment processed in Vari's thoughts. Through all the delicate moments she'd claimed for herself, she never expected to meet someone from another world still professing loyalty to House Severus. "You saw Lucan's mark. If there are others who oppose the Usurper, they must be united."

The hologram faded. "We'll be out of their patrol range in a moment. After that, we'll shift to Quantum mode."

Any trip at the highest speeds stole Vari's ability to stay out of the immediate conflict. Rather than fight for her people, she reached for her own ambitions. Justice for her father, redemption of her family's Sword, expression of her unrestrained self.

"We're in space," Solus said, still mired in his lamentation. "I cannot feel the sunlight."

"Maybe not, but there are billions of stars around us."

A cosmos drifted beyond the bulkhead, past the fighters and Imperial ships. Beyond quasars and nebulae, lay every star ever shaped by the creation of the universe. The Elagabal shaped itself, made a universe and life to inhabit such a realm. Any fortune of divinity waited at the farthest edges of the galaxy and the cracked recesses of Vari's heart.

The *Enchantment* flew beyond any floating remains of the previous Imperial ship. Geta had to die, but Lysandra? She'd opened doors of possibility Vari hadn't ever considered, not even with quiet discussion with Saran. If humanity had thrown off the yoke of one oppressor, why couldn't Vari dispose of another?

Caracalla waited in a dungeon. Saran lay in a crate. All because of four words Vari craved to say, but was forced to conceal.

If the Elagabal could create himself, then Vari would create someone worthy of her father's dominion.

Lucan's voice returned. "Brace for Quantum mode."

All inertia faded from the *Enchantment's* liftoff at last. Before any lack of gravity took hold, an absolute stillness surrounded Vari. The air turned chilly, though her breath remained invisible. Within the cold, she found only calm. She closed her eyes, wondering what insights came from traveling between stars.

Caracalla trampled through acrid muck and pungent sludge. The decline of New Brasilia's decadence slathered everything from his ankles to his knees. Slain bodies never lingered with such disgust in the general's sinuses, no matter how long a battle might go on.

The putrid stench of Brasilian waste gave Caracalla pause. Queen Fola allowed deception to annihilate the sympathy Caracalla struggled to maintain. Bassiana's little blades still stung thanks to the woman's unbridled malice. Such vile disloyalty seeped into the populace, corrupting their bodies with a rot that congealed in their secretions.

A hint of satisfaction quelled his lungs. Justice rendered the pretend Amazon in half. She may have worn a false heritage like a shirt, but her death restored a little balance to the galaxy.

Caracalla stung for his lost friend. Let the Amazons moan and cry for a mongrel-minded child.

The Non-Dead's crouched silhouette glared back. "You're falling behind."

"My apologies." Caracalla hadn't been scolded since his first months of military training. The shame of surrender magnified thanks to his languished cadence.

"Don't apologize. Catch up."

Something in the creature's words shrouded a hidden desire. Non-Dead didn't serve blindly. Their services were a premium. The wealthy pay for Non-Dead servants, the Non-Dead used those payments to support the impoverished.

Payment was always due. The Non-Dead weren't a charity.

"What do you seek, Non-Dead? You aren't doing this for free."

"My people are honorable citizens of the Empire."

"Who happen to identify the evidence our Imperator needs? My teachers warned me that coincidence was a fiction."

"We discovered a web of context clues that led to a wider conspiracy. Would you rather we not expose our enemies?"

"Your argument borders on propaganda." Caracalla shook his head. A spectrum of stink crawled through his soiled armor, sticking to the back of his neck, gluing the skin of his elbow joint. "The Imperator will ask for more concrete reasons. I recommend you have them ready when the time comes."

Within the confines of any battle is a shared language. In every moment of hate, there is a dawn of realization. Only two parties will ever comprehend this notion. The warrior and her enemy.

Queen Fola of New Brasilia
Private Notes

FIGHTERS STREAKED IN FROM above, firing guns mounted beneath all three wing foils. As two fighters annihilated Brasilians, arrows shot another from the sky.

At the ruined gate, waves of combatants crashed into one another. Metal clanged when the overhead explosions quieted for an instant. Enhanced roars tore through Brasilian warriors, leaving fewer to stand against the next charge.

Bassiana hovered over the Oval Desk, having been ordered away from the fighting. She'd seen such destruction before. Brasilians falling to the oppression of Imperial firepower. Scattered worlds throughout the Unnamed Empire experienced such fury a decade earlier. Many wanted to wait for confirmation, choosing to uphold the ancient Severus bloodline.

Yet the Usurper's hunger for power fueled so many torches, armed so many firing squads.

Marcrinus was capable of anything to cement his power. He'd be willing to steal Vari to Roma Vatica.

The Usurper would want to demonstrate his ultimate victory over Sextus. He'd see to it no one ever questioned him again.

Another volley of fighters swooped overhead. The few capital ships held firm. If their captains wanted, the large ships could position themselves to blast New Brasilia with exterminating force—something that would stir further agitators to rise against the Usurper. There'd been no further move to put centurions on the surface. Any steady fighting remained between Sparta and New Brasilia.

With so many dying between spear and shield, a new assault could disrupt the offensive.

Bassiana stood tall. Her nostrils flared with reborn determination. She commanded an update, knowing one of the nearby intelligence technicians would respond. "Communications?"

"Limited, but still active."

Bassiana nodded. "Put me through to the Imperial command ship."

Technicians adjusted controls while another pair of battle lines raced toward the shattered gate. "Princess, we can transmit to them."

With no guarantee of a response.

Bassiana focused the recorder on her face and voice. "Imperial Strategic Command, this is Princess Bassiana, Regent of House Severus. Respond."

The war room froze. Silence shook from the speakers.

"I repeat. This is Princess Bassiana, Regent of House Severus. Respond."

Nothing. None of the technicians near Bassiana spoke.

"I will proceed as though you can hear me and have chosen to remain silent." It was a final chance to provoke the distant Imperials into action. Bassiana hadn't expected a reply. "There are seven legions of centurions disarmed and in my custody. They are under the command of General Caium Caracalla. Cease hostilities and open negotiations, else the safety of these men cannot be guaranteed."

Bassiana slapped the switch, ending the transmission. She huffed for a moment before sitting. Her fingers eased a data chip from the seam of her left hip.

"Now, the skies will clear."

Blood splattered over Fola's face as she thrust her sword into another Spartan. Her weapon was little more than ceremony, but rituals often proved fatal.

A drumbeat shook her ribcage from within. Every muscle screamed to swing, thrust, rush at another monstrous man. Let any invader taste the price of soiling New Brasilia.

Conviction refined Fola's pace, tempering her desire to shed blood. Both sides held their shields firm while thrusting spears to catch an enemy's flesh. So long as both sides mirrored each other, the Spartan lines would never break.

New Brasilia had arrows. Sparta enjoyed an Imperial vanguard overhead.

Yet the explosions had stopped. The three-winged fighters flew in oval patterns over the city, keeping at a higher elevation than before. One last fighter exploded, having straggled behind while the others shifted away from the combat zone.

The olive-hued attackers slowed their approach. A booming shout exploded from their ranks, hastening their shift to defense rather than offense.

A rolling, cavernous voice called out from the Spartan lines. "Hold the advance. I must speak to the queen. Hold."

A Spartan emerged, carrying no spear or sword as he emerged to the front of the line. A simple braid hung under the edge of his helmet.

Fola lifted her sword to pause the attack. "Speak quickly. I have a battle to attend."

"I am Agis. Since Dion has fallen, I speak for Sparta in the absence of our King." Agis frowned under the shadow of his command helmet. "The Empire has asked us to pull back."

"Brasilians." The Queen saw a chance to strike a rival force, especially after it caused so much destruction. But she was not the Usurper. "Hold."

Combatants on both sides scowled under waves of hot breath. Hearts pounded under the race of adrenaline-fueled bloodlust. Only loyal minds restrained the fury of mutilation.

"Why do you hold?" Fola asked.

"The Empire is concerned you have prisoners of value. They wish for assurances of safety, especially for their general."

"Our battle makes that difficult."

"Yes. My Spartans will move back to the bridge so we can talk." None of the precision spearmen moved from their positions. They weren't stupid enough to show their backs to an enraged enemy.

Fola nodded. "I will allow your Spartans to move back to the bridge."

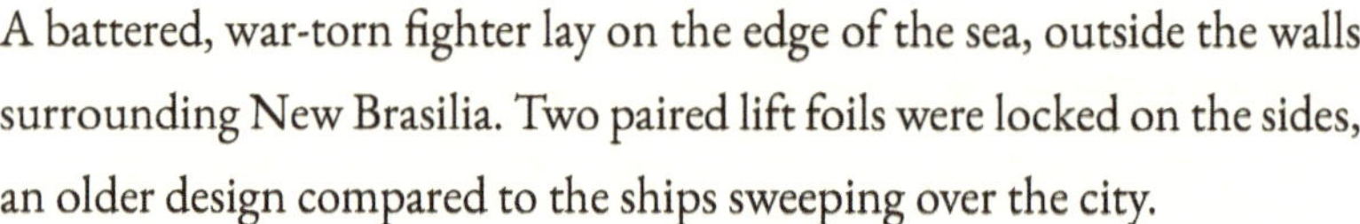

A battered, war-torn fighter lay on the edge of the sea, outside the walls surrounding New Brasilia. Two paired lift foils were locked on the sides, an older design compared to the ships sweeping over the city.

"This craft has a rudimentary stealth device." The Non-Dead primed external fuel systems and removed a detonator from the stubby fuselage. "It should carry us around the battle to the capitol ship currently in orbit."

Caracalla lifted and turned his head. The sky remained still, not even allowing thin clouds to pass. "They stopped firing."

"That will make our ascent smoother."

Caracalla's mouth tensed into a razor-thin line. "Not if the Amazons convinced Eldreth to stop the siege."

"Then I'll fly us with due haste." The Non-Dead opened the hexagonal cockpit and claimed the front seat.

Even though Caracalla knew the grade of fighter, additional modules were fused to the wings and the flight console. He resigned himself to the Non-Dead's care, taking the rear seat. As soon as he fastened the restraint straps around his shoulders and waist, the canopy lowered and hissed shut. A ripple of light showered over the fighter.

"Stealth mode is active. I'll route communications to you, General."

"That would be best." Once they approached the fleet, they'd need docking clearance in order to board any Imperial ship.

Both leaders stood on opposite sides of the ruined gate. The pungent ash of burned hair and seared muscle lingered in a thin haze between them.

Agis stood in a fluid pose, resting, but able to strike in an instant.

Fola sheathed her sword. Her shield clung to her left arm. Without arms, a queen still had weapons. "Did Caracalla send you?"

"We were asked to mobilize if we did not hear from the Imperial general. As we came, so did the fighters."

Scorched air rotted into ozone all around Fola. "What about the Non-Dead?"

"Dion said they would aid our engineering issues. We did not know he was one of them." Agis spat on the pavement, then stomped on the frothy moisture. "His name will not be written in The Glorious Book."

Fola echoed the gesture. A minor effort showing a shared disdain for the Non-Dead.

Agis gave a short nod before returning to his purpose. "Can you produce the general to negotiate?"

"General Caracalla surrendered to me, relinquishing his right to discuss military matters. His men are guests under my protection in compliance with the Nihl Accords."

"That is not what we were told."

"Please enlighten me." Imperial signals must have showered Sparta with propaganda. "I don't fear words."

"A poison has been administered to all centurions, denying them battle or a glorious death. If this is true, you will have violated the Accords—"

"Do not threaten my loyalty to humanity, Spartan." Fola's words raced ahead of her. She caught herself after taking two steps. A clatter of shields and spears braced for a return to battle. "I scowl at the restrictions placed upon me by the Imperator, but I will not tolerate an implication that I have betrayed my species. Such thoughts are the cancer left by our ancient captors."

Agis shifted closer, claiming the same space Fola stole a moment earlier. "I follow my orders and do my duty. I only repeat what I was told."

A shrill voice cried out from the Brasilian lines. "How old are you, Spartan?"

Mumbled commands shifted the ranks of Fola's warriors. Bassiana shoved her way through the battle lines. Tangles of hair flopped on her shoulder as her sleeves and skirts flourished.

"How much did you weigh when you were born, Spartan?"

Fola locked her teeth together. "This is not the time, cousin."

Still, Bassiana swayed closer. An exhausted strain pulsed through her neck and ankles. "Spartan, have you done anything but fight?"

"All Sparta fights for humanity."

Bassiana stepped past Fola without a glance. "Are you still human? When this planet split, Sparta lacked any women to bear militant children."

Tension erased Agis's mouth and narrowed his gaze. "We do not discuss this with Amazons."

"The Nihl Accords explicitly state no nation can maintain a rigid population. The Accords also say no nation using Nihl augmentation will enjoy Imperial protection. Is your King ready to endure the consequences of his nation's existence?"

If Bassiana had such proof, she could turn many against Sparta. She'd already manipulated the Imperials into stopping their aerial siege. That power did not belong to Bassiana. It barely belonged to her dead husband or missing daughter.

New Brasilia had one queen.

With a single hand, Fola eased Bassiana back into place. "I propose talks between myself and your king. If there is truth in my cousin's words, your king deserves the chance to keep those discoveries a private matter."

Agis thundered a foot forward. "I speak in the king's absence."

"Which is satisfactory under most circumstances. My cousin speaks of things that could endanger Sparta by way of Imperial scrutiny. This requires the king's direct involvement."

A stare burned the air between Agis and Bassiana. A curt, cordial nod possessed the Spartan when he faced Fola again. "In the name of my King, II Leonidas, the nation of Sparta will defend Fola of Virago, Queen of New Brasilia and Bassiana, Regent of House Severus until the King declares an end to our dialogue." Agis snapped out an open hand. "Agreed?"

Bassiana bowed with a grace that clashed with her demeanor.

Fola slipped the shield off her arm. "Agreed. I offer you my shield as acceptance of your protection."

Agis took the shield, holding it up with one hand. His voice rose in volume. "New Brasilia stands under Spartan protection."

The protected Queen offered her cousin an anguished glare and nothing more.

After humanity was stolen from its forgotten home, the
Nihl turned human culture into anathema. Every culture that rose through humanity's cultural ascendancy
embodied some fragment of our ancestral home. When
the topic of religion ignited among those reborn cultures,
they all threw away the glitter sacrificed to the notion of
Entropy.
Any god the Nihl slayed wasn't worth keeping.

William Pleiades III
The Modern Ascendancy of Man

WARMTH SETTLED OVER VARI'S skin as she opened her eyes. A swell of heat filled her muscles, drawing a smile on her face. Her body screamed that only an instant had passed.

Her mind knew better.

Lucan emerged from the cockpit. "You guys feeling warm?"

Solus gasped. "Yes."

"Thought so. Neither of you have protective suits, so we couldn't stay in Quantum mode long. You'd drown in your own sweat glands if we kept going."

Vari wiped her forehead. Liters of moisture clung to her fingers. "Where are we?"

"Lagrange Point 3-A-9. It's the most stable position between Brasilia and Gaulius. We'll drift here for about twelve hours so you two can recover long enough to survive the rest of the trip."

"I appreciate your wisdom." Vari had a thousand questions for Lucan. Why would a man choose a dead Imperator with no sword over a living Usurper still clinging to an ancient weapon? If there was loyalty in the galaxy, Vari needed to find it, learn from it. In so many ways, loyalty was like a child, waiting constantly to be reborn.

If only a willing mother could be found.

"There are a few things I need to explain." Lucan crossed his arms around his chest, allowing his body to press against the wall next to the sealed cockpit. "You guys got lucky. There haven't been many pilots willing to visit New Brasilia."

Vari tilted an eyebrow. "We welcome visitors."

The priest stretched his arms, popping both elbows. "I know what the captain means."

"A religious man with some sense." Lucan nodded. "Good."

Solus lowered his head. His eyes turned mournful. "Vari, you've spent your life surrounded by acceptance of the Elagabal. Even when your father was alive, there was tolerance for our faith that doesn't exist today. Macrinus lacks your father's liberal mindset."

"More like Macrinus wanted to set himself apart. He wouldn't let a single planet protect a religion that wouldn't obey him. He passed laws promoting Jupiter—even though I've never met a less spiritual man in my life."

A surge of shock forced Vari to her feet. "You know him?"

"I doubt anyone knows Macrinus." Lucan shrugged. "I've sat in his company, listening to him break promises over and over. His claim is distant and ambitious. His grandpa was the illegitimate son of the Twelfth General's granddaughter. Just as much a roughened officer as I am. Only I never benefited from a string of accidentally slit throats or relatives with obscure, undiagnosed fatal food allergies."

"He sounds like a madman." Vari's heart beat at the confirmation she'd always sought. The Usurper was undoubtedly the monster her mother claimed. Bassiana sometimes lamented the destruction of the Temple in Liberio, an act timed with the morning prayers of the faithful.

"Be careful not to mistake his ambition for foolishness. Too many have done that and died for it. Some say your father is one of them." Lucan bit his lip. "Do what you can to relax. I don't have any provisions on hand, so we'll all get to wait out the down time."

He pressed a button on his right wrist and levitated toward the ceiling. The captain swept his legs back before pressing the same button again. The helmet bubble sealed his gaze before polarizing into a mirror sheen.

Vari scowled, but there wasn't anything else. Her options were mourning or sleep.

Should she slumber, a measure of calm might visit her. She might even find herself slumbering in Saran's company, if only for an imagined moment. As long as she was awake, Vari lingered in a mountain of growing failures.

In a realm of dreams, Vari was a better person.

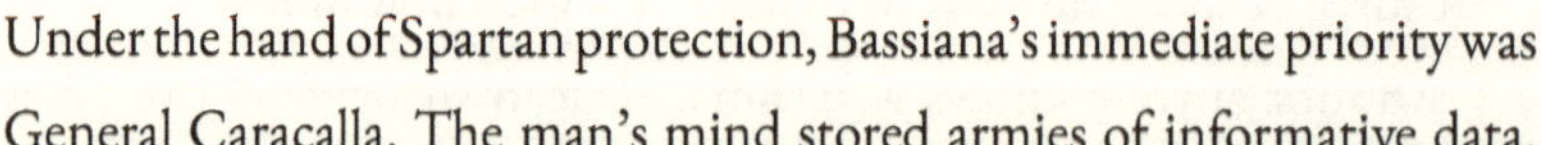

Under the hand of Spartan protection, Bassiana's immediate priority was General Caracalla. The man's mind stored armies of informative data.

She needed to extract what she could before any Spartans ventured into the dungeons.

Bassiana loomed through the halls, leading to the lowest floor. Tendrils of smoke curled along the ceiling, growing thicker with every step closer to the general's cell. The swelling cloud spat a guard at Bassiana's feet.

"Princess Bassiana." The guard choked on her coughs as she tried to kneel. "I apologize."

"For what...?"

A thick column of smoke whipped out of Caracalla's cell. Two more guards covered their faces as the blackened tendrils slapped their lips. Bassiana covered her own mouth before moving closer.

The floor of Caracalla's cell had melted, leaving an exposed tunnel of liquefied stone.

Once the docking bay sealed around the aged fighter, the Non-Dead released the ship's seals. As soon as the cockpit opened, Caracalla released his harness and jumped out of the fighter.

A quartet of armored troops carrying pistols approached. Another man followed, wearing a crimson and white cloth uniform. "General, I'm pleased to see you're well."

"Not as well as I'd like, Captain. My men are still incarcerated."

"That is unfortunate. Shall I order the Spartans to resume their attack?"

"No." Caracalla shook his head. "They stopped of their own volition. Ask if you like, but I suspect the Spartans may have been duped into offering their protection. That's a command only their King can dismiss."

"As Imperial subjects, they must obey."

The Non-Dead fluttered close to Caracalla and the captain. "They will not obey your orders. Their culture is strictly conditioned to follow their king according to their codes of conduct."

A snarl twisted the captain's face. "You will address me with respect, Non-Dead. Note the malfunction in your logs."

Caracalla lifted a hand, blocking the captain. "This is no simple Non-Dead, El. He is fully autonomous. Without him, I'd still be incarcerated." The General approached the docking bay door. "Order a crew to prepare the yacht, along with flight suits for myself and my companion."

The Non-Dead walked beside the captain. "I need no protective suit."

"Then for myself. See that the case stored in the fighter's hold is loaded onto the yacht, then signal Roma Vatica that I will bring gifts to the Imperator."

"What of the Spartans, my Lord?"

"Verify their status. Commence attack if they haven't offered protection. Otherwise, treat them as loyal allies as long as the Accords remain intact."

"And the Amazons? Didn't they kill Lord Geta?"

"They did." Somber eyes weighed down Caracalla's face. Savory vengeance whipped over his tongue. "I will take the proper evidence to the Imperator. Continue as I have ordered until I say otherwise."

Still armed, Fola stood in the heart of the plaza. She kept her bow and arrows stowed on her back as she walked among the scars carved by similar weapons. A strip of black cloth cushioned the wound on her face and the ruination of her eye.

She watched Spartans patrol her city, most of them securing defensive positions. She turned toward Mhati. "Stand for New Brasilia in my absence."

Mhati lowered her head, kissing the back of her hand. "Yes, my Queen."

Agis and another Spartan approached, both wearing similar vests and capes. "Queen Fola, I wish to present my second, I Dion."

The other Spartan's chin was shaved to a flawless, shimmering bronze. "This is not the same man I faced yesterday."

"No. Dion was the second of his name then. Now he is the first."

Fola nodded. The man she spoke to had been stricken from any place of Spartan glory. She held a hand toward her own aide. "This is Mhati of Hyppolyta."

Mhati briefly bowed. Her eyes darted to the side, tracking an approaching figure.

Bassiana made a terse march toward Fola. The Queen spoke. "Cousin, where is the general?"

"Gone. Unable to join our proceedings."

Agis crossed his arms. "Is he dead?"

"Not to my knowledge."

Agis locked his hands around his elbows. "What is the general's physical and mental state?"

"I do not know." Bassiana rubbed her right thumb over her ring finger.

Fola spotted the sign, interjecting herself. "General Caracalla's absence does not remove the need for our discussion with your King."

"It does not." Agis lowered his chin for a moment. "I shall escort you to my King near the border of the Sekht front."

Agis and Bassiana moved toward the spaceport. I Dion took a few steps toward the palace.

Fola gazed not at the scars of ruination, but at the shops and restaurants still largely intact after two rounds of immediate violence. She owed them safety and protection. She owed them a hope of peace and the possibility of discovering greater things.

A crisp hint of sea air raced through her nose.

Mhati bowed again. "Safe journeys, my Queen."

"Thank you, Mhati." Fola braced her right hand over her aide's shoulder. "Rule well in my absence. If I do not return, remember to keep our people safe."

A humble nod consumed Mhati. "I will not fail you."

Fola followed the others to the spaceport. She stayed a few steps behind, embracing the quiet as she looked upon her sun and sky.

During the months following the death of Sextus Severus,

his supporters rose up in droves, ready to support their

beloved Imperator.

Of all the systems and people who stood for Severus, none

of them could agree on how to go forward.

This proved to be the opening for Macrinus to rise to the

peak of power.

The Clarion

Unification and Power: A Study in Political Ascent

ANOTHER DISORIENTING WAVE WARMED Vari's bones as the *Enchantment* eased through a dark gray sky. She loosened her safety restraints, shifting toward a narrow viewing port.

An unvisited world expanded in every direction. An aged star washed cold light over thousands of steam vents lifting from a craggy surface. Any expanse not scarred by cracks and erosion lay victim to a host of ancient meteor strikes.

"Vari." Solus rubbed his eyes and massaged his robed knees. "Sit down until we land."

"This is only the third planet I've ever seen." Gaulius lacked the elaborate domes and columns of Roma Vatica. Any hint of natural beauty had been eradicated long before humanity met the Nihl.

A patch of navy blue ripped between the clouds. Flurries of black rippled through the rare spot of clear sky. "Saran told me about these holes. The atmosphere stretches thin enough to see the universe sometimes."

The sealed crate lingered behind Vari. Its presence kindly stroked her hair while threatening to slap her face.

Vari's admissions of sister-goddesses got Saran killed.

She sank into her seat, securing the restraints again. Saran's slight ponytail bobbed every time she swayed the slight curves of her hips. Her smile playfully admonished Vari.

"She was proudest on the day she became a warrior of New Brasilia." Vari's hushed tone pulled the images of Saran away from her heart. If she spoke of her, it wouldn't ache to think about her. "Saran kept grinning, no matter how serious everyone else was. It was the first time no one cared about her skin or hair. Her smile didn't fade when they took her breast so she could echo our victorious past."

"You miss her."

Vari stared at the sealed metal plates under her feet. "I'm empty without her. She's dead and I made it happen."

"You did not swing the general's sword. You did not create our people's enemies."

Solus didn't know Vari's secrets. The priest had no pulse on why Varius favored loose-fitting shirts and avoided the Imperial fascination with short-trimmed hair. Solus was never given a reason to suspect the palace's statue of Jupiter was anything more than a mandated decoration.

Some part of Vari remained locked in her illicit bed. The Gallae and their Temple of Cybele would never let Vari go now that she'd been seen. It didn't matter if Vari grasped the Imperial throne. She needed to feel an Imperial crown linking her own tresses. It was the seat of her own father she craved. When she claimed what was hers, no one would deny her ever again.

"Not everything is a choice," Vari said. "Some of us are driven beyond our guilt."

Solus frowned. "Saran's loss troubles you."

"If I can't protect Saran," Varius said, "how can I defend humanity?"

"Don't reach for burdens you can't yet claim—"

"Don't give me platitudes." A scowl anchored the sides of Vari's mouth. "I don't have the luxury of choosing what I can and can't claim."

"Varius..."

"They all have to die. Caracalla, Macrinus—" Vari shook her head. Every aspect within her agreed, no matter how latent or overt. "I will take what is mine, even if I have to drown their wives in blood."

"Seek the Elagabal, Varius." Solus shook his head voraciously. "Find the wisdom to bring justice, not cruelty or revenge. Any malice will turn you into the monsters you despise."

"Right." Vari glared down, looking at neither the priest nor the closing Gaulius landscape.

The *Enchantment* lay within the second-highest level of a skyscraper, one of the few buildings that grew upward instead of burrowing into Gaulius.

Both of Lucan's crewmen lowered the docking ramp before lifting the metal crate holding Saran's remains. Vari wandered behind them, pressing her tablet close to her thin slab of a chest.

Illustrations on every wall of the hangar showed an outline of the skyscraper. A yellow line stretched out near the top, noting an elevation hundreds of meters above the surface of the planet. Alternating posters swept into view, warning of precautions in the open atmosphere and the depth of Quantum operations.

Ships needed to travel between systems if the Unnamed Empire planned to maintain humanity's unity.

A man in a form-pressed black jacket and matching unitard approached with a clunky tablet, decades out of favor. Brown shadows noted the outline of his scalp. "Welcome to Gaulius. I am Customs Officer Tanimura Hidetaka."

Lucan extended a hand to the customs officer. "Captain Lucan of the *Enchantment*. We're here to deliver the remains of Judith Pollus."

Tanimura's eyes widened. He took a hard swallow. "The younger Lady Pollus?"

"Sorry to break the news this way." Lucan glanced at Vari. "I thought we'd be expected."

Vari stepped forward, bowing at the waist. "My apologies, Officer Tanimura. Communications from New Brasilia have been difficult in recent days. The situation became even more dire as we left."

"That is terrible news, young man." Tanimura lowered his own head, accepting Vari's gesture. "May I ask your name?"

"Antonio." Vari lifted her head. "I'm a student of many faiths, having studied with Solus most recently." She turned a hand toward the priest, sure that her fabrication carried enough truth to evade deeper scrutiny. "When Sar—Judith passed away, I volunteered to see that her remains were delivered to the Pollus family."

"I see." Tanimura's fingers typed faster than two hands could accomplish. "I'm sure the Lady Pollus will have questions for you."

Vari gazed absently at the monitor walls as she waited for her summons to meet with Lady Pollus. The visage of a seaside beach rolled at Vari without breeze. The latest wave crashed without a spray of elevated mist.

None of the coastline lay supported by security checkpoints or immense bridges. Gleaming gold sands soaked the unreal waters. A swaying mirror reflected a canopy of brilliant blue. None of the droplets carried a hint of salt or the soothing musk of aquatic life. The clear, cloudless sky left the mind free to relax and wander.

A syrupy chime further cast unreality upon the coastline. Vari took a deep breath before facing the door. "Enter."

Lucan entered, letting the door slide close behind him. He'd exchanged his flight suit for black utility pants and a matching vest. "Antonio." The captain nodded. "That's a good one."

Vari crossed her arms. "Did you think I'd give my real name?"

"No. Plenty of us remember that Macrinus forbade your family from travel. He can't have you going around recruiting friends."

Vari relaxed her posture, seeing the opportunity in front of her. "Isolate us so we can die faster."

Lucan nodded. "Let me prove my loyalty to your father."

After leaning in, Vari nodded.

"One legion of Brasilians stood with your father at the end, even after Macrinus froze the assets of every man in your father's army. This legion refused to break ranks, even when their accounts were overdrawn and their families were sold to the Spartan war effort. They only surrendered to Caracalla when they agreed your father was dead. It was the only way they could get fair treatment."

Pressure sealed Vari's lips and restrained her jaw. "Why haven't I heard about this?"

"The results of the inquiry made it impossible for you to know. Macrinus can't claim total victory without destroying the Eighth Quantum Sword. Your father's last bastion of Amazons supposedly know where the sword is, but they refused to tell Macrinus. Even when those Amazons were put to the knife, their leadership didn't falter.

"Since they'd surrendered to Caracalla, the general called for mercy. The Amazons refused the protection, but it put a stop to Macrinus's hunt for insects." Lucan shifted away from Vari, staring out at the illusory shoreline. A sigh swept away from him, shoving back the imaginary waves. "Macrinus wanted that sword so badly, he recruited Queen Fola to order the information from the remaining Amazons."

"She would have refused."

"Her loyalty is to her people first, no matter what. They say she gave the order. Since they refused their own queen, they were cast out."

"She wouldn't cast her people out." Vari slammed her fists to his sides. "She wouldn't do the Usurper's bidding like that." She breathed deep, cringing against her frustration. Then her eyes rose into pragmatic possibility. "Who told you this?"

"Smugglers. Other captains. Some of us who are loyal still talk, just not often. Word is that the outcast Amazons were sent to work in Quantum mines as long as they refused to answer. They aren't even allowed to die." Lucan shrugged. "This place has Quantum mines and produced an Amazon. If you want, I can ask around."

"If you're right, my aunt has already cast them out."

"Idiot. If I'm right, one of them knows the location of your father's Sword. At the least, you might find someone loyal enough to suffer for your father."

Vari's tongue landed along the base of her gaping mouth. She hadn't expected to find proof of her father's Sword. It was too much to believe. "I didn't think about that."

"You need to do a lot of thinking if you plan to rule humanity." Lucan dug a data card out of his pocket and tossed it to Vari. "Get some extra clothes for when you meet Lady Pollus."

A flat rectangle weighed nothing, yet anchored Vari's hand. She nodded. "Thank you, Captain."

"Don't change that line when you get on the throne. Everybody likes to be thanked."

A heavy black jacket and a tight blue shirt clung to Vari's chest. She waited in a pale white room lined with sterile florescent lights. The only sign of color was a small potted plant with three pale leaves.

The tablet in Vari's hand loomed around a single word. *Pending.* Saran remained confined by death, sealed in a cold vessel of flameless steel. She stayed there, slowly rotting along with Vari's heart.

In her decay, Vari lingered in a durable leather chair, scuffed from decades of use. Similar chairs waited in the rooms leading toward the stark bastion of oversaturated light. There was no drink to quench Vari's thirst for direction, no snack to fuel her ambitions.

Void-torn thoughts echoed through Vari. A shattered heart lay in a bed of agonized lungs. Every breath screamed for Saran or trembled for Bassiana and Fola. The deepest gorge in Vari's chest whined like a child deprived of a daily hug, half an hour of playtime, and absent of childhood friends. No tutor could have prepared Vari for the isolation of a soul.

Vari never expected to be a motionless statue pounding against an incorrect void.

If there'd been a view to watch, the wait might have passed with ease. But Gaulius had a single purpose, the refinement of Quantum. All things craved that Imperial power, so much that its refinement remained concealed, even after the fall of the Nihl.

All that Vari knew of Quantum came from broken whispers of Gaulius. Sporadic notes about a father or a sister crept out only in Saran's most unguarded moments. Why would Saran have made herself absolutely Brasilian only to have her remains sent to the family of her birth?

Such a magnificent general deserved a gleaming pyre to deliver her to the Elagabal. Depositing Saran on a broken ball of craggy smoke felt excessive.

The bland door hissed as it retreated to the side. A hooded woman with a breathing mask stomped a pair of battered boots before she stepped inside. "Sorry to make you wait. There was a surge two blocks over and no one else in the area knew the adjustment formulas."

She shoved back her hood and turned valves under the chin of her mask. Yellow hair lay bundled in a pair of rolls pinned to the back of her head. She yanked the leather gloves from her hands, exposing a set of dry, slender fingers with stubby nails. Strained eyes sank with exhaustion, leaving the rest of her skin in a cold hue. Her cheekbones weren't as high as Saran's, but their lips and nose were identical.

"Remind me," she said, "What was your name again?"

"Antonio." The syllables tumbled, dragging a coat of regret over Vari's tongue.

"Right." Her eyebrows lifted. "You came here from New Brasilia."

"I did." A deep breath filled Vari's aching lungs. Her heart screamed for relief against the tide of loss. Internal agony refused to be spoken, yet could not stay contained. "I wanted to talk to you about Saran—er, Judith. You're Lady Pollus, right?"

She chuckled. An amused smile lifted the right side of her face. "We're not big on titles here. You can call me Lady Pollus if you want, but most people call me Julia. You want something to drink?"

"I, uh." Vari shook her head. "It wouldn't be right of me."

Julia shrugged. "Suit yourself." She pressed the wall to the left of the potted plant. As a hidden cabinet opened, she tossed her jacket and mask aside. After filling two glasses, she held one out for Vari. "I don't care if it's right. I don't drink alone. The days on Gaulius are long and dark. The nights are twice as bad."

Julia tilted her head back, swallowing half of her drink in one gulp.

Vari didn't touch the glass in front of her, even if it might give her enough bravery of false confidence to say what she needed. A thread of desperation ensnared her sense of decorum, begging to chug the drink. Duty avoided such conflict.

"I come with bad news."

"About Judith." Julia slurped the rest of her glass. "Is she dead?"

Vari answered with a hollow croak. "Yes."

Julia shook her head. "I suppose she was playing Amazon when she died."

"She wasn't playing." Vari clamped both hands around her glass. Her fingers knotted together as her jaw tightened around her tongue. "She fired Quantum Arrows at a distant starship. She stood as brilliant as the sun."

Julia refilled her glass. "I heard she took another name. What was it?"

"Saran." A perfect soul had danced against Vari's lips. "Saran of Virago. She was adopted into the queen's household."

Julia drank again. The liquid appeared darker as each sip slithered between her lips. "If she was adopted, why are you here?"

"She left instructions to have her remains returned to you and your father if she passed away." She closed his eyes and drew in a long breath. "I'm here to fulfill her request."

"Why would she send her corpse back?"

"Tradition?" Vari shrugged. "I don't know."

"On this planet, everything goes to Quantum refinement. No grave-yards, no crypts. Most of our recreation is simple, direct. We'd have more, but the Empire wants so many balls of blue-white. Nothing else matters. Everything feeds the harvest vents. Trash, dirt, waste." She gulped down the rest of her glass. "Our corpses go, too."

Vari touched her glass against her lower lip. As she paused, she wondered why Saran would arrange such a waste. She drank.

Julia sat her glass down with an audible clunk. "You're not some kid, are you?"

"I'm a year away from acceptance." She put her glass down, caring little for the small burden.

"Acceptance? You sound like a rich kid."

Julia's voice echoed her sister. Both possessed the same direct, playful tone. Unlike Saran, Julia never altered herself to fit a cultural role. Every part of Vari coveted the purposeful self-conviction both sisters possessed. Julia's lack of overt display made her alluring. Her certainty echoed Saran's determination.

Vari turned her gaze, trying to not be indiscreet.

"No need to be shy with me." Julia relaxed her posture, tilting her head against her right shoulder.

"I'm sorry." Vari turned enough for her left eye to gaze upon Julia again. She wasn't Saran as much as she was an echo of who Saran might have been. "I should be more considerate."

"There's nothing wrong with looking. That's only natural."

Vari locked her eyes shut. Julia's assertive understanding was all too familiar. "You remind me of her."

Julia nodded before checking they both had full glasses. She pressed Vari's glass back into her hands. The coat of refinery weariness couldn't purge the reassuring shape from Julia's face. "Tell me more."

At the threshold of history, every being makes plans. Some
are great. Some fade from grandeur.
It is the quietest moment that precedes the storm.

Princess Dyanna, Champion of New Brasilia
Personal Journals

A DOZEN PAIRS OF columns marked the path to the Imperator's council chamber. Banners and two-headed eagle standards hung from each grand pillar. Matching streamers hung from the arched beams supporting the bronze dome overhead. Praetorians with glossy black armor and shields stood tall beside the path. The gleaming ebony wall kept any unwanted guests from touching the crimson carpet leading toward the heart of the Unnamed Empire.

A fresh suit of armor wrapped around Caracalla's body. His gaze locked upon the steps leading past the praetorians, centering his focus on the meeting ahead. The Non-Dead followed the general's approach, effortlessly carrying a bulky silver case with one hand.

Aside from a few short statements, the Non-Dead said nothing since leaving New Brasilia. The creature's name remained a mystery, assuming its nomenclature remained intact.

When the path came to its end, four more praetorians waited. Two on the flanks held their posts. The inner duo climbed the carpeted stairs, opening a cavernous pair of double doors. Each door bore half of an ivory carving of the Battle of Persephone. Quantum Sword-bearing generals led the charge against a host of Nihl. Amazons followed, shooting alien craft out of the skies, refusing any ability to escape.

Within the inner chamber, more banners proclaimed the eagle emblem of the Unnamed Empire. A two-headed eagle emerged from an enormous slab of polished onyx, dominating the chamber. Beneath the beaked gazes, a segmented round table dominated the circular room, casting a dense shadow over the ring.

Most of the seats in the chamber remained empty. The tallest chair, a lacquered frame of wood inlaid with gold, contained a rigid silhouette chiseled from stone and malice. A thick brow emerged between a head of short hair and a length of beard spiraling over a wide neck.

Crashing rocks broke the silence. "Caium, your expedition was less than fruitful."

Caracalla fell to one knee, clasping a fist against his heart. He lowered his head, accepting the shame of his defeat. "Yes, Imperator."

The Imperator's eyes burrowed past Caracalla. "I have not known you to keep a Non-Dead servant before." Macrinus batted his knuckles through the air. "Leave us."

The Non-Dead tilted his cowled head before retiring from the chamber.

"I've seen reports from New Brasilia." Macrinus lifted an open hand. "Reports aren't as valuable as the account of a trusted friend."

Caracalla stood, bowing his head for a moment. "Lord Geta found evidence of illegal weapons stockpiling on New Brasilia—hundreds of thousands of arrows, all ready for Quantum mounting. A chamber within the palace contained a Quantum Battery, along with Quantum Sword katas and training aids."

Macrinus unleashed a heavy exhale. "So, the brat wants to dethrone me. The council will review this. Caium, there are things you'll be interested to hear."

"Of course, Imperator." Caracalla glanced back to where the Non-Dead had stood. "I must make a request before then. It concerns the Non-Dead that accompanied me."

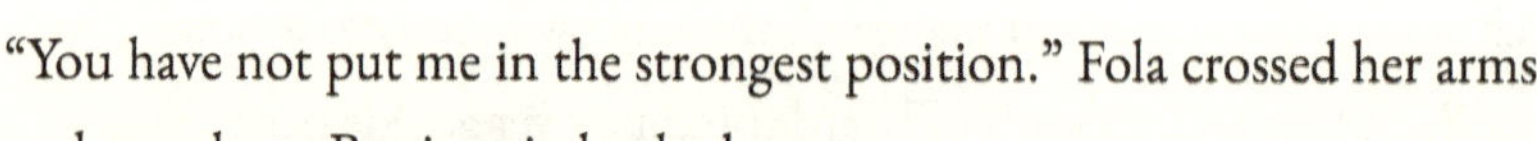

"You have not put me in the strongest position." Fola crossed her arms as she spoke to Bassiana in hushed tones.

The queen and her cousin shared a cabin on board the Imperial capitol ship that coordinated the attack on New Brasilia. Thanks to Spartan protection, the Imperial Captain Eldreth was compelled to take them toward Sekht space. It was the only way for Fola to meet with the Spartan King.

Bassiana glanced at the floor rather than meet the queen's angered gaze. "I apologize."

"When Vari apologized to me, I felt the weight of her heart. I cannot say the same of you."

"I swear to you, Fola, I'm sorry—"

"It's not your cousin you should apologize to. Your queen is angry with an impulsive Brasilian woman who had no place to speak."

A shared void pushed against them both. A single emotional gulf that promised to consume them both if they failed to navigate it.

Bassiana lifted her head with sincerity, rather than overwhelming pride. "What can I say to ease your rage?"

Fola shook her head. "Nothing. Any words that would calm me don't exist on your lips." Fola breathed out of her nose, assuming the role of a teacher. "You have no remorse for focusing on your daughter and yourself. Your only desire is to seat Vari upon the throne."

Bassiana squeezed her fingers shut and pushed her palms against her thighs. "Is it not right that I should advance my daughter to her rightful place? Should I not help our family reach the highest position possible?"

"There must be more beyond our family. Otherwise, we will become toothless and inept in a handful of generations."

"I am not blind to alliances."

"Even your rebuttals fail to see past your own blood. There is more than one family on New Brasilia, even among our warriors. We must be more than ourselves."

Bassiana shifted away from her cousin. "You couldn't understand. You have no child of your own."

After talking about Saran for almost an hour, Vari topped off Julia's glass. Every time her gaze locked with Julia's eyes, Vari wondered if she could stare at them in the same way she'd always watched Saran.

Julia tapped a finger against the vacant air. "You always seem to hold something back."

Vari shrugged. "Eventually, the bottle will be empty."

"True, but it's my bottle to drink. Did you drink often with my sister?"

Vari shook her head. "I don't have many chances to drink. Mostly wines on festive occasions." Her mind wandered to the palace wine cellar positioned across from the statue of Jupiter—and her hidden room.

"Your loss." Julia breathed in a gulp of liquid. "So are you going to hold back why you're holding back?"

"Saran always dug out my secrets." Vari smiled. "Maybe I like to keep my secrets so someone will pry them loose." Another sip of alcohol danced over Vari's tongue and coated her throat. "Someone always teases hidden things out of me."

In some cosmic hell, Lysandra surely laughed.

"I've seen you staring." Julia brushed her fingers across the collar of her wrinkled shirt.

"Sorry." Vari shied away, far too caught in old habits.

"What? It means you're human and you're interested."

"But—"

"But what?" Julia shrugged her shoulders and her half-full glass. "I'm just surprised. You came in here pleading 'Lady Pollus' only to check me out more than a little."

"I didn't mean to offend—"

"Offend nothing. You're hiding something. If you looked like a refinery worker, I wouldn't think that. A nice young guy? Knows my sister? Polite? Comes from New Brasilia?" She shook her head. "Doesn't add up."

Vari stood. "Perhaps I should go."

"Oh no, not yet, you don't." Julia pointed downward, a sly smirk rising over her face. "Sit. I'm going to figure you out."

The young woman sat, clinging to the role of guilt she'd conveyed. "I should go."

"Why?" Julia shrugged. "There's not much to do on this planet."

"Is that an offer?" The words burst from Vari's mouth, even though they'd been spoken by a far more assertive soul. It was the sort of thing Saran would say.

Julia tilted her head sideways. "Do you want it to be?"

A pause consumed Vari. From her heart, to her loneliness, to her insatiable cravings, no matter what form of aesthetic. Saran was always nearby, always prodding, even from the realm of death. "Saran asked me things like that. Always using that same sweet, invasive charm."

Julia's head shifted from one shoulder to the other. "Are you saying I'm invasive?"

"You're convinced I'm hiding something."

"You are. You have an eye for details, you're from New Brasilia, but that's not your whole ancestry. And you're attracted to my sister."

Vari stood up again. If she didn't leave soon, she'd reveal something else that needed to remain hidden.

"I heard a story from some girls in the refinery." Julia sat up. "When the last Imperator died, his family went into hiding. His wife was from New Brasilia." She tapped a finger against the edge of her glass. "Answer one last question and I'll let you go."

Vari withdrew into a whisper. "Ask."

"Are you part of that family?"

Julia pulled on Vari with her honeyed voice. Her plain demeanor and speech made her appear common, but her mind demonstrated a wealth of analysis and intelligence. A lie would be worse than an admission, if only for its denial. "Yes."

"What's your name?"

"I just answered your question."

Julia got up and circled Vari. "Don't be like that. You know how long it's been since I've been around someone who was clean? Someone who doesn't have refinery soaked into their skin?"

"No."

"I don't either. So, tell me your name. Let me brag about it later."

No one ever offered to brag about Vari. She'd been surrounded by teachers and friends. Mentors. Family. Enemies. Her circle was insular, failing to reach out far enough to meet others, much less have them brag about her. If Julia Pollus wanted her name, she would give it gladly—eventually. "Varius Antonio, heir of House Severus."

A full smile wrapped around Julia's face. "That wasn't so bad." She sat her glass aside, leaning back. "What's the sky like on New Brasilia?"

THE IMPERIAL COUNCIL CHAMBER glowed with additional rings of lights. The Imperator's chair remained empty, especially under the renewed radiance. More chairs filled the room compared to Caracalla's previous audience, allowing five men and two women to gather around the segmented table.

Beside Caracalla, another armored man with close-cropped red hair clasped a fist to his chest. "Caium, I'm glad to see you've escaped from the wilderness."

"Livius." Caracalla hammered a fist against his heart, returning the gesture. "It's been too long. Fighting makes you look strong again."

"It was my turn to wrestle with the Sekht. The fools don't know how to lose."

"At least the Spartans keep them busy on the ground." Caracalla made no hint of any order of protection rising from the hemispherical world.

"You haven't seen their devotion. The Sekht will do anything to remain divided from the rest of humanity." Livius scowled. "They have blind insanity but call it faith in their heathen gods."

"I've seen that devotion." Caracalla's spine twitched at the echo of a thousand tiny cuts. "The chief of the Sekht gods is worshiped on New Brasilia. I've seen Amazons gather at dawn to pray for the sun to rise."

Livius sneered. "Disgusting."

A gong erupted out of view, drawing all eyes to attention. Each stood with their heads lowered and fists clasped to their hearts. The elongated frame of Augustus Macrinus swooped in, wearing robes of maroon and gold. When he stood in front of the massive onyx eagle, a decorative plate of black armor became visible on his chest. Adornments of gold peeked through the layered robes, hinting at the Imperator's thirst for war.

He lifted his right hand. "Sit."

Everyone sat, moving as a single entity occupying multiple chairs.

Only the Imperator sat at a different pace, waiting for the others to be off their feet. No matter how bright the room turned, the depth of Macrinus's eyes still concealed their shape and color.

"We have a grave matter to discuss," the Imperator said. "The alliance of House Severus and the Amazons of New Brasilia is a rosebush with ten years' worth of thorns. I have discussed some of these developments with each of you, but the time has come for you to pool your information. General Artabanus, your report."

Livius activated a tablet. "Naval Command was sent a correspondence from Captain Eldreth of the *Arcturus*. He reports, in compliance with the Nihl Accords, that Queen Fola of House Virago and the Regent Princess Bassiana of House Severus have petitioned for a discussion of grievances with King II Leonidas of Sparta. Since the King is entrenched at the Sekht front, they will have to engage in negotiations there. In the interim, Spartan forces have entered New Brasilia as a defensive detail, protecting the Amazons from any advance on our part."

So much stirred since Caracalla left the Amazons behind. More cogs twisted in the dark, always ready to assert themselves with new and reborn threats.

The Imperator's shadowy gaze eased to the right. "General Caracalla, what is the most recent state of affairs on New Brasilia itself?"

The purified air of Roma Vatica filled the general's lungs before he spoke. "The Amazons have secreted caches of arrows primed for Quantum mounting. In addition, a chamber concealed behind the statue of Jupiter held Quantum Sword katas and a Quantum Battery, along with a collection of unsavory articles." The thought of Gallae-implicating clothing filled Caracalla's mouth with bile. He swallowed it back, forcing himself to choke on the death of too many comrades. "As Lord Geta's forces departed to deliver this evidence, the queen's household shot down their ship under a flurry of Quantum Arrows." Caracalla's brow sank as much as he dared in the Imperator's presence. "I led a failed defense of Lord Geta and the spaceport. For a time, I was captured and personally tormented by the princess Bassiana."

The onyx heads above the Imperator glared into Caracalla's chest. Each glossy eye narrowed in condemnation of failure. The standard offered no forgiveness.

From the Imperator's right, a twenty-something man with sunken eye sockets spoke. "Lord Caracalla, how did you escape your failure?"

An abysmal fragility tempered Caracalla's response. "I was visited by a Non-Dead agent who offered to help me escape. Without this agent's assistance, I would still be in the Amazonian dungeons."

"Did this agent bother to help the legions taken by your surrender?"

Only a whelp bearing the Imperator's name could imply such disgrace without feeling Caracalla's wrath.

"The craft that took me from that foul planet only seated two. Thankfully, my direct agony was the only target of the princess Bassiana."

"You should have freed your men and led them in a renewed offensive."

"With what weapons, Prince Diadumenian? The safety of my centurions deprived them of any arms they carried. Our shields were nothing but paper against the onslaught of Quantum Arrows." Caracalla stiffened his posture while relaxing his shoulders. He refused to allow weakness to destroy the Unnamed Empire, especially from a semi-entitled heir. "The *Arcturus* was better positioned to aid a contingency offensive I'd arranged from several Spartan allies. The only reason I left the field of battle was to inform the exalted members of this council of the treachery I'd witnessed on New Brasilia."

Diadumenian opened his mouth to speak, but the Imperator lifted a hand to signal silence. "I wish to hear more about the unsavory articles you mentioned."

A momentary sigh whistled between Caracalla's teeth. "Women's clothing, accessories, and adornments, all made for someone with two breasts, not one."

Adventus, a man at the extreme age to serve the Empire, lifted two fingers before speaking. "Many women on New Brasilia refuse to maim themselves. I'm sure the regent is among them."

Caracalla nodded. "It was the opinion of Lord Geta's Gallae-wife Lysandra that these articles belonged to the Severus heir, Varius."

Slight sounds erupted from many of the gathered voices. The women did not react. Neither did the Imperator.

"With that allegation," Macrinus said, "I would like to hear from Gallae Priestess Cybeline next."

A woman as tall as Caracalla straightened her pearl-shaded robes before parting the gold-trimmed veils woven around the sides of her head. "Thank you, Imperator. Shortly after the death of Lord Geta and his wife, I received a message illustrating Lady Lysandra's impressions of young Severus. At first, she'd chosen to woo him to aid her husband's quest for concealed information. After an intimate examination, Lady Lysandra discovered adhesive glue focused around both areolae. After this observation, Lady Lysandra successfully engaged young Severus in the shared rites of a Gallae initiate. If there was more to report, those lines never arrived due to the death of the Geta household."

A pause filled the chamber before Macrinus sealed the breach. "The loss of our friend, Lord Callium Geta, his wife, and the brave men serving with them, is a bleak tragedy. It is a testament to their loyalty that both of them continued their service in their final moments. Such a terrible loss."

To Caracalla's right, a man in maroon and white jumped to his feet. "Imperator, I do not profess the deepest friendship with Lord Geta, but I share in humanity's loss at his death. If I may, I wish to be the first to request vengeance for our fallen ally."

Another man stood from a seat further away. "I support this petition and cry for vengeance in the name of Lord Callium Geta."

The Imperator rose, bracing his hands behind his back. "Nestor, Ulpius, I appreciate your vigor. However, we should review another set of details before any decrees are made."

Both men in maroon and white sat under the Imperator's order.

When Macrinus sat, he lifted his left hand. "At this time, I wish to welcome a guest to speak to this council. General Caracalla, please introduce the next speaker."

Caracalla stood, duty compelling him through the lingering waves of disgust. "I mentioned in my report that a Non-Dead rescued me. While most of these servants are docile and capable of only rudimentary reasoning, my rescuer possesses a keen mind and a cunning acumen. I present to this council Roker of the Non-Dead."

The gong rang out again, freezing every tongue in the room. The doors opened, allowing the hooded silhouette to flow inside. Roker still carried his bulky silver case. When the entrance shut, Roker knelt, clasping his hand to the right side of his chest. "Hail Macrinus, Imperator of the Unnamed Empire and Defender of all Humanity."

"Welcome friend." Macrinus flexed his hand. "You may rise."

"Thank you, Imperator." Roker stood, extending a spindly set of legs to elevate the case. "I present to you and this council articles of physical evidence validating the claims presented prior to my entrance. These items are officially entrusted to General Caium Caracalla. General, with your permission, I will reveal the contents of this case."

Caracalla nodded. "Granted." He only had Roker's claim of what lay sealed inside. There was no reason to start doubting the Non-Dead.

Roker typed an extensive sequence of buttons on top of the case. Half of the vessel unfolded, exposing a shroud of black fabric. "I have sealed each item in a clear, sterile pouch for observation and uncontaminated assessment." He unfolded the fabric, laying out a mountainous red wig full of plump curls, an azure and violet dress, a gold and vermilion corset, matching undergarments, and formal heeled shoes. "These items all fit the physical shape of Varius Severus, especially when combined with an accompanying prosthesis." He lay out another set of pouches, all flesh-toned padded masses.

Caracalla scowled at the foolishness laying in front of him. A greater sword in his hand sang a better song of justice than this parade of pageantry.

"I also have a sample of Amazonian arrows bearing requisite gaps for Quantum fittings." Roker lay out an array of vacuum-sealed projectiles.

Macrinus stepped down from his throne, eclipsing Caracalla's shoulder. Dried, scarred fingers lifted an arrow for a moment, then rotated the feminine heels. "Amazing. The Non-Dead have fulfilled the dream that has haunted me this past decade."

A gleaming smile sparkled from Roker's hood. "What is that, Imperator?"

"You have given me the tools to end House Severus."

"Should we be so hasty?" An older woman seated across from Caracalla stirred in her seat. "Do we know, without dispute, that these clothes belong to the young heir?"

Macrinus glared at the woman. "I shall order them tested."

"And if the results are wrong?"

"Then this Non-Dead and the good general will be punished for their deception. All record of this meeting and its proclamations will be stricken."

Roker's smile never faded. "Imperator, I detected natural hair fibers in the clothing and wig. The articles may also contain other secretions. Surely these can be compared with any records from the young heir's birth."

Macrinus snorted. "Amusing. I don't think heir will be appropriate for much longer."

"I must protest." The older woman sat up from her chair. "We must not act rashly."

"You forget yourself, Maesa. I remember your relations, as much as you would prefer. Lady Cybeline?"

The towering woman stood. "Yes, Imperator?"

"Should the evidence be confirmed, would you accept young Severus into the Gallae?"

"Of course, Imperator. We gladly welcome all who would join our benevolent order."

"Excellent."

Maesa stood. "Again, Imperator, I protest. It is unprecedented for a religion to annex members in their absence."

"Your concerns are noted." Macrinus pinched the coiled mass of beard under his chin. "I have decided upon a course of action."

Caracalla gripped the ends of his armrests. His fingernails dug into the dense wood. Any debate was in the past. What Macrinus said next would tilt the trajectory of the Unnamed Empire.

"General Caracalla will travel to Ardesiel." The Imperator clasped a scarred hand over the general's shoulder. "Upon the conclusion of any talks between the Amazons and Spartans, you will take Queen Fola of House Virago and the Regent Princess Bassiana of House Severus into custody. From there, you will retrieve the regent's child and bring all three here to Roma Vatica.

"Lord Nestor will travel to New Brasilia. Once General Caracalla's prisoners are in custody, you will destroy every arrow on that planet, confiscate every drop of Quantum, and strike down their heathen temples. From there, you will serve as Interim Governor until a permanent official can be installed. Your primary mandate will be the forceful integration of all New Brasilians into Imperial life. At the first sign of disobedience from the population, you are to poison their waters, burn their grain, and volunteer the planet for Quantum weapons testing.

"Lady Cybeline, you will file a writ of acceptance for the Severus heir, accepting his female designation and abdication of formal titles and rank.

"House Severus itself will be surrendered as a wedding gift from the Lady..." The Imperator's gaze locked upon Roker, expecting a response to some unspoken question.

Roker grew excited at such a formal glance of attention. "Varia, according to her journals."

Macrinus nodded. "A wedding gift from the Lady Varia to the House of her betrothed, Lord Diadumenian Macrinus. As head of House Macrinus, I will sell the rank and title of House Severus to the young Lord Alexander Aurelius, provided he swear the fealty of his House to my own."

Those named clasped their hands against their hearts before speaking in unison. "It will be done, Imperator."

"Lady Maesa, do you still protest to any part of my decision?"

The aged woman did not shrink in stature. Instead, her hand pressed her heart as she tilted her head forward. "No, Imperator. I have no protest." She was as wizened and bold as her years suggested and more. A gray-haired woman did not counsel or protest an Imperator without having equally old and noble blood pumping through her veins.

Like Diadumenian and Varius, the masses called Maesa's father *Imperator.*

Caracalla wondered what sort of Imperator would rise from one Imperator's loins only to suckle a failed Imperator's tit.

Julia's blissful face reminded Vari of lying across a sofa. Monitor panels on the walls showed rainy forest scenes, complete with a gentle patter of water.

Vari leaned over Julia, tickling her fingers through the unbound swoops of her blond hair. Each fiber, rough from exposure, enticed her to savor every liquor-steamed breath. They both bobbed in and out of consciousness while they talked. Julia told silly stories about Judith; Vari beamed about the sorceress called Saran.

While listening to the recorded tones of rainfall, Vari tugged the band restraining her own hair. An elated sway of midnight brown fluttered over Vari's cheeks. A pocket of seaside breeze drifted into her nose.

"It looks better that way." Julia smiled within the golden shroud, brushing a finger through Vari's hair. Her fingertips glazed over Vari, shifting from chin to collarbone. "There's a grace about you. Something pretty about your eyes."

A puff of laughter crept through Vari's mouth. "I haven't heard that one before."

"Most people I see are exhausted from working refineries. Nobody's royalty pretty."

A full burst of laughter erupted from Vari. "Nobody's ever called me pretty." It was a tiny lie.

Julia snorted a strand of hair away from her nose. "At least I'm not noble."

"Let me judge that." Vari kissed the tip of her nose. The sting of sweat pierced her tongue, sobering Vari to the reality that it was Saran's sister in front of her.

"You want another round?" A disheveled lioness was still a great cat, even if she wobbled from drinking.

A tiny beep shook Vari's clothes. "Damn."

"Leave it." Julia tugged on his hip, pulling him closer. "They can call back."

Duty compelled Vari into a fog of sobriety. She stretched an arm away from the sofa, dragging her transceiver from the end table. Vari groaned at the display. "Captain Lucan is looking for me."

Julia loomed over Vari before she could get up. "Don't even think about flying away. Even if you have to wait for me to get out of the office or a refinery." She flopped her arms around Vari's neck and shoulders.

Vari inhaled deeply, locking the fragrance of oil and alcohol within her lungs. "I... uh..."

"Close that pretty mouth and go about your business. Find something else to hide from me." Julia offered a droopy smile. "It'll give me a reason to be curious again."

"I will." Vari leaned close. An echo of Saran's warm set a tingle in Vari's neck.

"Don't forget." Julia slipped onto the couch, playfully waving as Vari stepped away.

Any leader needs allies, not just emotional guidance, but
those trusted to serve on the field of battle.

Imperator Sextus Severus
Spear Point Academy Commencement Address

LUCAN LEANED AGAINST THE dull silvery-white wall outside of Vari's room. "I guess Lady Pollus took the news well enough," the roguish captain said. "You were gone for a while."

Vari straightened a stray wrinkle along the front of her shirt. "She took it as well as an estranged sister would. How did your contact work out?"

Lucan bobbed his head toward the door. "Inside."

They entered. Vari sealed the locks. Lucan juggled a shadowy green data card between his fingers. "This will get you a breathing mask and exposure gear. You need to go to a bar called Tartarus. It's in Refinery Complex 14."

"OK." A blank weight hung over Vari's cheeks. Every hallway on Gaulius looked the same.

"This is Refinery Complex 1. If you want to get to Complex 14—"

"I have to go outside." Vari nodded. The directions sounded isolating. If it weren't for the tattoo on Lucan's arm, Vari wouldn't consider going at all. "What's happening at the bar?"

"Ask for Diana. She's a regular there. Buy her a drink, then say, 'I'll never have sex with you.' Then put your right hand over your eyes."

Vari shrugged. "Odd code, but whatever works."

198

The decayed atmosphere of Gaulius chilled Vari, even through layers of protective gear. Her gloved hands clamped over reinforced handrails. Clouds and mist condensed miles beneath the lattice of walkways connecting one complex to the next. Bursts of light ripped through the condensation below. Rumbling howled from the cracked surface, though never from the same direction twice.

No visible sunlight pierced the muddy bank of diseased clouds. The horizon took on a sickly green glow, radiating light from distant refineries and the distant tease of daylight. A cargo shuttle blazed into the air, taking Quantum to an empire ravenous for power.

Vari understood why Saran wanted to leave such a world. There was no life. No sculptures defined a plaza, since there were no parks. No homes lined non-existent countrysides. No seas released salt to the air, nor did they hint of savory fish waiting to be caught. There was only Quantum and the machines that toiled to extract it.

Only a few planets had Quantum refineries. Tests took place on asteroids desperate to extract a drop of purified energy. Every test failed to reproduce the cornerstone of Nihl technology.

Humanity may have disposed of the Nihl, but the Unnamed Empire needed every oppressive advancement to keep star systems connected.

After twenty minutes of winding through the exposed walkway, Vari reached a soot-stained tram. A tarnished metal kiosk blocked the entrance. A frayed, dented speaker took the place of gate controls.

The speaker crackled. "Where to?"

"Complex 14." Through so many coverings, Vari sounded as distorted as whoever controlled the gate.

A grating buzz wrapped around Vari before the gate unlatched, allowing her down one of half a dozen sealed passages. Like everything else on Gaulius, leaving one complex for another was abrupt and forgotten.

Tartarus was a large room with bleak beams of blue and purple light aimed at an industrial tavern far from the entrance to the Complex. A withered man poured drinks for the sedentary souls seated in isolation. Groups of friends sat at tables, crowding close to keep their conversations intimate. Ripped leather benches tumbled against the walls, serving as the only refuge for those too drunk to walk back to their quarters.

A mob gathered in one corner. Mostly men, though a few women stood among the mass of bodies. From behind, they all looked soiled, from their unkempt hair to stained jumpsuits that would never be clean again. Several held up luminous drinks radiating a cosmic hue of pink.

Vari swerved the other way, approaching the bar. The withered bartender waddled close. "What're you having?"

Palace events on New Brasilia had dishes paired with complimentary spirits. Wine lists were for peasants pretending to enjoy alcohol.

Clueless, Vari gave the best response she could manage. "What do you have?"

The bartender rolled his eyes. "We've got Macrinus Ale, Imperial Best, and Refiner's Delight."

"I was told to ask for Diana. If she's here, I'll have what she's having."

"Ugh. Kid, the swarm is already big enough." He hooked a thumb at the crowd. "You should try after her next shift."

"What do you mean?"

"Asking for Diana and doesn't know a damn thing." The withered bartender filled a slender glass with luminous pink liquid. He sat the full glass in front of an empty barstool. "Have a seat and I'll enlighten you."

Resistance tightened Vari's jaw, but she recalled how forward Julia had been. Vari mounted the stool with a nod. "Enlightenment is good for the soul."

"At least you're willing to learn from your elders." The withered bartender took a swig from a dingy glass mug. A trail of amber crawled around the deep lines of his mouth and chin. "Diana works thirty-six hours at a time, twelve more than most people in these parts. She gets twenty hours to herself and spends the first two of those auditioning who gets the rest of her time. Even stuck in a refinery, she's quite the lady, so people line up to buy her drinks."

Vari swallowed a fifth of the gleaming liquor in front of her. "Sounds like she can change the galaxy."

A sigh in need of a breath mint rolled across the bar. "You may as well wait."

"I may have to leave before her next shift ends."

"So be it." The withered bartender put another luminous glass on the bar, scanned Vari's data card, and walked away.

Vari took both drinks and squeezed against the mass of oily jumpsuits. Puffs of soot rose from every set of feet, no matter how far they stayed from the refineries. A few voices mumbled as Vari passed. Most chanted, "Drink, drink, drink…"

At the core of the gathering, a brick-shaped woman chugged one of the luminous drinks. Her chest and nostrils remained still as she finished. She swung the empty glass like a sword, slamming it against the edge of the closest table. With a clunk, the glass popped out of her hand and rolled onto the floor.

An unseen woman spoke. "Another one bites the dust."

The brick-shaped woman flared her arms out in protest, wobbling as she failed to stand. "Really?"

"Really. Thanks for playing, Trudy."

"Damn." Trudy shambled through the crowd. Vari turned sideways to let her pass. A burst of applause rang out from every direction.

The unseen woman stepped forward, posing her buxom hourglass figure with every step. Dusk-shaded hair framed an ageless, olive-skinned face. "I've got enough in me to take on a few more contestants. Who wants to make a go of it?"

Dozens of voices screamed in desperation. An olive finger pointed at individuals among the crowd. "You won two shifts ago. A month ago. Also, a month ago."

Her finger froze. Her eyes widened with warmth. "Who is this?" She pointed at Vari. "A new player?"

"I heard you were a vision." Vari returned the woman's smile. "I had to see for myself."

"Anybody can look, but I'm sure someone wants to play." Her finger tapped Vari's chest. "Is that you?"

"I don't mind, but you should know something."

She smirked. "What's that?"

Varius shifted both glasses into his left hand. "I'll never have sex with you." She covered her eyes with her right hand.

Diana groaned. "Dammit."

More voices shouted. "If you don't want her, get lost."

Frustration whipped around Vari. "Go to 22 if you want someone to stick you."

"Diana ain't a Gallae. Get the fuck out of here."

Vari lowered her hand, curling his fingers toward his palms. There wasn't a weapon in her hand, but she could throw a punch. If she shoved her palm fast enough under someone's chin, she'd shatter their hyoid bone, thrusting fractured shards into their brain.

Diana lifted a hand. "Shut the fuck up." Her finger pointed into Varius again. "I decide who's turn it is." She pointed at the chair Trudy used two minutes earlier. "If you want my attention, kid, earn it."

Varius sat, placing both glasses into an intricate web of moistened rings.

"Since you're from out of town," Diana said with a smirk, "I'll make the game a bit more fair. Usually, you'd have to drink more than that. Just for you, I'll let you stick with those two glasses. Drink them both, one then the other. Don't leave a drop in either glass. When the second one is empty, ram it against the edge of the table. Crack it, you get to go again. Shatter it, you win. Got it?"

She nodded. "Got it."

Vari took a deep breath.

The crowd chanted low. "Drink. Drink."

Guzzling anything broke decorum, something Princess Bassiana scolded every time Vari tried it. The first time Vari tried it, her father had muffled a laugh.

"Drink, drink. Drink."

Vari shoved the first glass against her lips, turning it upward. The liquid pressed through her mouth, squeezed through her teeth. Her throat churned to consume more glowing vitality.

A certainty flowed through Vari's eyes. Power flooded her lips.

She would have smiled, if the luminous stream didn't keep flooding her stomach. The tangy sting coated her tongue, freeing her to swallow deeper than her dreams. Shedding restraints freed Varia more than any coupling or acceptance. She took on so many burdens, accepted roles upon roles.

But her father's throne had been stolen. Varia had to steal back what was hers by birth, by right, by a childhood of lessons. Varia damned her male skin every night for keeping her from what she deserved. From her throne, she would make humanity praise her, no matter what extreme she needed to assert to make that happen.

Varia snatched up the full glass with one hand. She slammed the inverted empty vessel on the freshly exposed ring.

Diana's eyes widened at the impact. The crowd cheered in shock before setting back to their chant. "Drink. Drink. Drink..."

As her hostess stared harder, Varia chugged faster. She had dreamed of pushing her mouth between Saran's legs, biting and kissing with an intimate intensity that would have denied both of them the ability to breathe.

Pretending to be male made her so forgetful.

No matter what she called herself in silence, Varia craved the same vengeance as a woman that she did pretending to be a man. She let the crowd see a silly teenager gulping at a glass of alcohol.

Varia knew the truth. She was the rightful Imperator of the Unnamed Empire. No stupid drinks would keep her from that.

Her gaze locked onto the edge of the table. The crowd's fanaticism swayed like Lysandra's hips.

Vari stopped breathing, swept up in the last part of the challenge.

If a foolish man ever wanted to rule the universe, it was time to woman up with the full force of her Brasilian ancestry.

The glass dripped empty. Vari turned it in a sharp circle, lifting it overhead before swinging it at the point she'd been watching. An instant before the glass made impact, Varius slammed her left fist against her right hand, doubling the force.

Clear, jagged splinters scattered over the table.

Quiet muzzled the crowd. Faces transfixed with gaping stares.

Diana clapped. Her expression remained calm and steady. Her voice remained low. "That's a Brasilian method." She parted her hands and paced along the edge of the crowd. "It seems we have a winner, after all."

"But he doesn't even want you."

"That's his loss." Diana's eyes patrolled Vari from head to toe. "He met the challenge, so he wins. Maybe he'll change his mind when you're all not looking." She held a hand out for Vari. Only when her dry, cracked fingers locked in her grasp did Diana lift Vari's arm in triumph. "Let's hear it for tonight's winner, Antonio."

A few people clapped. Most of the crowd stumbled away, languishing with disappointment.

Without letting go of Vari's hand, Diana went to the bar to run her data card.

The withered bartender shook his head while accepting Diana's payment.

Once the transaction finished, a toothy gleam filled Diana's smile. "Shall we?"

"Sure." Vari wasn't sure who should lead the way. "Back to your table?"

"Gods no. We're going to my room."

The deepest of marital arrangements are built on the same
foundations: Mutually beneficial alliances and sex.

Old Sekht proverb

DIANA'S QUARTERS HAD NO calming display panels. Like the walls, her tables were bare. Unlike Julia's quarters, Diana only had a partition dividing a cooking area from the nest of crumpled blankets over a sofa bed.

When the door hissed shut, Diana pulled a latch. Locking restraints clicked, sealing the door from any intrusion.

"You look like him."

Vari tilted an eyebrow. "Who?"

"Sextus Severus, the last Imperator." Diana sat on most of her blankets. "Lucan said you're after the Eighth Quantum Sword."

"Yes." Saying anything more would reveal more giddiness than Vari had ever expressed.

"Up front with it, too." Diana shook her head. "I swore never to say where the damned thing is. That way, a giant asshole can't have it."

"Macrinus." The taste of bile swirled in Vari's mouth.

"The way you say his name, Antonio, I'd swear you hated him, too."

"He killed my father."

"He killed a lot of fathers. Asshole had to have his throne, didn't matter how thin his claim."

Vari slapped her palms on a table. "Macrinus stole my father's throne. Big chair? Carved from a giant mass of black meteorite?"

Diana pulled out a sealed leather flask. Cracks dug into the seal of a graceful, single-headed hawk fused into the front of the container. "You're awfully good at this, Number Three. Send the fucker my compliments."

"Excuse me?" Vari shrugged with her hands and shook her head. "I'm not a number. I have a name."

"Yeah, yeah." Diana screwed the cap onto her flask. "You're the third Varius Severus that assmonger has sent to con me. You know a few things about pretending to be from New Brasilia. If you live, I hope you find a good theater company."

"I've only had ten years to learn about New Brasilia."

"Really?" Diana leaned back on the sofa, crossing her arms. "Where did you complete these magnificent studies?"

"New Brasilia."

"Shit for brains must be desperate. Conning some Brasilian kid and Lucan to swindle me out of my last scrap of pride."

Direct arguments did nothing for Vari, especially on such an abrasive world as Gaulius. "Why don't you think I'm Varius Severus?"

All joy drained from Diana's face. "Varius Severus has his aunt's legions to back him up. He doesn't need me."

A sigh sapped away all resistance. The weight of continuing failure stopped tugging on Vari's chest. She flopped onto the opposite side of the sofa. "If it was up to me, I'd have every legion backing me up. Not just Brasilians, but Spartans, centurions, praetorians. None of that matters without the Sword. The Sekht could beg to join the Unnamed Empire under my rule and I'd still be disputed—unless I have *that* Sword. I might be able to make Macrinus's Sword work, but he can't empower the Eighth Sword. I can, if I can find the warrior who hid it."

"Isn't that why you're here?"

Vari shook her head. "Lucan said you'd know where to find this warrior. He only told me that once we landed on Gaulius."

Diana's mouth twisted. "If you didn't come here for the Sword, why are you here?"

Shards of a broken heart clattered in Vari's voice. "My friend died. Her will said to bring her body here."

Diana's eyes widened. Worry lines betrayed an age hidden behind pride and years of labor. She eased a hand over her mouth before tilting her head in disbelief. "That sweet girl."

"Sweet doesn't say half of it."

"Huh. Did you know Judith well?"

"No. My friend is Saran of Virago."

"Saran...?" Two leathery vices clamped around Vari's wrists. "She took a Brasilian name? Fola claimed her?"

"Yes."

"It wasn't for show? Or to curry—"

"Every Brasilian warrior looked at her as another sister in arms."

So many had wondered why Saran swerved away from her chosen glory in death. The answer lay bound within Diana, a truth hidden with the Eighth Sword. Saran must have hoped Vari would meet Diana, then find the Sword. "Thank you for sending her to me." Vari lay a hand over Diana's scratched knuckles. "Saran was the best person I'll ever know."

Vari's head slumped low for an instant, long enough to sense rising tears, but short enough to fight the moisture back.

"Did she die in battle?"

Vari nodded. "Just after shooting down the Imperial assessor's ship."

"Saran." A smile crept over Diana's face. Two tears moistened her left cheek. "You followed the tradition of visitation? Full armor and arms?"

"No helmet." How could one face the Elagabal with a helmet blocking her view?

"Bring me her weapons."

Venom saturated Varius's mouth. "I won't let you desecrate Saran for your drinking games."

"Fine." A languished exhale drew Diana to her feet. She unzipped the top of her jumpsuit, snapped off her shirt. She unhooked her vinyl bra and dropped it on the pile of blankets.

Diana clawed into her skin, digging all of her fingers into the lighter mass. Her teeth grunted together. She pulled, her throat winced. Knuckles blazed whiter as she pulled harder, yet there was no blood. The mound snapped free. Diana dropped the prosthetic into Vari's lap.

As she caught her breath, Diana sat on the armrest beside her bra and blankets.

Vari tenderly rubbed a thumb against the warm, realistic skin. The tender mound reminded her of similar, less impressive versions she'd worn on her own. Vari envied Diana's natural shape. "This is the most impressive artifice I've ever seen."

"That's great." Diana snatched the fake tissue away from Vari. "This is what I want you to see."

A knot of scar tissue twisted in a mass of unstable curves resembling a starburst. Additional hardened spots crusted the skin between the erratic arcs. No one cut the flesh from Diana's body. Quantum arrows had atrophied the most exposed extent of her body. Such a design only existed on the bodies of veteran Brasilian warriors. "Satisfied?"

"Are you satisfied that I am who I claim?" Vari had never given her full name, only the portion she'd officially listed when they landed.

Diana snapped a blanket around her chest. "Bring me Saran's weapons, then we'll talk about yours."

Ardesiel was an ancient aquatic world whose swaying surface lay painted with dense threads of coral. Three conjunctions of color fused enough material to form a star-shaped swirl of islands.

Of those islands, few had the strength to hold a full Spartan transport. Artificial struts expanded the makeshift landmass, bonding multiple islands together into a larger structure. A decade after coalition forces first converged around The Enlightened Kingdoms of Sekht, Ardesiel's frail ecology became the most active military bastion since humanity toppled the Nihl.

Bassiana frowned at the angular beams anchoring each building to the ocean floor far below the reefs. "A terrible place to stage an attack or a defense. Nowhere to fully gather phalanxes or to base siege weaponry."

"They have food and water." Fola breathed in the cool, sweet air. "The only supplies anyone needs here are fresh soldiers and arms. Unlike food and water, those are easy to come by."

Five pairs of Spartans flanked the brick path ahead of Agis. The honor guard all wore red capes and carried scratched shields. Broad helmets bore scars and stains following years of plasma-kissed battle.

Agis made a coarse grunt. The honor guard drew swords, holding the blades at the same angle as the braces around the neighboring buildings. "Follow me," Agis said. "He is waiting."

They followed the brick path to a small cargo bay swept clean of debris and ships. Four chairs waited in the center of the chamber, all facing the others. Of the four, a single chair was already occupied by a Spartan with thick braids extending from under his helmet. The center braid reached to his waist while the others wrapped around his shoulders.

Agis knelt. "My King, I present to you Princess Bassiana, Regent of House Severus."

Bassiana stepped forward, performing an immaculate curtsy. She'd made the motion thousands of times as a child.

Agis spoke again without moving. "My King, I present Her Royal Highness, Fola of House Virago, Queen of New Brasilia."

Fola offered a slight nod of respect. Only the Imperator or the Elagabal could ask for more.

Agis stood facing Bassiana and Fola. "I am honored to announce His Royal Highness, II Leonidas, King of All Sparta."

Leonidas stood. "Welcome." He snapped his hand out to the seat across from his own.

Fola approached the offered chair, little more than a hunter's stool reinforced for use in the wild. "I thank you for meeting with us."

He responded with a quick nod.

Bassiana placed herself behind the chair on Fola's right. Agis moved to the remaining position. No one sat.

The King and Queen studied each other in silence. Two hardened gazes searched for the smallest sign of a mortal threat. Leonidas relaxed his shoulders. Fola nodded. They both sat simultaneously, followed by the aides each kept in attendance.

Leonidas lay his hands across both armrests. "Shall we begin with the facts?"

As Vari returned to Julia's quarters, the pragmatic lady greeted her with a smile. "Get done early?"

"No."

She pulled Vari forward, luring her toward her bedroom. "Want a drink?"

Waves of regret filled Vari's head. "No."

Julia frowned before pulling out a fresh pair of glasses. "Don't be like that."

"I actually need your help with something."

"Oh?" Julia unscrewed an amber bottle. "You don't seem to be in a kinky mood."

Saran had wielded the same kind of subtle humor. The first time was when Vari needed to express the truth hidden inside her drab, rigid body. Something needed to be spoken. Only Saran was willing to listen.

"I need to open your sister's casket."

Julia scowled. "Please tell me you're not into necrophilia."

Vari cringed. "No."

Julia pushed a full glass in front of Vari before taking a drink.

After taking a cordial sip, Vari licked her lips. The liquid tasted like brutal fire. "As a Brasilian warrior, Saran was adorned with armor and arms, even in death."

Julia fiercely clanged her glass onto the closest table. Her face ruptured with hateful lines. "Jupiter, save me. That bitch is still down there."

"I never called Saran—"

"Not my sister. Diana of Hippolyta. Our Imperially designated refinery worker."

The answer hung in Vari's open mouth. "Yes."

"She wants the weapons to blow up my refineries. Once she's ruined everything here, do you know where she'll go?"

"Roma Vatica?"

Julia shook her head. "New Brasilia. She won't be going to join up. That bitch'll shoot up the palace, the temples, everything. Macrinus burned her, but Fola left her to rot. So, no, you can't open my sister's casket. In fact, take that coffin with you when you go back."

She snatched the glass out of Vari's hands, pouring the liquid back into the bottle. "You've come a long way for nothing."

A hollow rebuttal whispered out of Vari's throat. "I need her."

"You can do better than that bitch."

"She knows things."

"There's only one thing she knows." Julia shook her head enough for hair to tumble over her eye. "I don't think she'll ever tell anyone, not even you."

"I still have to try."

"You won't get to. I have my own Imperial assessors calling. They show up twice a year and someone always goes looking for Diana."

"I've lived under the same specter, the thought of doing something harmless to unleash Macrinus's wrath. That's been half my life." Vari clawed her fingers around the back of her chair. "If I had something to offer to make it worthwhile, I'd give it to you in an instant."

The legacy of House Severus depended on it.

Saran's memory depended on it.

"All I have is this." Julia turned her hand toward the walls around them. "My mother died of inhalation when I was a kid. My father has been hooked on a ventilator for three years, leaving me to run this dump of a planet. In less than fifteen years, the pathetic atmosphere on this planet is going to collapse. No atmosphere, no Quantum. Then the Empire gets to foreclose on all my contracts. They'll buy my family name for cheap and that'll be the end." Julia flopped back into her chair, sprawling one leg over the armrest.

"I'd do anything for Saran. I'm sure she'd do anything for you."

"I haven't talked to her in years. Judith left long ago and died somewhere." Julia twisted the side of her mouth. "I don't know this hero you keep talking about."

Vari crouched beside Julia, bracing against her own knees. "I'm sorry for what's happened to you. It seems like the galaxy has stripped everything from you one thread at a time."

Julia took a slow drink from the bottle. "Pity from someone who still has a noble name."

"I'm just as discarded as you."

"I've seen pictures of your paradise. Go back to New Brasilia. You can breathe there."

Vari lowered her head. "We had our own Imperial visitors. Want to know what happened to them?"

"They enjoyed a week of luxury before going back to their mansions on Roma Vatica?"

"Not this time."

Julia took another swig of liquor. "Two weeks then."

"They got nothing. Saran killed them to save me."

"Good for her. Judith was a second daughter. She spent years dodging family obligations, especially when my father started coughing. The only way I'll ever be finished with this rock is to marry some rich jerk and become his doting housewife."

Julia had enough good humor. She might have been direct, but so had Saran. Since Saran saved Vari, she had no choice but to see some level of gratitude delivered to her friend—Saran's next of kin.

Vari looked up. "I can make part of that happen. You have too good of a head to waste on being a simple housewife."

"You don't have to humor me."

The solution was in hand. Vari only had to prove it.

She knelt low, taking Julia's hand. Her eyes closed as she pressed Julia's fingers to her own forehead. "Julia of the House Pollus, will you consent to join your House to mine, through an alliance of resources, and a joining of our bodies?"

Julia leaned closer. "What are you offering?"

"The Ancestral Mansion on Roma Vatica. What about you?"

"Fourteen years of Quantum production." She eased her hand away and stood. A laugh chimed from her as she put the liquor bottle away. "It's a cute idea. I don't suppose you have an imperially sanctioned priest who could validate this clever idea of yours?"

Vari smiled as she stood. "I might."

No matter how much we loathe our neighbors, we are still part of the same community.

Queen Fola of Virago
Remarks prior to attacking a Sekht settlement

S OLUS KNELT IN THE center of his room. His fingers wove together with his thumbs pressing against his lower lip. He stared beyond the ceiling, searching for a star to guide his answer.

"It's a simple yes or no," Julia said with her arms crossed. "This planet is screwed. House Severus could use a decade's worth of Quantum."

Vari stood closer to the kneeling priest. "If we're lucky enough for my mother to object, we can always state this as a union of Severus and Virago interests."

"I'm Pollus, not Virago."

Vari shrugged. "With the fighting when I left New Brasilia, you might be both."

"Great." Julia rolled her eyes. "Babysitting one Amazon is bad enough. A whole planet of them...?"

"It would make you a queen."

Solus parted his hands and stood. "We do not know the state of things on New Brasilia. The Queen and the Regent are resourceful. They may yet live."

An overwhelming frown lowered the sides of Vari's face. "And if they don't?"

"Then this is a wise course of action. Lady Julia, I promise nothing as binding as full marriage, especially since the two of you are de facto heads of Houses, not the official reigning leaders. Given what each of you have told me, I see an advantageous arrangement for you both."

Julia nodded her head. A moment of contemplation filled her eyes in a way Vari had never seen from Saran. "What do you need to get the documents in order?"

"Time and the use of your offices."

"Done. That'll give me and clean boy time to sort out the rest, especially that bitch in the basement."

No matter how much Fola adored her cousin, Bassiana excelled at grinding on the queen's nerves. Even while holding a rigid tone of voice, Bassiana proved grating. "Modification using non-human material is an egregious violation of the Accords."

"We are what we are." Agis spoke in the same unmoving tone. "It is part of who we are."

A drop of passion flooded Bassiana's voice. "Do you have no concern about the welfare of our planet? If the Imperator were to learn of this—"

"He may already know."

As the aides argued every point, Fola watched her Spartan counterpart. Neither spoke, allowing the others to bicker while the rulers acted as the adults in the room. When her eye met the aggressive gaze of the Spartan king, Fola let her silence break.

"What about the Non-Dead?"

Leonidas lifted his head.

Agis turned. "What about them?"

"Non-Dead were fighting among your forces." The bandage around Fola's head stung. "A Non-Dead Spartan exploded and took my eye with him."

Leonidas tightened his mouth. "His name will not be written in the book."

"I've heard that already."

Bassiana spoke with growing fury. "The use of Non-Dead in a military capacity is strictly forbidden. They aren't permitted to equip themselves in a combative nature. Despite that, they marched from Sparta in lock-step with Spartans."

"Such things would carry less weight if they occurred on Sparta alone." Fola eased her fingers into a fist. "These Non-Dead marched with your men in a campaign of war."

"That was not war." Storm and thunder rose from Leonidas's voice. "War happens between here and Sekht space. War is constant conflict without a moment to speak. The Non-Dead have not marched to war with or without Spartan aid."

Fola rapped a knuckle against her chair. "We must assume Spartan modifications have been made in concert with Non-Dead technicians. If this is the case, it would be an illegal synthesis of both groups. However, you can buy our silence on the matter."

"We do not barter. We make war."

"Then we have nothing more to discuss." The queen stood. "Bassiana, let us go."

Without a word, Bassiana followed Fola to the door.

"Stop."

Fola crossed her arms before she straightened her posture. She applied a stern visage as she turned.

Leonidas dug his fingers into the central weave of his beard. His exhale echoed throughout the vacant room. "The Unnamed Empire is ravenous for your heads. Inside of a month, New Brasilia will be under an endless siege. Glory is your only hope from here."

Fola turned her eye onto Agis. "Come over here." She faced Bassiana and said, "I want both of you to verify what I am about to do."

Leonidas nodded to Agis in approval.

Once both aides stood beside Fola, she pulled a yellowy, aged scroll from her quiver and unrolled it. "This is the deed for the hemisphere known as New Brasilia." She took a lengthy pen from the quiver and scrawled on the bottom of the rolled paper. "I have signed ownership to King II Leonidas of Sparta. Verify this."

Bassiana's eyes locked open. Her lips clamped shut. Her fingers trembled.

Agis tilted his head as he read over the paper. "It's genuine."

"Princess Bassiana." Fola kept her words stern and civil. "Is this genuine?"

A tiny gasp whimpered from the pale-cheeked princess. "Yes."

Fola rolled the scroll and returned it to her quiver. "King II Leonidas, I will give you the scroll and public verification of the transfer on one condition."

The Spartan King shifted his fingers away from the braid of his beard. "Name your condition."

"Varius Severus was taken by an unidentified party. I wish for his safe and free return to his mother, especially if the Houses Severus and Virago are to face glory against the Unnamed Empire. While you locate and secure the young man, my cousin and I will remain your guests." Fola extended her open hand. "Is this satisfactory?"

"One young man for a complete Sparta?" Leonidas stood, nodding.

Both rulers approached each other. Their hands clasped halfway between the door and the chairs.

Leonidas may have thought he'd bought half a planet at a discount.

Fola knew she'd bought a new line of defenders.

The depths of Refinery Complex 14 swelled with steamy vents and pungent, mechanical scents. A lattice of elevators and trams sent Vari and Julia deeper into Gaulius. Even though they were indoors, the array of bright and muddy vapors forced them to keep wearing protective gear in order to breathe.

Under metal walkways, large scoops dug into deeper layers of crust. Industrial lasers blasted erratically into the dense rock, loosening each section before a scoop threw the mass onto a broad nest of battered conveyors. Each belt tugged deposits toward a central nexus, the massive compressor where pressure converted solid mass into hyper-dense plasma.

"It gets up to sixty degrees down here." Julia waved a gloved hand toward the mechanical dance beneath them. "Going into the compressor area is impossible without another layer of safety equipment."

"Right."

She stopped, grabbing Vari by the rubberized seal around her collar. "Don't go in there by accident. Most of this is automated. Every half hour, there's a three-minute pause in the cycle. One airlock closes, the next opens. That's when shift changes happen, so that's when we drag that bitch out."

Beads of sweat already clung to Vari's brow. Another rush of droplets squeezed through her sticky joints, only to congeal behind her ears and under her jaw. She'd only been near the refinery for a few minutes. Some spent lifetimes toiling in such molten conditions.

Within an enclosed, grimy security booth, a man in dense protective gear lowered his cracked tablet.

Julia held out her data card. "I need to speak with Diana of Hippolyta at the next interval."

"I'm sorry, Lady Pollus." The man shook his head. "An armored Imperial assessor showed up an hour ago and sealed all the staff doors. No one comes or goes until he gives the all-clear."

"Damn."

Vari leaned toward the booth. "Is there a way to speak with the assessor?"

"Transmitters are staticky, but they work."

Julia pushed Vari back. "What are you doing?"

"Provoking my opponent." Vari connected a wire from the security booth to the side of her protective mask. "To all who hear my voice. This is Imperator Varius of House Severus. I order the staff doors opened at the next interval. Failure will be treated as a violation of Imperial decree and subject to death. Respond." She disconnected the wire and stepped away from the door.

"What the fuck was that?" Julia's hands lifted as she shook her head.

"You'll see. Play along."

Several moments later, the door hissed open. A bulky figure in a milky white armored bodysuit stepped out. "Who's the clown?"

Julia stomped forward and crossed her arms. "You will kneel in the Imperator's presence."

"And remove your mask." Vari stood as tall as possible while bundled in protective gear. "I have not given you permission to conceal your identity from me."

"Idiots." The assessor drew a thick, boxy pistol from behind his back. "Both of you will step inside the refinery chamber." He flipped a tab with his thumb, causing the weapon to whine with life. "Now."

Vari shrugged, lifting her hands. "I suppose there is no choice."

Julia shook her head. "Knew I should have brought a gun."

When Vari reached the door, she stomped on the armored man's instep. The man stumbled for an instant, allowing Vari to snatch the pistol away. She aimed the weapon at the reinforced shoulder joint.

Julia's hand clamped over Vari's wrist. "I've got an idea." She connected the transmitter wire to her mask. Her voice crackled over every speaker. "This is Planetary Administrator Julia Pollus. I am enacting an emergency shift change. Everyone out of the chamber now."

A stream of bodies flowed through the doorway. Excited postures and confused motions dominated every masculine figure. Of the female workers, only one reacted. Those who stayed in line appeared wrapped in dense cellophane under their protective gear. The woman who reacted possessed a smooth gait betrayed the burdening layers of protective gear.

She stopped near Julia and Vari, glancing back and forth at each. When she turned to Vari, Diana asked, "Where are the weapons you promised me?"

"Still locked away," Julia said. "Insurance that my refineries stay intact."

Diana sighed through the filters of her mask. "Give me that pistol." Her wide hand opened toward Vari.

Julia shifted between them. "Don't."

"You want that Sword?" Diana shifted her head around Julia to face Vari. "I want that gun."

"First it was a bow?" Julia's hands flared up in anger. "Now, you want a gun. Sounds like you—"

"You ever read my personnel file, Lady Pollus?"

"I've seen it."

"But have you read the damned thing? Every word."

A cold moment pierced the swelling refinery heat. Julia broke the ice with a single word. "No."

"Then you missed where I ended up with a Non-Dead contract. Weird thing to have for someone stuck on a refinery world."

Vari pulled a hand over Julia's arm. "That's strange," he said. "Brasilians don't take Non-Dead contracts."

"If Macrinus hates someone enough, they get a contract anyway." Diana's thumb curled behind her at the female Non-Dead. "There are few people Macrinus hates more than me and the women I served with. Let me give them death."

The Imperial assessor barked from the floor. "Treasonous Amazons don't deserve death!"

Julia kicked the assessor's waist.

Vari lowered her finger over the trigger. Generations of military leaders weighed on her knuckle, giving her permission to fire. "Why?"

"Those bitches defied the Imperator. They refused to give him the Eighth Sword. Kill me if you like, but do not let them—"

No thought bound the pressure on the trigger. Searing heat washed around Vari's ankles as the assessor's head burst under a pulse of liquefied plasma.

Vari turned the weapon around, offering it to Diana. "I give you this courtesy, Diana of Hippolyta. If your intention is sincere, prove it."

Julia hissed for an instant, but Vari lifted her hand, begging for a moment's pause.

Diana stared at the slain assessor until the smell of molten bile crept through every filter. Her gaze returned to Vari as she wrapped her fingers around the weapon. "You have your father's honor."

"Thank you." A timid wave of relief pierced Vari's lungs, even as Julia scowled.

Even as Diana euthanized the fallen warriors.

None of us chooses her name. We are all shaped by the
tales we've read and the labels of our old lives.

Lady Lysandra Geta
Personal journal

F OOTSTEPS CLANGED ACROSS THE final walkway as Vari and the others left the cruel surface of Gaulius behind. Diana stomped her boots, knocking away snowy tufts of powdery ash. "Why didn't you just bring me the weapons."

"We need to get off the planet before we make our next move."

"We, Lady Pollus?" Diana tilted an eyebrow down at Julia. "Since when are we on the same side?"

"Since I realized I need you both." Vari didn't restrain her vulnerability. She needed Julia to get access to Diana, as well as the remaining Quantum on Gaulius. Vari needed Diana so she could claim the Eighth Sword and the birthright that came with it.

Rather than reveal any detail of her motivations, Vari stepped away, having seen Solus enter the chamber once the air quality pressurized. The priest clasped his hands and bowed. "It is done."

"Thank you." Vari lowered her head in an instant of reverence. When she lifted her head, she saw Diana and the priest sharing unfamiliar glances. "This is Solus, High Priest of the Elagabal. Diana of House Hippolyta."

"I know that name," the priest said. "I should know..." His eyes swelled open as he took half a step back. "Varius, this woman is a liar and an enemy of your family."

Diana crossed her arms. "Most of my friends died fighting for House Severus."

Vari lifted a hand. "That's enough. There are larger enemies to deal with."

"Who?" Diana tapped a finger against her left arm.

"Imperator Macrinus." A visible tremor flowed through Julia's shoulders. Hints of pale glowed throughout the blonde's face. "Yeah, I just said that."

Diana relaxed. "You're shutting down the refineries? He'll send the heavens to crush this place."

"Which is why I'm putting out an open call to hire off-duty workers to keep Macrinus from restarting production."

"You're serious. Maybe I misjudged you, Lady Pollus."

Vari broke the discussion. "We misjudge each other all the time. For now, we need to get off-world."

"And get away from the fight?" Diana shook her head. "That's no good."

"I need you to take me to the Sword."

"Oh." The large woman stopped. Air seeped out of her voice before she spoke again. "Oh. If you need more fighters, call anyone from Hippolyta. Tell them to do it for the Son of Sextus. That title will tell them it's an order from me."

Solus glared at Diana. "Or it's a trap."

"I stood with Sextus Severus, priest. I stayed loyal to my oath to serve him even when my own queen sided with Macrinus to break that oath."

She loomed over Solus, turning her scowl into an unending eclipse. "I haven't seen a sunrise or a star in a decade because I stayed loyal to my oath. Have you ever done the same, priest? Or have you basked in the light without fear?"

"We need to get to the *Enchantment*," Vari said. "Lucan's waiting."

The displaced priest frowned up at Diana without looking in her eyes.

"Everyone has to do their part." Vari never imagined delegation. Any fight had always been her own burden, or one she shared with an immediate ally.

Saran did her part. Time for Vari to do hers.

Even if Varia's heart curled into the cold dark to do it.

Julia spoke up, following her part of the plan she and Vari had forged. "Solus, we need you here to keep the refineries from coming back on. If you want to serve or minister, this is your chance to do it."

Solus turned with a deferential bow. "It will be done, My Lady."

Julia shivered. "I'll never get used to that." She stepped away from the priest, bobbing her head at Diana. "Let's go, bitch."

"Glad you haven't forgotten me." Diana followed Julia toward the hangar deck.

When they were alone, Solus wrapped his fingers around Vari's shoulders. "May your venture prove fruitful, Varius."

The young woman nodded, lacking the words to inspire Solus.

Instead, the priest offered a benediction. "Power does not seek greatness to wield it. Power finds those who have the strength to keep it. Seek the Elagabal, you'll find the strength you need."

"Thank you." Vari didn't have another response. If she ever saw Solus again, it would be as Imperator, not as an aspirant or one seeking congregation.

Even if Vari threw every rule aside to stand as Imperatrix Varia, there wouldn't be another moment. There would only be defeat.

Better to find the Sword. With it, Varia had hope.

She ran, following Julia and Diana.

Vari settled into the same seat she'd occupied before. Julia nested beside her, playfully tapping callused fingers on Vari's knee. Diana sat as close to the exit ramp as possible.

Lucan stood beside the cockpit door. His face torqued in a frustrated scowl. "You might want to see something before we meet any... Imperial conflicts."

A heavy breath filled Vari's lungs. She lay her hands over her knees, accidentally trapping Julia's fingers. They both exchanged a glance, opening each other to something more a growing personal understanding. It was an empathy similar to Saran's without stinging that wound.

"I've got to ask," Lucan said. His brow lowered. His lips tightened. "Are you violent when you get angry?"

Vari shook her head. Rage didn't come quick for her. When it came, it burned deep and low. Her fires begged to burn the Usurper for stealing her father's holdings. The same fires flared in hunger for Caracalla for having taken Saran away.

Lucan nodded. "I'll leave you to it." He triggered a recording before sealing himself in the cockpit.

The Usurper's two-headed eagle washed across the view. The beast's dim eyes gleamed at humanity, deciding which mouse to pluck off the bare field. A bombastic fanfare rolled around the heartless avian visage, fading only when the shadow-eyed gaze of the Usurper replaced the eagle.

"Citizens." Macrinus spoke to humanity as though they were his servants. One word betrayed his assertion that every other being was less than him. "Ten years ago, our Empire was torn by violent, savage conflict. Today, I seek to end that enmity once and for all."

Diana snorted. "Only thing that's savage is you."

Julia batted her hand to regain a sense of quiet.

Macrinus leaned forward on a carved throne of burned meteorite. He locked his fingers together while leaving his elbows on the armrests.

"In recent days, terrorists have attacked the good people of New Brasilia. In their rampage, they killed Lord Callium Geta and his wife, Lysandra."

Custom held that Lysandra should have been referred to as *Gal-lae-wife*. She'd been elevated beyond the chains of her physical birth. She'd earned the Usurper's praise.

"As such, the ruling Houses of New Brasilia have come to me with a token of peace." Macrinus paused, allowing his words to circulate like vocal poison. "With the blessing of the Temple of Cybele, Princess Bassiana, Regent of House Severus has offered her sole heir as Gallae-wife to my son, Diadumenian. So, there is no doubt, behold the Lady Varia's garments."

The Usurper motioned to a mannequin shrouded in white. Two servants wearing robes of the same cloth withdrew the covering in a single flutter of cloth. An exquisite blue and purple dress hung from an artificial figure bearing Vari's proportions. A crimson wig full of large curls dominated a facsimile of Vari's face. A golden crown lay nested elegantly within waves of spiraling scarlet.

Fury enveloped Vari. Her nose flared at the sight of the most beautiful dress ever worn on New Brasilia. Saran had the dress ordered not to fit her, but specifically for Vari. Such a fine, delicate garment didn't belong in the Usurper's presence—unless she asserted herself fully at the bastard's execution.

Rage locked Vari's teeth together. Steam blistered from her eyes as she glared at the Usurper. Macrinus had stolen from House Severus once more. An empire, a throne, a home, a wardrobe, an identity.

The broadcast burned Vari's soul with the same ferocity that chopped Saran away from the living world. An angular wound tore through Vari, depriving her of the satisfaction of opening herself, allowing futility to fall away so a better shape might unfurl over her body.

Yet the same unwanted shape metastasized in her flesh. Every joy it offered was stripped away thanks to the unwelcome presentation of honesty and faith.

Vari squeezed her eyes shut. Agony swelled within her eyelids, refusing to flee. Curls and shimmering soft fabrics were a reward, the perfect assertion. A moment of adoration meant to fill the galaxy as the truth proudly rose from stained lips. *I am Varia Antonia Severus, Imperatrix of the Unnamed Empire.*

That moment had been stolen, like too many emotions and possessions. Vari hadn't been given a choice or had time to process what might come. She couldn't prepare herself to emerge with pride. Macrinus snatched away what should have been triumph. Vari stayed in the shadows while the Usurper spoke a proper name of glory.

Humanity heard the name Varia, but it was the Usurper who enlightened them, not Varia herself.

"It is my fondest wish," Macrinus said, "that my son may openly wed his Gallae-bride in due time. Yet we all know every great Lady requires preparations before making her debut." A gleeful grin pierced the Usurper's shadowed face.

A thunderous fist raced upward, punching the hated visage. "I'll make my debut when I damn well please!" Ruptures exploded within Varia's chest, her lungs screamed to take in enough air to fight for calm.

Julia said nothing. Her posture shrank into solemn repose.

Diana's face bore a deep scowl. A faint smirk broke the ages of resentment she still held. "We'll see what he thinks of a debut when he sees the Eighth Sword again."

It should have been the thought that inspired Vari the most. But there was nothing for her, not even her father's legacy.

In silent anger, Varia sat again, plotting how she would make Macrinus and his son pay for their theft.

When he isn't consumed by the affairs of state, our new
Imperator enjoys taking his beloved son to any number of festive games. During the week I spent with him,
Lord Macrinus quietly attended a last-chance qualifying
event for the upcoming Grand Chariot Season. He favored none of the racers, nor did he scowl upon them.
Each driver and defender absorbed their own share of the
Imperator's notice. When I asked who his favorite chari-
oteers were, he offered a timid laugh.
"I have no favorite," he said. "I love the thrill of the
moment. It reminds me of triumph on the battlefield."

Aelius Valka, Jr.
Macrinus: Forging a New Dynasty

T HE REEFS HOLDING UP the Spartan camp on Ardesiel shook. A
blowing storm of exhaust slapped sea spray and particulate over
every face. Heat and cold kissed Bassiana's cheeks with equal ferocity.

Fola drew her sword. The Spartans found their spears and rifles.
Bassiana freed the blades concealed within the folds of her dress.

A reinforced steel rhombus struck the landing pad. Angular panels
hissed before unfolding from the massive metallic heart. Boots thundered as a wall of centurions emerged from the troop transport, blotting
the scent of moisture from the air. Most of the Imperial soldiers took on
escort positions rather than forming a sealed defensive wall.

At the core of the procession, Caracalla approached the armed dignitaries. He smiled at the Spartan king. "King Leonidas, thank you for helping to collect these criminals."

Fola scowled. Bassiana steamed with a maternal glare.

Caracalla deserved a lifetime on Bassiana's table. Several lifetimes.

As the one person who didn't draw a weapon, Leonidas crossed his arms. "I have collected no one."

"Modesty doesn't suit the strongest of warriors." Caracalla bore a hint of amusement as he spoke. "You've stopped a war before it could start."

"This is a Spartan base," Leonidas said. "State your purpose."

"I'm here to collect two criminals, Queen Fola of House Virago and Princess Bassiana of House Severus." Caracalla's gaze shifted toward the Brasilians. "Where is the young heir?"

Bassiana tightened her grip on each blade, shifting one behind her back. The other pressed against Bassiana's abdomen. "I was about to ask you the same."

"As was I." Leonidas tugged on the central braid in his beard. "It is imperative that I find the young man."

"I appreciate your help—"

"I do not seek to help you, General. I have made a pact. I will see to its completion."

Caracalla remained quiet long enough for any joy to seep from his face. "Perhaps you have not heard the decree. The Imperator has made peace with House Severus. I need the heir and these two criminals to come with me to Roma Vatica."

Bassiana shifted a step forward, though she allowed her others to stand ahead of her for once. "Does Macrinus intend to abdicate the throne he stole from my husband?"

A rigid pause entrenched the general's posture. "Hardly. With the collected evidence, the Temple of Cybele has already accepted your child."

Leonidas tensed his fingers. "A pitiful claim for a great man to make."

"I have seen the evidence. It was enough for the Cybeline to permit the Lady Varia as Gallae-wife to Lord Diadumenian Macrinus."

A fraction of a grunt shifted the Spartans into an aggressive defensive barrier. "I do not care who the Imperator's scion marries. My pact with Queen Fola requires me to retrieve the young man for his family, delivering him safe and free."

Caracalla approached the front row of Spartans. "Stand aside, Leonidas. You do not wish to make an enemy of me."

"I have no enemies. Sparta has crushed them all."

The centurions stepped forward in unison and braced their shields.

Leonidas never glanced at the Imperial soldiers, saving his focus for Caracalla alone. "Sparta fights the Enlightened Kingdoms of Sekht for you, but they are not my enemies. Do not give me a reason to turn my spears away from them."

"Such a shift would be a mistake—one I will not allow." Caracalla made a curt nod. "I'll leave until your pact is complete. Queen Fola. Princess."

Bassiana lifted a knife, slowly turning it. If the chance came, she knew exactly which nerve to sever next.

The general turned, gesturing for his centurions to board the transport once more.

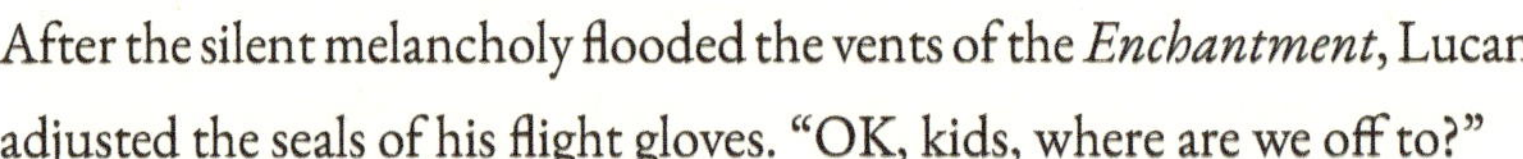

After the silent melancholy flooded the vents of the *Enchantment*, Lucan adjusted the seals of his flight gloves. "OK, kids, where are we off to?"

All eyes turned to Diana, who shrugged her right shoulder. "Artaxata."

Sour bile beaded on Vari's tongue. A parent's tomb was never an inviting place for a child.

"I never moved it." Diana grinned. "I saw no reason to take the Sword anywhere else, especially since everyone decided the planet was dead."

Julia glared at the olive warrior. "Are you saying Gaulius is dead?"

"No. You've still got an intact atmosphere."

Lucan crossed his arms and leaned against the edge of the door. "Macrinus would look there."

"There's more to getting the Sword than being on the same planet. It's impossible for him to find it." Stares seared toward Diana. She hardened her voice. "It's still where we need to go."

Vari breathed deep, stirring together fresh waves of rage and despair. If she meant to purge those sensations—

If she meant to reclaim her father's throne—

If Vari wanted her pride over a defeated Macrinus—

Varia needed the Eighth Quantum Sword.

She tapped her knuckles against the *Enchantment*. "Artaxata."

Lucan laughed. "Never a smooth ride with you, is it?"

"We seek victory, not comfort."

Lucan nodded. "You sound like your father."

"More like a Brasilian warrior," Diana said.

Relief touched the inner curves of Vari's nose. "I've known both."

The exchange seemed to restore Julia's relaxed assertiveness. She'd bound her family to Vari's fate. If House Pollus fell, any sense of order on Gaulius would go as well.

Two worlds depended upon Vari's victory. Without the Eighth Quantum Sword, both New Brasilia and Gaulius were bound to the oppressive hand of the Usurper. Julia was enough of a mystery to make Vari curious. She had enough in common with her sister to make it worthwhile.

As the *Enchantment* lifted from its berth, Vari and Julia watched each other from the corners of their eyes. Something should be said, an explanation to a future spouse, a partner in all things. Even if Saran had bought the dress Marcrinus showed off, there was no guarantee Julia would accept that reality, especially with the decrees hooked around it.

"Have you met Diadumenian before?" It was the last question Vari expected Julia to ask. "He's a shit. Can't do any wrong in his father's eyes. Just as malicious."

"If I ever meet him," Vari said without hesitation, "I'll have to kill him."

"Why is that?"

Vari didn't have a reason, not one that mattered to anyone else. A firm swallow stiffened her throat. "As long as he's alive, there's a chance he'll try to see this decree through. I don't belong to him."

"Do you belong to me?"

Vari flexed her lips inward. "We have a partnership."

Julia leaned closer. Her brow tilted downward. "That's it? Just a partnership?"

"It's a beginning."

She nodded. "I can do that. Just make sure you have an heir before you go cutting anything off."

Julia's meaning hovered like a guillotine swinging by a frayed rope. Vari touched her lower abdomen. Her fingertips stroked her protected navel with hope and wonder. "I can do that."

The *Enchantment* shifted upward, breaking free of Gaulius.

Everything jolted left. A surge of momentum smashed every passenger against their seat. The fading pull of gravity spun all around the ship. Lucan's voice crackled through the speakers. "Fighters in pursuit. Brace yourselves."

"Dammit." Diana threw off her restraints, bracing herself against the ceiling as she walked to the back of the ship. "Tell him to straighten this ship out."

Vari twisted against her own seat. "Where are you going?"

"I still need those weapons—unless you'd like to explode."

Julia grumbled, following Diana to the back of the ship. "One of these days, I'm going to kill you."

"Make it another day, Lady Pollus. We can drink each other to death."

Vari freed herself and followed the others. It would take multiple hands to open the crate holding Saran's remains.

A second polished steel box loomed next to Saran's remains in the cargo hold. Diana gripped the side of Saran's crate, tugging and grunting against the sealant Vari fused around the box. Another roll pushed the trio sideways. Vari clawed her fingers around the sealed corners containing Saran's remains. Within, her friend stirred under the *Enchantment*'s evasive turns.

Julia pressed the sides of Saran's crate, snapping the sealant loose from the top. Diana climbed beside Julia, grimly waiting for the enclosed casket to open. The lid split in half, each section unfolded like a pair of wings sliding downward.

Saran still closed her eyes within her eternal sleep. Her hands clasped the edge of an ornate Quantum Bow. A quiver of arrows lay proudly against her armored hip.

In so many ways, Saran seemed alive. Beautiful, pristine, relaxed.

In others, she was empty. None of the vibrant snark or playful attitude that always charmed Vari. None of the proud valor Saran exhibited in her slightest motion.

The crimson arc of Caracalla's attack slashed through Vari's memory.

"Sweet girl." Diana lay a hand against a heroine's chest plate. "Your soul was always Brasilian."

Julia eased Diana's hands away from Saran. "She's still my little sister."

Diana nodded, gently guiding the bow and quiver away from Saran. "Seal her up. I'm going to prime these arrows."

Vari snapped toward a polished steel box similar to Saran's. It didn't unfold like Saran's casket, even if it held the same shape. A palm-sized door opened on the end, allowing a round fuel connector to emerge. Diana plunged the tip of an arrow through the metal ring. Blue-white light washed over the once-confined warrior with uncanny brightness.

"Consider it my dowry." Julia reached for Vari. Her hands pressed the controls to enclose Saran once more. Julia peered at eyelids matching the shape of her own face. Worried lips marred her typically pragmatic expression.

Two gleaming arrows dangled from Diana's grasp before she pulled a third loose. She slapped the palm-sized door shut. Once she stomped to the back of the hold, Diana braced her hand on a call button beneath a speaker. "Fly straight and open the bay doors."

Vari and Julia braced protective masks over their faces. The cargo doors opened like the short beak of a squid. Four Imperial fighters swooped around the *Enchantment*, allowing a small troop transport to draw closer. All five ships fired over and around the *Enchantment*, trying to herd them back to the planet's surface.

"Asshole picked a great time to squeeze," Julia said.

"Stay back." Diana locked her legs apart at an angle. "I'll handle this."

Light blossomed around her arms, threatening everyone nearby with blindness. Diana held her first arrow in place, glowing like a star. The glowing burst flew outward, plunging the cargo hold into a nest of dull shadows.

Once more, Diana smacked the call button. "Close it."

As the cargo doors groaned shut, an elliptical burst devoured the troop transport. Azure shockwaves ripped through the rest of the formation, tearing at least one wing away from a fighter.

The *Enchantment* jerked ninety degrees. Vari fell into Julia, knocking them both to the floor.

Diana hadn't budged. She clamped a hand over the quiver as she powered off the Quantum Bow. "Come on." She walked to the opposite end of the cargo hold. "Let's go get your Sword."

Caracalla marched across the command deck of the *Arcturus*. Those free from their duties clasped their fists to their chest as the general walked past. Most nearby screens were absorbed with some view of the aquatic world below.

His duty lay below, even as diplomacy forced him away. The fiendish woman's dirty knives had dug into his flesh. She'd found another blade to dig into the Spartans, twisting them away from their duty.

"Eldreth, have fighters on standby to engage the Spartans."

Eldreth gave a curt nod before drawing close enough to speak discreetly. "Sir, the Imperator has been signaling for an update on our status. He wishes to speak directly to you."

Caracalla nodded. "I need access to your transmission projector."

"Yes, General."

A curved pane lowered near the tactical console. Lime green rings of light surrounded Caracalla, muting all sounds from the command deck, even Eldreth's breathing. Two emerald lenses basked light on Caracalla and the curved pane.

The Imperator and his son appeared within the arched surface. Their shrouded eyes burrowed darkness toward Caracalla like they all shared the same space. "General, have you taken the Brasilians into custody?"

Air surged through Caracalla's nostrils before he replied. "No, Imperator. King Leonidas has forged a pact with Queen Fola. I don't know the full terms, but part of their agreement requires the Spartans to locate the Severus heir."

Diadumenian's lips frowned in a rigid crack. "My Gallae isn't on Brasilia."

Caracalla shook his head. "I don't believe so."

"This is an issue of fact." Macrinus knotted his fingers together. "An Amazon attacked a patrol pursuing Lady Julia Pollus. An Elagabal priest, acting under her authority, halted all Quantum production and exports from Gaulius. I had already sent an assessor to review Diana of Hippolyta's condition, but I lack further confirmation."

"It seems like Young Severus has found allies on Gaulius. With your permission, I'll continue my search there."

Macrinus tilted his head. "Pursue them at once. Instruct the fleet near Ardiesel to stop ferrying Spartans until further notice. If the Eighth Quantum Sword still exists, do not let Sextus's heir obtain the weapon. We have a peace to maintain."

Caracalla locked his fist against his chest. "Yes, Imperator."

The lights shut off, and the curved pane lifted back into the ceiling. "Plot a course for Gaulius. A Gallae wants to steal the throne."

WITHIN THE STARK RECEPTION hall, four Spartans approached their King and his guests. The soldiers exchanged glances with each other.

Agis stood from his seat. "Speak. Your King has given his guests our protection."

One of the four stepped forward as the others knelt. "Forces engaging the Lesser Kingdom have been abandoned by their escorts."

Another of the quartet stood. "The next wave meant to deploy to the Lower Kingdom has been refused transport clearance."

Leonidas slapped the edges of his chair. The impact echoed through the hall. "Do all of you possess similar reports?"

The first Spartan nodded. "Yes. Imperial ships have stranded us throughout the theater of war. The campaign in contested Sekht space continues without delay."

Leonidas turned toward Fola. "Is General Caracalla so cowardly?"

"Possibly." Fola rubbed at the bandage covering half of her face. "Whoever gave the order wants to make sure Bassiana and I can't leave."

"He does so at his own peril. Agis, send word to every division. Fall back to yesterday's position and remain there until I give contrary orders. After the order is sent, I want all reserve transports unlocked and ready to move."

⸻◈⸻

"Take a look." Lucan pointed ahead. "Artaxata, what happens when someone screws up a Quantum Bomb."

A fractured tan and brown globe lay adrift in a swirling galaxy. Abandoned flecks of communication satellites floated on the fringes of Artaxata's gravitational pull. Cracks ran through the surface and the atmosphere, webbing like fractured glass. Continental plates bobbed up and down on a dying molten sphere.

The *Enchantment* drew closer to the surface, dodging sections of buildings, both tall and short. Miles of space separated each crumbled structure. Heat vents blasted debris through the acrid sky, plunging everything into a bland sepia glow.

Diana pushed herself through the cockpit door. "Go to X-minus-26. 238 by Y-plus-118.301. Land wherever you can." The olive-hued woman turned to Julia. "Lady Pollus, when we land, will you infuse any of the arrows I don't take?"

A semi-amused huff snorted out of Julia's nose. "That's the nicest thing you've ever said to me."

"Get used to it. People are only going to get more formal with you."

244

Julia shook her head.

Vari clamped her fingers around the edge of the door. "This is where I take back what the Usurper stole." No one present seemed to notice Varia's conviction. The dividing line wasn't a piece of clothing, nor was it a hairpiece. When every piece of Sextus Severus's heir spoke, those words belonged to Varia.

An impetuous tone filled Diana's lips. "Your father wanted this planet to be a monument to his greatness. Now, it's a monument to his failure."

"Only because of the Usurper's praetorians—"

"Never happened." Diana shook her head. "It was a stalemate at that point, but Macrinus was running out of funds. Rather than hire fighters, he recruited miners to set up antiquated drilling operations to dig deep into each planet. When they drop in a few drops of Quantum..." She lifted a hand to the ruined view around them.

"If he was out of funds," Julia asked, "where did he get the Quantum?"

The answer came as Vari congealed a thousand tiny facts from a decade in her aunt's palace. "The Usurper rarely shows anyone his Sword. He never uses it as anything but proof of his claim."

Some weapons were too powerful for a modern battlefield.

"You got it, kid." Diana's frown deepened. "After that fuck found out your father was on Artaxata, Macrinus made sure one of his grubby Quantum bombs made it here. By the time we found the drilling station, it was too late." A meter-wide hunk of rock floated past the *Enchantment*. "We fell back to the complex so Sextus could secure his Sword." A stillness colder than the rusted sky froze the recycled air before Diana spoke again.

"Your Sword."

Encased in a sealed environment suit, Vari stepped away from the *Enchantment*. Erratic sections of crust rose and fell like a sleeping beast. Dust fountains exhaled from elongated fissures.

Vari glanced at Diana through the oval dome of her helmet. "Are we in the right place?"

"No buildings around, right?" Diana moved forward at a steady pace. "We did this just so Macrinus wouldn't find it. Once this planet cracked, most people were afraid to fight him. They didn't want their planet to be the next target."

The impossible reality caved on a confused kid. Her father came and went like a stiff breeze, fading for months at a time. Vari cared little about the ongoing strife with Macrinus, only that someone from a Noble House wanted planets screaming out for reform among waves of self-inflicted chaos.

It wasn't war that Vari knew as a child.

It was a kind smile, a reserved laugh.

Diana drew her bow, firing an unprimed arrow away from the *Enchantment*.

Vari narrowed her gaze at such a waste. "We only have so many of those."

"Brasilian arrows are attracted to Quantum. Makes a bigger target, especially if the arrow doesn't have Quantum of its own."

A glint from the arrow swept through the desolate sky, shooting past plumes of dirt and floating clods of debris. Every particle ran from the shaft, cutting a thin path forward.

Angular cracks tore through the surface of Artaxata. Some lines intersected, throbbing with a pale glimmer of azure light.

If the Sword hadn't been promised, Vari would have lingered near every crevasse, every flake of broken society. In two days, she'd visited as many planets as she'd ever known through her life.

But the Eighth Quantum Sword was close. A stiffness filled Vari's wrists. She fought to keep her breaths steady. In another day, vengeance might be reality.

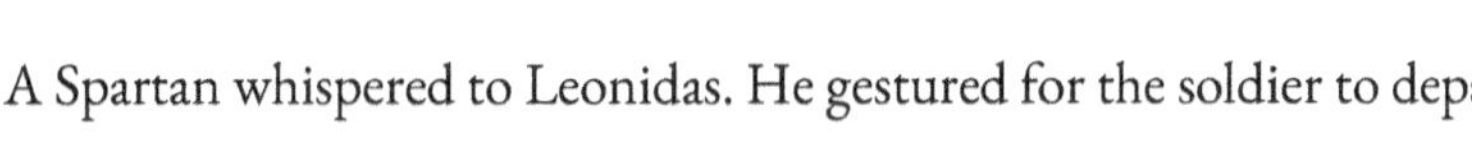

A Spartan whispered to Leonidas. He gestured for the soldier to depart. "Queen Fola, New Brasilia has been contacted by the acting Quantum refinery administrator on Gaulius. It is a priest named Solus."

Fola's eyebrow ticked upward. "That's odd."

Bassiana turned rigid. The last she knew of Solus, he'd been helping Vari ready Saran's remains for transport.

"Your General Mhati is working to clarify the situation." Leonidas faced Bassiana. "I think your son went looking for allies of his own."

"What happened?" Bassiana's knees and shoulders sloped. Her breathing quickened. She hadn't forced herself to imagine what might have happened to her precious daughter, her determined child. "Is Vari all right?"

"The message said he was going to Artaxata."

Half a gasp filled Bassiana's throat. "That's where his father died." Bassiana spoke of her daughter in the masculine, ensuring the Usurper's smear campaign didn't root in Spartan minds.

A proud smile washed over Fola's face. "Perhaps he's gone there to live." She gently rubbed her bandaged cheek. "When I stayed with my aunt on Roma Vatica, I saw much of the Imperial elite. Every time I saw something odd, I asked my aunt about it. She always told me to watch closer. She wanted me to see the servants along with the nobility. The servants treated their work as a great honor. The nobles rarely did. Anyone who bothered looking past themselves often had a better understanding of humanity." Fola wrapped her fingers over her cousin's wrist. "Elagabal grant him a spark of wisdom."

Leonidas rose from his seat. "If we know this, Caracalla and Macrinus will soon. We must act."

Icy dread constricted Bassiana's posture. "Does he have a chance?"

"Maybe," Fola said. "Vari must have a plan."

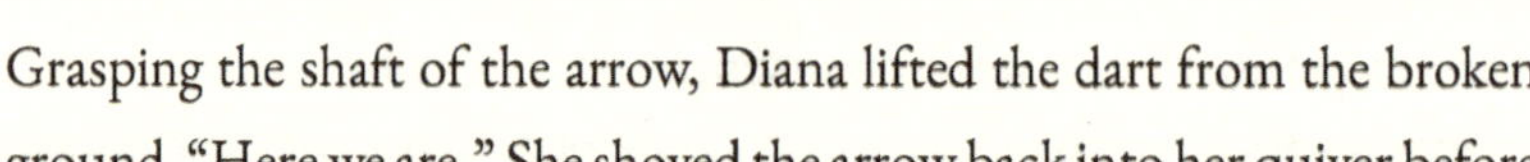

Grasping the shaft of the arrow, Diana lifted the dart from the broken ground. "Here we are." She shoved the arrow back into her quiver before pushing aside brown soil and thick clumps of desiccated mud.

Vari crouched, letting her fingers plunge through the resentful dirt. Scoops of particulate, both soil and powdered buildings, scraped away from the surface. "What are we looking for?"

"A metal door." Diana shoved more handfuls of dirt aside.

A decade of debris drifted away from them. Angry handfuls reached into the soil, ripping into the depths of Artaxata. Each strained grasp brought them a fraction closer to the heart of a dying world. The dimly polarized domes covering their heads kept them from the scent of decay years after rot arrived.

Instead of learning more, Vari and Diana dug. Through huffed breaths broadcast through short range radios, they toiled through the corrupted soil. No worms squirmed away from their fingers. Absent moles couldn't scurry from their grasps.

They may as well have been robbing a grave without tools or a map. On Artaxata, any tomb would need metal reinforcement, demanding a door share such construction. Perhaps a crypt lay within, maybe a dank pit bearing a weapon, an environment suit, and a hermetically sealed corpse.

Diana's middle finger unveiled a steel line pocked with tiny abrasions. The revelation drove them onward. Hands flailed, gloved palms cupped into makeshift shovels. The surrounding air thickened with particles that refused the call of gravity.

Tension filled Vari's fingertips. Calcium drained from her bones, replaced with strain and inflamed nerves. No matter how much it hurt, she kept dragging dirt away from the door. If she didn't, the Severus birthright would remain in darkness, leaving Vari alone in her ambition, divided from her revenge, shackled to flesh outside of her design. Without the Sword, justice remained a dream, Varia's grace contained only nightmares.

The door came free, offering a stale gust of pressure from within. Diana twisted the long lever bar, opening a rectangular pit into darkness.

A rusted ladder crawled into the opening, reaching into the unseen depths.

Varius needed the Sword for justice.

Varia needed the Sword for acceptance.

The Heir of House Severus nodded. "Let's go."

Every time I hold this Sword, I feel my birthright, my duty,
and the responsibility to protect humanity.

Imperatrix Varia Severus
Last recorded words

I N THE DEPTHS OF Artaxata, darkness obfuscated every shadow.

Sprinkles of dust skittered against the ladder rungs and skipped over the solid floor. Every inhale echoed within Vari's skull. Each exhale echoed in a thin fog over her domed helmet.

She tapped a button on her left wrist. Lights sprang alive around her collar and over her shoulders. A haze of forgotten gloom drifted through the barren chamber. Dense layers of gray clung to a dented transmission connector.

Diana landed behind Vari. She leaned around her and nodded. "It's still intact. Jack into the transmitter and say your name. Speak clearly when you do."

Vari approached the connector, dabbing dust away from a cable hanging from the dented terminal. After opening the communication port on the arm of her suit, an electronic chime whistled inside Vari's helmet. The weight of a thousand worlds pushed upon her lungs as she committed her most egregious deceit.

"Varius Antonio Severus."

Death curdled under her tongue and soured her lips. But such fictions were all the former Imperator knew of his heir.

The wall clicked, ejecting another stream of dust into the chamber. A curved transmission pane twisted into position. A motor whirred behind a wall. Flickering light struck the pane.

When the light steadied, a masculine shape emerged. Dark hair spilled from his scalp. Scratches and dents ripped through the tarnished exterior of his centurion armor. Fresh cuts lined the left side of his face, but failed to smother a weakened smile.

"The hour grows dark," Sextus said, "but my love for you will never fade. Know then, Varius, that on this last day of my reign, your destiny begins."

Vari reached forward, unable to make contact. "Father."

"None of this has gone the way I wanted. You will see soon enough, there are few choices available to an Imperator. Every choice carries a grave consequence. My worst decision was siding with House Macrinus against the Sekht. I didn't realize the Sekht shared your mother's religion. I didn't think Lord Macrinus would refuse all efforts at peace."

The pale image of Sextus Severus revealed tired eyes hovering over a smile that refused death.

"On the Imperial Council, your grandmother has taken her emeritus position seriously. She keeps herself away from your mother, even though both operate from the highest seats any woman could occupy."

Varia's lips hardened. She held her tongue rather than miss something vital.

She planned to win the unspoken argument against the dead.

"If you need aid, seek the Lady Julia Maesa. She has many accounts held in trust. By the time you see this, those funds will have useful value."

Vari hadn't heard from her grandmother in years. She had no reason to doubt the Lady Maesa supported the Usurper in outing Varia. The old woman might even be dead as far as Vari knew.

"Make peace with the Sekht. As defender of humanity, you must protect all people, not just those who swear fealty to you."

Sunlight sparked in Varius's heart.

"When this message ends, the Eighth Quantum Sword will be yours. House Hippolyta has sworn to defend the Sword and its owner from all enemies, even if it angers their Queen.

"Be strong, Varius. Stand proud in your convictions. Embrace your allies."

The heir grinned. "I will, Father."

"I love you, son. Now stand strong, for your enemies are drawing near." Sextus clasped his fist to his chest and knelt. "Hail, Imperator."

Behind Vari, Diana made the same motion. "Hail Imperatrix Varia. Long may she reign."

The projection ended, allowing the pane to turn away.

Vari hadn't given the oppressed warrior reason to see the truth. A fact Vari hadn't been able to share on her own terms thanks to the Usurper's meddling. When Diana had spoken, she'd done so with a respectful grace Vari had never witnessed from another person. It was equal parts loyalty to her father and pride in following Vari herself.

Vari reached toward Diana. "Rise."

Diana took Vari's hand and stood, leaving the young ruler longing to share the moment with someone dear.

A bulbous onyx capsule slid out of the gap holding the transmission pane. The capsule burst open with a hiss that shook Vari's suit. A handle as long as a leg connected to three interlocked structures. The first was a gold blade traced with silver, bearing a cutting edge as high as a grown man. Beside it, a wider plate of metal as tall as the first, separated by a finger wide gap of space. The last structure was a spiked ring bound to the base of both blades, reaching beyond the sharpened boundary.

The glory of Humanity's triumph over the Nihl lay before Vari. An unbroken chain of conqueror-soldiers and willful insurgents had carried the massive weapon.

It was Vari's birthright, even more than an accepting home among the people of New Brasilia. Respect, and honor belonged to whoever could operate the grand Quantum conduit, even if it was sealed behind a genetic lock.

Sextus had bequeathed the weapon to his rightful heir. The kind Imperator never knew that it was the key to his daughter's power and dominance.

Vari claimed the Eighth Quantum Sword, brushing a wisp of dust from the surface. "Let's get back to the ship."

Diana lowered her head and clutched her chest. "Yes, Imperatrix."

A digital outline of Artaxata emerged before Caracalla seconds after his ship shifted out of Quantum mode. The planet lacked any intact settlements, only the desolate remains of the former Imperator's bases. Without the previous maps, those structures were beacons of dust.

Eldreth snapped to attention after checking another console. "Sensors detect a small ship on the surface. It matches the make of the ship that attacked our forces on Gaulius."

Scar tissue stung along Caracalla's spine. "Keep our larger ships back. I don't want to make easy targets for any Quantum arrows."

"Sir?"

"Release an escort of fighters, but have them approach Artaxata on an attack vector. While they approach, our transports will land in flanking positions. Assemble two legions to accompany me to the surface."

"General, it's only one ship."

Caracalla had tasted raw ozone and coppery mist when he fought on New Brasilia. Such flavor would not infect him again. "All parties will prepare to advance in three minutes."

Vari followed Diana up the ramp of the *Enchantment*. The Eighth Quantum Sword hovered within Vari's grasp, lacking the strain of the sizable weapons she'd trained with.

Julia slid a gleaming arrow out of her tank of Quantum. She eased the shaft into an identical collection. "I'm working as fast as I can."

"I need this." Vari lifted the Sword with a graceful hum, laying the slab over her betrothed's Quantum.

Julia froze. Visible awe stretched her eyelids open.

Diana stowed a few of the prepared arrows in her quiver. "I can hold off a few ships with these."

"Um..." Julia blinked, finally turning herself away from the Sword. "You'll need those soon. The captain picked up several ships in orbit."

"Do we know what kind of ships?"

Vari lifted a hand. "Wait." Her father ordered her to protect all of humanity. Vari triggered a call button. "Lucan, close the cargo bay door. I need to open my suit."

The speakers replied for the captain. "You got it." The ramp growled upward.

Julia forced herself to examine the Sword again, bracing her hands on the edge of the box. "The central ring acts like a Quantum Battery." She leaned close to the blade, tapping the protective dome of her helmet against the spokes. A smile stretched over her face as she stood again. "When the hold is sealed, grab the handle with your bare hand, then press the tip against the access point. Everything else should be automatic."

The ramp locked with a rumble before the seals exhaled. Vari normalized her suit and disconnected her right glove. Her dome lowered automatically, removing any remaining barrier between her and the weapon.

Silver lines ran along the edges of the Sword, meeting at the spiked ring fused to the hilt. Tiny ports ran through the handle. Each small hole forged a network of grooves, increasing the friction against her skin. As she lifted the blade, her heartbeat grew faster, pounding beyond her expectations.

Vari never touched the Sword as a child. Her father said it was too dangerous for a child to handle. History danced beneath her fingers, connecting her to her progenitors. Far in the past, the Eighth General held the same grip. Oppressive Nihl died against the might of Vari's Eighth Quantum Sword, slain by waves of destruction and cleaved by the cutting edge.

Before moving further, Vari glanced at Julia. "Can you record this?"

"Sure."

Diana passed Julia a tablet. Julia frowned for an instant before offering a nod and taking the tablet. She tapped the screen a few times before aiming it. "Posterity awaits."

For three seconds, stillness dominated the cargo bay. The *Enchantment* wasn't the ideal locale for an Imperial proclamation, but there was no stronger alternative. No one would care about the room Vari occupied, only that she held the birthright of her father and the entire Severus line. Vari pressed the tip against the Quantum valve, allowing the radiant light to swell around her. Her eyes widened as the engraved edges excited beyond life. In the heart of the Sword, a sphere of blue-white light swelled like a growing fetus, small at first, before growing at an exponential rate.

"I am Imperator Varius of the House Severus, Embodiment of the Unnamed Empire, Bearer of the Eighth Quantum Sword, and Protector of All Humanity." If she meant to topple the Usurper, Vari needed the lie of her birth name a little longer.

A jolt surged through the Sword as vibrations shook the handle. Vari lifted the weapon, aware that the galaxy would see she controlled the most ancient claim within the Empire. "This is the Sword of my Imperial forefathers, given to me to deliver justice."

Julia tapped the tablet. She nodded with a proud grin. "Not bad."

"Good." Vari relaxed her arm. "Send that to the ships in orbit."

When Marcus Octavian, the First Praetorian flushed out
the last nest of Nihl, he became the greatest hero of his
age.
All it cost him was his brother's life and the Second Quantum Sword.

William Pleiades III
Preface, The Modern Ascendancy of Man

T HE OVERHEAD SPEAKERS RUMBLED with Lucan's voice. "Fighters coming in."

They'd escaped Gaulius because the *Enchantment* was already moving when they were chased by Imperials. By the time they got off Artaxata, the fighters would swarm them.

Everyone in the cargo bay sealed their suits. Diana opened the ramp, ducking her head outside. "That's odd." She pulled herself back inside while the ramp continued to lower. "It's an escort cluster flying on an attack vector."

Vari had been told to protect all of humanity. The uncanny grace of her Sword reminded her of her father's warning. An Imperator had precious few choices.

"I've got more ships coming along the horizon," Lucan said. "If we're getting out of here, we'd better do it now."

The fighters drew closer, twisting so two foils extended from the bottom, the third rose over each small fuselage. Gleaming lights stared down from each foil's cannon. None opened fire.

Artaxata groaned. Steam lurched powder and smoke away from the surface. Withered chunks of former streets or sidewalks drifted upward, never to succumb to gravity's embrace.

Before he'd consciously decided on a course of action, Vari pressed her call button. "Captain, find the closest place where a transport can land. Diana, don't attack the fighters."

"I don't have a ton of arrows, but I can take out—"

"Summertime gnats sent to waste your arrows." The avenue of attack and defense was another of those rare choices Vari now had. Managed destruction was something she'd have to deal with as well.

Lucan's voice crackled through outside wind and static. "Half a kilometer port and stern, there's a clear path. The next closest spot is over ten kilometers away."

"Wait here. Keep eyes on me and that next closest spot." Vari shifted the Sword over her shoulder before walking down the ramp. Katas shifted within her thoughts. Reminders of muscle memory flexed in the presence of her Quantum-infused weapon.

On a day long past, Sextus Severus declared a celebration on Roma Vatica. A blanket of waterlogged clouds hovered over the capitol and neighboring palaces. With a wide, patient swing of the Eighth Quantum Sword, every moist cloud and drop of rain fled the charged shockwave, leaving behind a flawless, clear sky.

Vari closed toward her destination, a bare patch of desolation marked by the faint outline of where a park and playground once stood. Strength filled her arms. Quantum shook deep beneath her feet. Abrasive particles skittered into the air, chasing the tip of the Sword as it reeled back.

The speckled presence of approaching fighters filled the air. If they opened fire, everyone on the *Enchantment* would die immediately or be abandoned on Artaxata.

The only choice: Death.

Vari kicked her leg forward before anchoring her weight on the opposite foot. Power filled her arms. Quantum shook beneath her feet before rolling through her knuckles. The Eighth Quantum Sword sliced through the air, pulling Vari toward the ground while stretching any tactile sensation toward the approaching fighters. Every weathered rivet holding the fighters together shook. The armed cannons warmed Vari's wrists like a drop of fresh perfume.

The expanse faded from Vari as quickly as it arrived. A blue-white band seared the air and sky. It annihilated the smallest specks of dust and cleaved any clods shaken loose from Artaxata's gravity. Fighters burst in tiny wads of fire. The grimy atmosphere beyond grew dark, fading into cosmic oblivion.

Vari fell to her knees, staring up at the widening disintegration. No kata sheet ever mentioned a wake of absolute destruction.

A broad azure curve ate the nearby atmosphere.

Of the three transports in Caracalla's coterie, two evaporated in a single crimson breath.

"General! All fighters and transports are caught in a Quantum wave!"

"That's history, boy." Caracalla's lips hardened, even as his transport rumbled within the sapphire wake. "There's a Quantum Sword down there. Let us claim it for our Imperator."

"Yes, sir." Wide eyes and panicked excitement filled the inspired pilot's face.

Caracalla pressed his fingers against the seals of his armor. Uniform code was a constant for any soldier, no matter if they fought in a tropical paradise or upon an inhospitable landscape. Behind him, a decade of centurions checked their own weapons and shields. Every rifle had to be ready to fire, every spear and blade capable of tearing through unarmored environment suits.

Outside, faint sapphire sparkles fluttered about. The last embers of an attack not meant for atmospheric use. Moments earlier, every particle had been a brick, a cloud, some extant structure. After tasting the fury of a Quantum Sword, there was only cosmic dust.

For the survivors, it meant a chance to strike. The greatest warriors exhausted themselves fighting the Nihl. Two Swords had been lost to bickering and poorly chosen attacks.

A greater sword wasn't just a replacement for a devastating weapon, it was practical in application. The blade, cold to touch. The handle was sturdy, bracing a consistent level of mass.

The transport shook, colliding with Artaxata's surface. Caracalla rose first.

"Come with me. One fight to solidify an era of peace." He held his immense blade out with both hands. "Long live Macrinus."

A singular voice rose from a company of bodies. "Long live Macrinus."

Alone, the Quantum void dispersed. Glowing dots fluttered downward, sprinkling hints of fading blue across the cracking surface of Artaxata. A chill rushed through Vari's skin whenever a pool of tiny bits settled on her atmosphere suit.

Heat radiated from her chest. A band of tympani rolled within her heart, beating the rhythm of war.

Caracalla approached in the distance. A company of centurions followed his quickened pace.

"I can fire," Diana chimed in Vari's ear.

"You may need the arrows to escape."

"Escape is worthless if you're dead." She sighed through the speaker. "Imperator."

"Hold your fire." Vari pushed her breathing into a more controlled pace. "I have to try for peace."

Caracalla lifted his greater sword, slowing the speed of his entire company. Shields braced. Rifles filled defensive gaps.

Lucan's voice broke through. "He wants to talk to you. One to one communication."

Vari gave a timid nod. "I'll hear his secrets."

"You'll be isolated."

"I told you to do it."

A pause filled the connection before Lucan replied. "Don't get killed."

Several beeps plunged Vari into silence. Only low breaths and the tinkling of Quantum dust echoed around his half-oval helmet.

Another beep shattered any thought of solitude before it settled. "A fine strike, young Severus. You've resurrected your father's legacy."

"Thank you, General. Are you ready to serve your Imperator?"

Caracalla chuckled. "That's a clever verbal trap."

"Do you refuse?"

"I refuse mindless fighting. I reject aimless carnage." He pointed a finger in the distance. "As long as that Sword exists, humanity will be in chaos."

Vari held the Sword higher, ensuring it remained visible, though not actively aggressive. "I spent my life looking for this. Why would I give it up?"

"Because you are Varia Antonia Severus."

Vari clamped her hands against the handle, praying it would give her the Elagabal's resolve.

Caracalla relaxed his stance. "Your hatred of Macrinus runs deep. You've had a decade of isolation, unable to see what he's built across the Empire. But I was there when he saw your clothing—just as I was present during your father's reign. The cycle of destruction cannot continue." He opened his arms to the ruined landscape. "This happens in the wake of such enmity."

The ground shook. A hiss of blue-white steam spewed from a growing fracture.

"Your men respect you, General. They'll follow you when you follow me—"

"Varius Severus will never be Imperator and you know it."

Vari froze. The Eighth Sword pulled her arms downward.

Caracalla stepped closer, though his men did not move. "You are Varia Antonia Severus. Varius Severus can't be Imperator, because he doesn't exist."

A moment of fog steamed Vari's helmet. "I'm not so fragile to succumb to you deadnaming me."

"Consider this, Lady Varia." Caracalla gestured upward to the dissipating void. "What if this was the first gesture from the most powerful woman in the galaxy?"

"I don't see the purpose of your question."

"What if you kept the Sword—and submitted yourself to Macrinus's decree?"

"No."

"No, what? No to peace? To your own desires? You chose to be a woman, so use your gender for what it's worth."

More cracks scattered through the desolate surface. A pyre of Quantum burned louder beneath the surface of Artaxata.

Varia squeezed her lips tight. "You would have me submit to Macrinus."

"I want peace. You want your birthright and your chosen gender. Think of the future. There has never been a Gallae-Queen before. Your grandmother is a shrewd woman, but she would endorse it. Keep your Sword, Lady Varia, but be the woman you know yourself to be."

"This is why you wanted to speak alone." Varia shifted her stance. Quantum hummed within the Sword.

"I wanted to offer you a way out, especially since you haven't had time to refuel."

Varia swept her Sword back. With the transport and the centurions ahead of her, none of her enemies would escape.

"That attack is meant for limited atmospheric use. Your father used a few drops of Quantum to part a few clouds. You spent the same effort with a full charge." Caracalla shook his head. "It's not an attack you'll make again, at least not without refueling. You'll have to run back for that. And I will catch you."

The general approached, holding out his left hand. "Surrender, Lady Varia. Rise as a prominent and proud queen. Forge an even stronger dynasty allied with the full authority of the Throne."

"But never on it."

"No woman can hold the Throne, Lady Varia—"

"Stop calling me that." She snapped the Sword downward, feeling none of the tactile sensation the came with her earlier attack. "I am Imperatrix Varia of House Severus, Defender of Humanity." She shifted for a close quarters attack. "I have not come this far to kiss the Usurper's feet."

A barb of blue-white whistled past Caracalla.

Artaxata exploded in Quantum light.

Lt. Piter Mitchell

Attempted poetry taken from personal journals

D EATH CALLED OUT TO Varia, begging for her to rest.

Throwing away her last chance for peace, prosperity, and an open persona, she saw no other road forward.

Spiral whips of pale light snapped in every direction. Each tendril was the width of a commoner's house. Pale energetic cords raced from the horizon to the heavens, tearing through the tattered hole high above.

A rumble shook her environment suit, quaking through the ground around her. Gorges of light cracked through the surface, spraying steam mixed with gleaming dust. Half of a centurion spun overhead, still clutching his shield after his legs and manhood had melted away.

The explosive intensity dimmed, leaving only a sunburst of radiance flowing up from where the centurions once marched. Thirds of the Imperial transport drifted within the active storm of Quantum desolation, dancing in a swelling cloud of floating crust.

Upon the largest nearby section, a broad silhouette stood waiting. A greater sword stretched out from his left hand, shadowing the Imperial figure into darkness. Smoke rose from the decorative plume of his helmet. Hate pooled within the angle that should have revealed a face.

"I will not surrender humanity to war."

Varia shifted her Sword. Thanks to the communication link with Caracalla, the general was still the only voice she could hear speak.

"Only Diadumenian will mourn you."

The toxic thought of the Usurper's son squeezed between Vari's thighs. "An unwanted husband I've never known." Varia braced her posture, unable to see anything more than the storm tearing through the surface of Artaxata. "The only power he'll ever know is death at his father's side."

A shadow of tarnished bronze rippled through steam and dust. Metal sliced through the electric torrent, slashing for Varia.

She spun, using the balance she'd been born with to roll against Caracalla's chest before kicking off the general's thigh. Varia rose. Her ascent refused to fade.

Gravity's dying breath turned Artaxata into a maelstrom. Hunks of years-dead civilization tore loose from their ruined grave. Rusted pipes, electrical posts, and cellular towers vomited into the air, all migrating around Varia.

When the frame of a high-rise ripped free, Caracalla ran up the building's jagged outer corner.

Without footing, Varia had no response. Without an answer to Caracalla's attack, she would never be herself, much less the creature witnessed by her deformity.

But that deformity provided her an education an Imperator's daughter would never have otherwise. Vari's environment suit was wet tissue compared to a greater sword, while no weapon of the Unnamed Empire could push through a Quantum Sword.

Varia lifted her weapon, bracing a hand behind the wide blade.

An empire slammed against her. Battle rage locked Caracalla's grimace within the shadow of his relay helmet. The atmosphere rumbled. Cadres of centurion training, and the residual hate of an ambitious man rained upon Varia, shoving her from the sky.

Impact might tear through her environment suit. A collision could knock her out. Caracalla had neither weakness. The General loomed closer, steady in his approach. "I will end your plague."

Friction and pressure shook Varia's grasp. Light flickered through the engraved patterns on the Quantum Sword. The same glow flowed through her eyes.

Azure radiance arced from the Sword as it shoved Caracalla back. All force, no damage.

Caracalla spun backward, flinging toward the rising ruins he'd leapt from.

Varia swept her Sword at the approaching ground. Newborn gravel sprayed around her in the instant before she rose again.

Had she ascended through a breathable atmosphere, the sky would have been cool against her cheeks. Her eyes would strain against a snap of dryness. A fabulous, mythic shape would fly high, full of life, beauty, and wonder.

Artaxata was not that place.

Varia still lingered in the angry cage called Varius.

She was Imperatrix by right, by force. Only Caracalla came close to crying out to her. *Lady Varia* should have been a kindness. The general came to the title by spite.

"Say my name." Varia snapped her wrist, flinging another bolt of azure at her enemy.

Caracalla lifted his greater sword, letting the surge of Quantum ricochet away. Magnetic thrusters glowed under his feet. He shoved against a whip of energy chewing through the atmosphere. Hollow breaths echoed through their private connection. "Long live Macrinus."

No kata taught Varia how to measure the fuel in her weapon. She swung the widening sharp plane back and forth, steering herself.

"I am my birthright."

They clanged against one another, bouncing toward the drifting remnants of a world her father imagined. Sapphire radiance and a spark of metal blinded the luminous vortex.

"Sing my title, General." Varia slashed through Caracalla with all power and might. A deep gash appeared in his armor. "Let humanity know my name."

An armored fist bruised the dome protective Varia's face. Caracalla's finger smashed against the dome again, forcing a jagged crack through her field of vision. "I would have made you a great man."

Caracalla swung his greater sword at a downward angle. The same angle that met Saran. An angle that ate through human flesh for a power-hungry fiend.

Varia's hands locked together, Her Sword ripped the greater sword in half. The extensive tip fluttered into the distant abyss.

Varia danced with her Sword and the sky, much like she'd danced with Saran while hiding her truth. Brilliance swelled from the tip of her weapon, boring through the line she'd cleaved in the general's armor. Agony echoed through her ears, shaking her skin from nose to ankle.

A breath of blood sprayed over the protective pane of Caracalla's helmet. Thousands of crimson marbles raced away from the definitive soldier of the Usurper's reign.

Gurgling suffocation surged around Varia. "Your Imperatrix sentences you to death." She swung the Sword in a flat arc, severing the drowning sound.

Vari ended Saran's killer with justice and cruelty. The awful gurgling was more than Saran had been offered.

Caracalla's suffering ended as his head and relay helmet drifted away from each other. Varia reminded herself not to give Macrinus such a mercy.

Under a whirlwind of exhaustion, Vari dragged herself back to the *Enchantment*. Her Sword still weighed little, growing lighter as Caracalla's blood drifted away. Only the intensity of battle lingered in her burning muscles. Rage was gone, purpose evaporated.

Under such a blanket of strain, only one thing remained.

"Vari." The name crackled through the transmitters in her helmet. She cringed, unwilling to crawl back into that guise. Static thinned enough to identify Diana's voice. "What happened?"

Vari groaned as she climbed upon the cargo ramp again. "Everything blew up."

"That was me. Those centurions were getting twitchy."

"Caracalla can guide them to the underworld." Vari lay her Sword upon the wealth of Quantum that fueled her victory.

A flicker of joy dawned on Julia's face. While she stood by Saran's remains, for an instant, the elder Pollus daughter embraced the role of

Varia's chosen bride. "No alcohol," Julia said. "Work's almost done." She reached for Varia, stretching a hand toward the Sword-wielding wrist.

Artaxata shook beneath them. A burst of static swelled through the cargo bay. "Blockade."

"You'd think they would have run." Vari stomped toward the interior of the *Enchantment*. "Lucan, can you get me a visual?"

"They're everywhere. Fighters are spreading out. Command ships are taking positions for orbital bombardment."

"I need to refuel." As soon as she spoke, a nearby impact flung Vari forward. Her helmet banged on the wall, widening the crack made by Caracalla.

Diana howled in her helmet. "Dammit, Lucan. Get us out of here."

"Try telling that to the planet you blew up." The *Enchantment* lifted. Its ascent quaked as much off the ground as it did while Vari climbed on board.

Until cannons knocked the ship further off balance. Vari braced herself. Diana fell backward. Julia tumbled over her sister and her Quantum.

Before she could brace one foot against the floor, another cannon volley shook the *Enchantment*. Vari slipped into a seated position, crashing her tailbone against the floor.

"They're not letting me get any higher." Lucan's voice pitched higher, growing increasingly frantic with every syllable. "They're going to blast us back to the Nihl Age if you can't kill those fighters."

Diana crouched to look outside. "Damned fighters are staying too high. I can't get a clean shot."

Julia pulled herself over her sister's casket. "Take a dirty one, dammit."

"It'll rip a hole in the damned ship."

Another lack of choice circled around Varia. She crawled around the Quantum tank, lifting the tip of her Sword against the nozzle.

The *Enchantment* rumbled under another cascade of cannon bursts. Every impact screamed with the rage of every desperate old fool who failed to accept a new generation had to rise. The *Enchantment* spun in a corkscrew, knocking the Sword away from the nozzle.

Vari rolled along the inverted ceiling. Julia's wealth of Quantum struck the crack Caracalla's fist started.

An erratic hiss fogged Vari's helmet. Beads of moisture rolled along the jagged glass canyon.

"Tape! Someone tape my helmet!"

Diana braced Varia's head. Olive lips screamed something. Her words only arrived as a serpent's threat.

The *Enchantment* rocked to the left under the muffled puff of impact.

Varia gasped. She stared up at the seam connecting the top of her elliptical helmet with the environmental systems behind her head. Her eyes spun and grew heavy. If she still wanted life, she shouldn't have placed it before a tunnel of darkness.

Bassiana clutched her hands around her shoulders as the transports exited Quantum mode. Restraints nested her within a protective seat close to Leonidas.

The Spartan King insisted on keeping Bassiana close as long as Fola was occupied with other matters.

Pretending to be a hostage meant nothing, not as long as Artaxata remained intact. The crumbling planet steamed with glowing cracks, all fuming like heavenly volcanoes.

Among all those fountains of death, Vari needed her.

"Signal Eldreth." Leonidas squeezed the front of both of his armrests. "Tell him I am here."

A cluster of large Imperial ships spread around Artaxata's orbit. Clouds of debris held them away from the positions they needed to blockade a planet.

A Spartan with a narrow beard turned from his console. "He does not reply."

"Advise the queen." Leonidas remained still, frozen, almost cold in his commands. For a Spartan, stoicism meant relaxation.

The view of Artaxata, another eruption of blue and white, shook the Imperial blockade. This one came not from the fractured planet, but from the destruction of a peripheral wing of Imperial ships.

The narrow-bearded Spartan turned again. "Eldreth is signaling you, my King."

A transmission pane slid ahead of Leonidas. The flickering image of a half-panicked officer came into view. "—dammit man, what are you doing?"

"I want the Severus heir." Leonidas did not tense, nor did he shift his posture. "He is on that planet. You will leave so I can retrieve him."

Eldreth shook his head. "I think not. You need us to ferry you—"

"Did you miss the explosion that killed your men? I told you to leave. I expect you to obey."

"You wouldn't dare."

"I don't dare. I take. Leave, or I'll take your lives."

The transmission pane remained active, even though neither man spoke.

Stony Imperial eyes struggled to match the King's constant stare. Even mountains trembled ahead of greater powers. "I stand on the Imperator's order."

"Then you are blind." Leonidas remained as calm as a waveless sea. "I shall ask the queen to enlighten you."

"What queen?"

Bassiana leaned against Leonidas's seat, ensuring Eldreth saw her.

"The mother of the bride." Eldreth's fear wavered. "I thought Spartans were pragmatic, not—"

Another eruption rang out. Sapphire fractured into a million bolts of azure as another wing of the Imperial blockade died.

Bassiana touched the back of the Spartan seat. "Are you pragmatic? I came here with my cousin. I'm sure she has enough arrows for you."

Eldreth scowled. "This is treason."

"Only if my son says it is."

"Your child will die under my thumb—"

"As you will die by Queen Fola's decree."

Leonidas rapped his knuckles against his right armrest. "Are you so loyal as to die for a false Imperator's command?" His left hand mirrored the motion of his right. "Can you guarantee your gunner's success before the Brasilian Queen strikes you dead?"

Eldreth pondered the answer for two seconds before his image vanished from the transmission pane.

A ping of static pierced all three blooms of light hovering over Artaxata. Specks of Imperial ships drifted between the Quantum petals, scurrying like insects taking flight as their home tree burned to ash. "I didn't trust him not to fire," Fola's voice said through an intercom.

"They will never trust you with peace again," Leonidas said. The pits of his dark eyes glared up at Bassiana's wayward hand. "No one will take your hand in virtue."

"It doesn't matter." Bassiana took her fingers away from the seat. She stood tall, unwilling to bend to the Spartan warning. "You have an accord with my cousin. Perhaps the Imperator will reward your wisdom."

"Let's find out. Deploy landing craft to retrieve the Severus heir."

The generals who freed humanity prided themselves
upon their wisdom.
Such thought demanded they use the same level of force
as the Nihl who'd subjugated them.

The Clarion
Criticisms of Humanity's Ascension

SOMEWHERE IN OBLIVION, A nest of voices screamed at one another.

A muscular pit of thunder rolled between Queen Fola's protestations. Julia groaned as Bassiana huffed on about proper wives.

It wasn't the cosmic embrace of the Elagabal. Life hadn't abandoned Vari. It only left her clinging to a tense back and a sore neck. Her right elbow whined for a long pair of seconds before popping like a wet balloon.

She sat on the edge of a meager, unfamiliar bed. Looking at a pillow drove stabbed pain into her mind. She rubbed her tired eyes. Her features remained too rigid, her shape far too bulky, even as others might claim she was small for her lineage.

Few would ever say such things directly as long as the Eighth Quantum Sword waited for her hand. All it took was a single activation for the weapon to know her touch. As long as it held ambient energy, it would gravitate toward her grasp, if close by.

Varia opened her hand, feeling nothing approach.

Her eyes filled with alertness, certain that Caracalla's death hadn't been a dream. The massive blade sat outside her reach. The hole in the center of the Sword had been filled by dull shadows.

Caracalla said it had to be refueled. No matter how hard Vari had tried, the weapon hadn't been fed. The only meal present was the continued rumble of angered voices quibbling over mysterious disputes.

Varia tossed the sheets away from her wiry frame before draping bits of a loose robe over her shoulders. The pants and boots of her environment suit would work until she found something better.

Unsure of her location, Varia had only one path to follow: Why were so many people arguing? Her father's last message had been right. Choices fled from her embrace.

A dim metal hallway lit by thin beams of florescent yellow cut a path through the darkness. None of the light reflected off the surface of the Sword, much less the edges of her cheeks. The voices grew louder, through proximity as much as unquenched fury. Sonic pressure steamed through every joint in Vari's skull.

"What is all this screeching?" Varia forgot the brusqueness of her own voice. She'd spent too long sealed within a protective helmet.

A broad body of Spartan muscles and elaborate braids rose at Vari's question. Fola snapped her head, even if it was webbed by a roll of bandages. Julia relaxed for an instant before Bassiana smiled smugly.

"The heir is delivered," the impressive Spartan said. "Give me the deed."

"What deed?" Vari approached Fola and the Spartan, glancing at both for any hint of an answer.

"The deed to Sparta's second hemisphere. It is the price of your safe return."

"Yet it was my arrows that sent Eldreth running," Fola said.

"While you stood on my transports and hid behind my protection."

"After your people attacked mine, King. And after we discovered your... stagnation."

The last word froze the room. Julia's eyes flickered with the same confusion rolling in Varia's thoughts.

Since her mother lacked any reaction to Fola's assertion, Varia turned. "Explain, Mother. What's going on?"

No time for gratitude, hope, or reassurances of safety. The universe overflowed with friction.

"Our Spartan neighbors are genetically stagnant. They are no longer born, but grown by mindless Non-Dead to perpetuate a legacy of clones."

"We are not clones." The few Spartans in the room grunted in unison at their King's words.

Varia hoisted her Sword over her right shoulder. "King II Leonidas, yes? This is a grave claim."

"It is not your concern."

"Then I underestimated your greatness. No one told me you lacked the ability to see."

"Consider your words, boy."

Varia lifted her hand. Her eyes fixated on the King's almond-shaded irises. "Consider yours as well. If you've protected me so far, Macrinus will call you an enemy. Make sure the next Imperator you address is a friend."

A faint glimmer of a grin shone through Leonidas's lips. "You have conviction, heir—"

"*Imperator*." Varia tapped a finger on the grip of her weapon. "Caracalla forgot himself, even when I impaled him on this Sword."

"Then, Imperator, in the spirit of friendship, adjudicate our dispute." All pleasure faded from Leonidas's face. "Your kinsman queen claims she does not have to pay for your return, despite her pledge to deliver the deed for her half of our shared planet. You are returned. I request due compensation."

"It is a service you have completed." Varia lowered her head. "You are due compensation."

"Thank you." Leonidas lowered his head. "Imperator."

Fola tensed her fists. "Varius, with that deed, you will have no home—"

"You should have thought about that before." Varia tightened her mouth before fixating on the most constant ruler in her lifetime. "You sold your fellow Brasilians to Macrinus."

"Varius!" Bassiana stormed closer. "Why do you say such lies?"

"Have you asked my betrothed about the warrior with us on the *Enchantment*? Diana of Hippolyta has some interesting things to say about loyalty."

Fola's stoic temper squeezed her words tight. Her breath turned low and narrow. "That woman would say anything to save herself."

"I thought so for the longest time," Julia said, "but she proved me wrong."

"How can a traitor prove facts wrong?"

"Still yourself, Queen Fola." Varia dragged a fresh breath into her nose. She shoved used air out of her mouth. "Julia is not only my betrothed, she is also your kinswoman."

Fola's eyebrows tugged at her bandages. "What idiot decreed that?"

"You did. The moment you declared her sister legally your daughter. Julia's younger sister is Judith Pollus."

Julia stood tall. "You called Judith by the name Saran of Virago."

Fola scowled. "Then silence yourself, little niece, before I remind you who is the head of our House."

"Yes. Do be quiet." Bassiana snorted.

Varia tapped her knuckles against her Sword, releasing an ominous chime. "All of you, be quiet." She glanced at each waiting stare, measuring all four and their arguments. "I hold the Eighth Quantum Sword, thus, I am Imperator." Varia cringed. Her swallow turned sour. "My betrothed has proven her word and her worth." Varia extended a hand to her side, inviting Julia to join her.

Once Julia moved, Varia turned her gaze back to Bassiana and Fola. "You have claims against Sparta, yet one of my loyal servants has claims against you." Varia held the Sword out, keeping the blade parallel with her own body. "Diana held true to her word, so I will ask, did you sell your warriors to Macrinus so he could deprive me of my birthright?"

"You still have a lot to learn about leader—"

Varia swept the Sword downward, cutting a high-pitched slash into the floor. "Did you do it? Yes or no?"

Fola took a deep breath before a scowl anchored the corners of her mouth. "I did it to keep you safe. Those warriors were never going to break their oaths, but I had to keep the Usurper away until the time was right."

Varia lifted her left hand. "Did you offer King II Leonidas the deed to New Brasilia in exchange for my safe return?"

The queen's scowl deepened. "I did. To keep you safe from the Usurper's claims." Her intact eye widened with fury. "You know which claims."

Varia snapped a glare at the impressively bearded Spartan. "King II Leonidas. How many mothers does your nation have?"

Leonidas lifted an eyebrow. "How would I know that number?"

"Then I'll ask another way. Who will mother your sons? Who is your mother, for that matter?"

"No mother's name is written in Sparta."

"Out of disgrace?" Varia approached the King, curious about his workout regimen. "Or do those women not exist?"

"Tell him," Bassiana said. "I'll prove—"

"Quiet, Mother." Varia spared her mother a momentary glance. "I'll ask when I want that evidence."

Bassiana lowered her head. After an instant of consideration, she descended to her knees.

"King II Leonidas, your answer to my question."

The Spartan nodded once. "We have no need for mothers. We have only soldiers and battle."

"And a grievous violation of the Nihl Accords."

"Then forgive me, Imperator, for saying I could buy the favor of Macrinus and make any such claims vanish."

"I already killed Caracalla with this Sword." Varia held the weapon in a relaxed position. "Do you actually think you can take it from me?"

"I can be dissuaded from trying. Your war is not my fight."

Vari saw an opportunity to quell the dispute and widen her base of allies. "What if it was your fight?"

Leonidas clasped his arms around his chest. "Do you wish to sell me something?"

"A solution. Queen Fola owes you half a planet, but she doesn't wish to vacate." Vari glanced at the Spartan's chiseled neckline, eerily similar to the same neck every Spartan possessed. "You need to prove to the Imperator that you aren't violating the bonds of fellowship that keep all humanity united."

"Tease your solution if you like, Imperator. I am curious."

"Do not sell me like a dog," Fola hissed. "I am not a bitch in heat."

Varia shook her head. "What would you prefer? To send every Brasilian into exile or will you realize you finally have an ally?"

Vari found Julia's hand grasping her fingers.

Fola huffed. "Is that what you want for our world? A shared kingdom under Spartan rule?"

Varia faced Leonidas again. "That's my solution, King II Leonidas. You and Queen Fola of Virago, two of the strongest leaders humanity knows today. What could Sparta and New Brasilia do as a single, united force?"

Leonidas massaged the center braid of his beard. "Do you mean for Sparta to write such a contract?"

"You will write it together."

"I have a condition, one that will dissuade me from ever caring about Macrinus again."

"What is it?" Varia eased away from Julia, standing parallel to the Spartan King.

"I have an unfinished war. I do not leave such things incomplete. If you want me to fight your war, you will help me finish my war first."

Some part of Artaxata crumbled further, obliterated by the years-old grief of Sextus's last plea. "You want us to fight the Sekht."

"It will remove any doubt."

"He's right," Julia said. "Macrinus couldn't finish that fight. If you fight the Sekht, you will show the Empire—all of humanity—that you are the rightful Imperator."

Varia passed the Sword to Julia. She'd need her to refuel the weapon in either case. Varia held a hand to Fola.

"You're too good of a learner," the queen said. She took Varia's hand.

Varia made the same gesture to Leonidas. "We will fight the Sekht together. A single family of warriors."

Leonidas clasped a fist to his chest before slapping the same hand into Varia's grasp. "Hail Imperator Varius."

Bassiana sprang to her feet. "Hail Imperator Varius." She grinned with a fountain of pride.

Fola shook her head. "Hail Imperator Varius."

United, the collected Spartans followed the same gesture. "Hail Imperator. Hail Imperator."

Varia linked Fola's hand with Leonidas's. She'd forged her own peace. All it cost her was her father's final plea and the hope of uniting with the Sekht.

ACKNOWLEDGEMENTS

Loyalty of Severus has been a long labor of creativity. What started as a simple NaNoWriMo project to express my love of the classic scifi novel *Dune,* has taken a long time to gestate into the text you've just read.

Part of that gestation took place through an initial serialized version of this story on Patreon.com/LenBerry to reward my supporters there. Thus, my first round of thanks have to go to the following supporters: Jacob Ressel, Jessica Guernsey, Jack Johnson, Ruby, Angie Ratliff, Mike Jack Stoumbos, and Star & Duck.

I was fortunate enough to have two fantastic allies who swept through different versions of this story, each doing their best to shed editorial light into the shadows and help to sand off any rough edges. October K. Santerelli guided me through the oddities of the earlier versions, up to and including referring to our protagonist as Vari. Mar Fenech showed me how to make this book more internally consistent while proving there's a real audience for my work beyond my own circles—a powerful realization for any writer to feel. Without them, I wouldn't have the book before you.

My amazing cover was assembled by Leraynne S., who provides the pinnacle of perfection when it comes to custom art. My words can go so far in delivering my ideas. Leraynne's art proves that I can fully reach others.

My fellow author Novae Caelum and the entire Robot Dinosaur Press community have been more than reassuring and helpful with guidance. Also, Novae let me use their Atticus to get the formatting done.

Many thanks as well to you for reading *Loyalty of Severus*. I hope the story has proven worthy for you to mention it to others. If you were to leave a review, I'd be greatly honored.

Also by Len Berry

Vitamin F

Scars Of Shadow

ABOUT THE AUTHOR

Len Berry is the Writer of Ethereal Darkness. Len greatly enjoys watching anime, reading X-Men comics, and playing existential video games. When he's not writing, Len is probably drawing weird worlds into existence, watching red panda videos, or contemplating too much philosophy. Learn more at Len-Berry.com

www.ingramcontent.com/pod-product-compliance
Lightning Source LLC
Chambersburg PA
CBHW022112310726

48972CB00007B/2001